BONE CHIPS

A COLLECTION

Keith Hopkinson

REGENT PRESS
Berkeley, California

Copyright 2015 © Keith Hopkinson

[Hardback]
ISBN 13: 978-1-58790-248-2
ISBN 10: 1-58790-248-6

[E-book]
ISBN 13: 978-1-58790-323-6
ISBN 10: 1-58790-323-7

Library of Congress Control Number: 2014931220

Printed in the U.S.A.

REGENT PRESS
Berkeley, California

CONTENTS

SHORT STORIES

POETRY

BRIEF ORATIONS

FOUR ONE-ACT PLAYS

Short Stories

THE TROPHY

"**W**HEN WILL YOU tell him about us?" Benjamin asked. They were sitting together on the sofa in the sunroom, their arms tight about each other.

Clarisse moved luxuriously. "When do you want me to tell him?"

"The very instant he returns from that absurd safari," said Benjamin. "Don't even allow him to stamp the dust from his feet."

"Dear Bunny, you are funny, do you know? Funny bunny!"

"Please." He squeezed her. "Be serious."

Benjamin Whipple had at last turned lucky. Clarisse Burgess, an unbelievably attractive and wealthy woman had fallen into his arms. Soon confessing her loneliness, she had whispered to him how she longed for a delicious honeymoon on some quiet summer beach—after a quick divorce.

It was a bit of luck long overdue. The ocean crossing from Merry England had been made long before, followed by too many years spent drifting through the gardens of the rich, relying upon a spurious Oxford manner and the credulity of the American nouveau riche. Tether's end had very nearly been reached when he met Clarisse in the San Francisco home of a mutual friend.

Benjamin, or Bunny, as his temporary friends called him (and he had no friends who were other than temporary), was not handsome. His face was too round for the full mustache he affected, and when overexcited, he had a tendency to slaver through an unfortunate gap between his front teeth. Still, he had developed his charm to an effective degree and he was an easy mixer. Fortune hunting, though, depends largely upon luck, and Benjamin's luck had been abominable. Luck is a matter of meeting the right person at the right time, and he always seemed to happen by either too early or too late. He had begun to wonder if the cultured Englishman had gone out of fashion. Or perhaps—and the thought brought a clutch of fear—perhaps he was getting old.

His miraculous conquest of Clarisse Burgess while her husband was off in Africa had suddenly put everything right. Once more, his naturally sanguine thoughts had begun revolving around what delights he would indulge himself in once he had married rich. He had insisted upon divorce. "How impetuous you are for a cold Britisher!" Clarisse had taunted him, but a few kisses later she had agreed, and they had commenced making detailed plans.

How completely his luck had turned! Herbert Burgess was as wealthy as any man ought to be, and with California a community property state, Clarisse would control, besides this handsome mansion on the Peninsula, large chunks of stocks, bonds, real estate, and cash. It was just such a coup that Benjamin had dreamed of on that long ago ocean voyage, as he breathed in salt spray and watched the sun hanging brightly over the New World.

Clarisse grew nervous about the servants. They left the sunroom and wandered together through the great house. They came to a closed door.

"What room is that?"

"His den."

Benjamin tried the door. It was locked.

"He locks it each time he leaves. And takes the key with him."

"A den of iniquity, no doubt, heh, heh."

"His trophies are there. All the poor animals he has slain and beheaded." Clarisse rubbed her wrist where a diamond bracelet cut into her flesh. "There are so many trophies."

"In my view, trophy collecting is a barbaric custom."

Hands clasped, they moved out to the western terrace and sat side by side in chaise lounges, talking low, promising each other the delights of paradise once the divorce business was done with. They were waiting for Burgess, due to arrive from Africa early that afternoon. Their murmuring talk trailed off.

Benjamin's mind drifted back to early that morning, when he stood alone on the patio, breathing deeply, watching the mist lift from the grass. Beyond the impeccable lawn was the swimming pool and then the tennis courts; all his, one day soon. His, a mansion among a colony of mansions. And the servants—how quickly he had become accustomed to the servants—that charming Latin girl; plump, ripe curves....Well, not now, of course, but soon, as the new master of the house, he would enjoy certain discreet amenities.

Benjamin took in another deep breath.

"What is it?"

Benjamin's reverie vanished. "What?"

"I heard you catch your breath."

"Oh. Nothing." Benjamin leaned over and kissed Clarisse's ear. "What if he should return early?" he whispered.

"Not Herbert. He lives on a strict schedule. His motto is Time is money."

"Oh, dear—is he really so dull? My poor, poor Clarisse."

Herbert Burgess arrived at 2:12 p.m., four minutes later than he had planned. He plunged through the front door and into the guest reception area, where Clarisse and Benjamin were waiting. He brusquely waved more speed out of his chauffeur, who followed, carrying a bulky crate.

"Herbert!" Clarisse presented her cheek to her husband. Benjamin stood behind her and to one side, grinning cheerily.

"Get that right to my den!" Burgess called out as the chauffeur entered the house. "How are you, Clarisse?" He grasped her shoulders and pecked her cheek.

"Herbert, this is Benjamin Whipple."

Burgess broke away from his wife and looked at Benjamin; his eyes were gray and quite cold. "Yes," he muttered. "Yes, yes—"

"How do you do, Mr. Burgess?" said Benjamin.

They shook hands.

"You must excuse me," Burgess said. "My chauffeur is carrying the frozen head of a gnu, and it must be treated immediately, lest it spoil." He started after the chauffeur and then stopped, glancing at Benjamin. "I do my own mounting."

They watched him hurry down the hall to his den. He unlocked the door, motioned his chauffeur inside, and quickly followed, slamming the door after himself. A few moments later, they heard the door opening and closing—the chauffeur leaving the den.

"I say," said Benjamin. "He is a bit abrupt."

"Yes," said Clarisse. "Sometimes I think he lives for those trophies of his. We must give him time."

An hour or two later, Herbert Burgess sent word that he would receive his wife and her guest in the den. They went immediately.

"Well," said Burgess as they entered. "Well, well, well." He was still wiping his hands with a towel. "You must forgive me, Mr. Whipple, for being such a poor host, but it was quite essential the trophy be prepared properly with arsenical soap. The head of a white-tailed gnu, Mr. Whipple. Or black wildebeest, as some prefer." A smile came and went. "That means nothing to you, of course. The animal is practically extinct. It was quite a find."

Benjamin had stopped a few steps beyond the threshold. The "den" had the dimensions of a baronial hall and was festooned with objets d'Afrique: the colorful, glaring, and shaggy heads of carnivora and ungulata; the spindly bodies of large African birds; drums and spears and shields and skins and unhatched eggs—an indiscriminate outpouring of Africa's mysteries. Benjamin swayed before the chaotic display, faintly hearing the barking, cawing, roaring of numberless beasts in extremis. His hand touched his forehead. He felt faint. "It is a bit overwhelming," he murmured.

"Never you mind," said Clarisse. "Herbert, why don't you fix us some drinks?"

A small zebra skin–covered bar occupied a niche among the trophies. Burgess was already there, handling bottles. "What do you prefer, Mr. Whipple?"

"Bourbon and water, please. I have acquired a taste for fine Kentucky bourbon."

"Democratic of you," said Burgess. "Clarisse and I have acquired a taste for fine British gin. So it is hands across the sea."

Clarisse had settled into an armchair upholstered with impala skin.

Benjamin, recovered somewhat, was moving among his host's trophies. He stopped before a snarling leopard's head. "Meow," he said tentatively. "Big pussycat."

"Your bourbon, Mr. Whipple."

Benjamin took the drink from Burgess and sipped at it. He winked at Clarisse and, glancing back at the leopard, said, "Meow," this time more strongly. "I wonder why a man does it," Benjamin mused. "Hunts for trophies, I mean."

"I would be interested in your opinion." Burgess had provided his wife and himself with martinis and now leaned against his bar, staring impassively at Benjamin. Since they had last seen him, Burgess had changed into a sport shirt and slacks, the shirt open at the collar, baring his sun-bronzed bull neck.

"Perhaps it makes him believe for a moment he is God. Power of life and death, you know. There he is, stalking through the jungle—the Great Hunter. Bang! Bang! And life drops dead."

Clarisse tittered. "Oh, Bunny…"

Emboldened by the bourbon, Benjamin continued. "The poor beasts actually haven't a chance. Really, old fellow, isn't trophy hunting regressive behavior? Don't you agree that it is atavistic?" Benjamin grinned disarmingly. "I don't really expect you to agree with me. I am slashing away at ideals you hold sacred."

"Yes, you are, Mr. Whipple. And most effectively." Burgess's expression had not changed; his broad face remained cold and controlled.

"Do you know, I always thought trophy collecting was like those head-hunting natives—where is it? South America somewhere? They shrink the heads of their enemies into horrid little balls and hang them about their huts by the hair. Perhaps my analogy disgusts you?"

"Not at all, Mr. Whipple."

"It disgusts me," said Clarisse. "I didn't know you could be so nasty, you naughty Bunny!"

Burgess said, "Perhaps you are right about hunting. I have been thinking lately of giving it up. It takes me away from home too often. And too long." He glanced at his wife. She was looking at him, her eyebrows raised. "Oh, I might hunt for an occasional pheasant now and then, but big game no longer interests me quite as much as it once did."

"Now you are coming around," said Benjamin. "It really isn't humane, old man."

For a moment, no one spoke.

With his empty glass held out, Benjamin approached Burgess. "I believe I should like another bourbon."

Burgess studied him closely. "Aren't you wearing one of my ties, Mr. Whipple?"

Benjamin clutched at his throat. "Dear me, so I am. I had hoped you would not notice. Yes, as a matter of fact, this is one of your ties. Clarisse offered it to me. I do hope you don't mind."

Burgess impassively handed his guest a fresh drink.

Benjamin said, "I haven't a decent tie left. And this is a bit of an occasion, isn't it?"

"Is it?"

"Of course he doesn't mind, Bunny," said Clarisse.

"You seem to be on quite intimate terms with my wife, Mr. Whipple."

Benjamin cleared his throat. "Well...yes...I suppose—"

"I am divorcing you, Herbert," Clarisse broke in casually. "Bunny and I are to be married." She speared the olive from her martini with a fingernail and popped it into her mouth. "Make me another martini, won't you?"

Burgess's bland expression did not change. The man seemed to have no emotion.

"After all, old fellow," Benjamin explained, "you are off on these hunting trips of yours, and poor Clarisse is alone for weeks on end. A warm, vital human being—and you just walk away and leave her to herself. What else can you expect?"

"Yes," said Burgess dryly. "Thoughtless of me."

"Well. So you see it is all settled. No point in fighting it now, old fellow. Clarisse has a perfectly valid case. Desertion. There isn't a judge in the state of California who would deny her justice. You must bow to the inevitable, old friend."

"I am sorry, Mr. Whipple, but it is not my nature to bow to the inevitable."

"No?"

Burgess shook his head. "No." He handed his wife a fresh martini. Clarisse returned to her antelope chair and sank into it, her eyes brightening.

"You have never been to Africa, Mr. Whipple?"

Benjamin shook his head.

"No? That's a shame."

"Yes. Isn't it odd? An Englishman quite ignorant of what was once the empire? But there you are. I find civilization more congenial."

"Yes. Civilization agrees with your kind. You should know, Mr. Whipple, that Africa is a great instructor. Africans have their own way of solving these age-old problems."

"Oh, quite, old man. But we are not in Africa, are we? This is America, you know. Courts, juries, lawyers, and such—we do not do as the savages, do we? No, we talk over such things as the civilized human beings that we are."

"We are not all that civilized." Burgess straightened and looked at him. Benjamin suddenly saw that his host's character was not impassive at all. "It is a shame that you don't know Africa. It is a magnificent land. Savage. Wild. And the home—the family—is man's sanctuary from that wilderness." Burgess was fingering a giant, steel-barbed assegai. "Do you have any notion what would be the end of a conversation like ours in the bush?" The spear flashed swiftly in the air, and in an instant it was pricking the flesh over Benjamin's heart. "The native would thrust his spear through the chest of his rival!" he shouted.

"I say!" Benjamin cried out. "Oh, I say!"

Clarisse sprang to her feet. "Herbert!"

Benjamin fell back, but the sharp point still pressed his skin. "Careful, old man!" he said. He indicated his chest. "You'll tear your tie! You don't want to damage your own tie!"

Clarisse grasped the spear and pulled it away. "Really, Herbert. How boorish! I don't know why you insist upon bringing all these silly things home with you from Africa."

Burgess replaced the weapon in its holder against the wall. "For object lessons, dear."

Benjamin pressed his palm against his chest, but failed to smooth the crease left in his host's tie by the spear tip. "I'm afraid you've ruined your cravat, old man. Hang it all, why make a scene? Divorce courts settle this sort of thing."

Discreet knuckles tap-tapped on the closed door of the den.

"Yes?"

A servant entered. "Dinner is ready."

"Very well. In a few minutes," Clarisse said.

"Yes, madam." The door closed again.

"Would you care for another bourbon and water before dinner, Mr. Whipple?" Burgess asked, his face impassive once again.

"Yes, I would, rather."

Burgess prepared another round of drinks. "I know nothing about your background, do I, Mr. Whipple?"

"I expect you don't."

"I'm sure you'll pardon my interest in my possible successor—have you been in America long?"

Benjamin told Burgess as much of himself as he had thought fit to tell Clarisse. Burgess handed the new drinks around, and after a moment's consideration said, "Then you are alone here—no friends, no family..."

"Oh, dear. Yes, it's true. I'm afraid not. It's so sad. Clarisse is all I have. She is my life."

"You seem without roots."

"Yes, yes. I've been knocking about for so long. But rejoice for me. At last, I've found the person with whom I want to live the rest of my life."

"Yes, and live well, I should imagine."

"Really, Herbert!" Clarisse exclaimed.

"That was a bit of a crude job, old fellow," Benjamin said with a grimace. "You Americans are so materialistic. You reduce everything to the holy dollar."

"If you mean to marry Clarisse, you will find money quite important," Burgess said with a smile. "Perhaps you have noticed her fondness for diamonds. What my trophies are to me, diamonds are to Clarisse."

"Ah, well, there are more important things in life than diamonds."

Burgess smiled again, for the first time with a hint of friendliness. "Have you discussed that point with Clarisse?"

Clarisse moved to the door and opened it. "Let's not talk anymore now. I'm hungry. If I have one more drink on an empty stomach, someone will have to carry me out of here."

The two men followed Clarisse into the dining room.

The dinner was quiet. Benjamin tried several times to open a discussion, at first concerning the status of the three of them and then upon general topics—the state of the country, of the world—but neither host nor hostess made a response more than perfunctory. The dessert, a lemon flan quemado with brandy sauce, was consumed in dead silence.

Burgess pushed back from the table, his chair noiselessly sliding across the deep-piled rug. "Please excuse me." He nodded curtly toward Benjamin and walked out of the room.

"After dinner he goes to the library to take his wine and smoke a cigar," Clarisse explained. Her eyes were clouded with some contrapuntal thought.

"I say, Clarisse," said Benjamin brightly, "he is a weird one. I thought I was to be skewered on the spot when he got that spear against my chest."

Clarisse nodded her head absently. "Yes."

"Really, if he returns that savage from each hunting trip, life must be touch and go around here for a day or two." Benjamin left his chair, and moving swiftly to Clarisse, knelt beside her. "Darling, we must make serious plans. Do you think he'll fight us? Do you?"

She looked at him, her fingers toying with a coffee cup. "I don't know."

"But darling, you must know. You know him better than anyone else does. Please think."

She was tapping a spoon upon the lip of her coffee cup.

"Do I make you nervous?" Benjamin asked.

"No." Her eyes turned upon him at last. "I see no reason why I should become involved in any negotiations. You work it out, you two men. If he asks to talk with you, go with him and talk to him." She sighed impatiently.

"Darling, what is it? You seem upset."

"Nothing."

Benjamin rose from his knee and looked down upon his love. "I have never seen you this way. You are as restless as the proverbial cat on a hot tin roof. Is it something I've done? I know how obtuse we British can be at times."

Clarisse sighed again.

A servant discreetly cleared his throat behind them. "Madam, Mr. Burgess will see you in the library."

Clarisse leaped to her feet and scampered out of the dining room.

Benjamin gaped after her for an instant and then followed her. When he entered the library, she was upon her husband, tugging at his sleeve. "Come on!" she cried. "Come on! Come on!"

"Find it yourself! Look around—it's hidden! Just as it always is." He was laughing.

She broke from him and her glance, bright as a terrier's, darted about the room. "In here? In this room?"

"Yes!"

"Where? Where? Where?" She pounced upon a chair and tore the cushions out of it. "Where?" She flew at the bookcases and scooped books off their shelves, stumbling among them as they crashed about her feet. "Where, Herbert, where?"

"What is it?" Benjamin cried, completely befuddled.

A table banged across the room, a chair overturned, a lamp shattered on the floor, and eager fingers sifted among its shards. "Come on, where?"

"You're getting warm!"

She stopped, her cheeks flushed, her lungs gasping for breath. A handsome vase, colored a delicate rose pink, embossed with golden figures, caught her eyes. She fell upon it and smashed it to the floor. A small jewelry box that had been concealed within it clattered against the wall.

"Oh, God! Oh, God!" She dropped to the floor. "Yes!" she moaned. "Yes! Yes!" She lifted the box tenderly and opened it, cooing gently.

Benjamin lifted himself onto his toes, but could not see what it was she was sighing and moaning over. Then she lifted the object and held it so that it sparkled, catching the light, and he saw that it was a magnificent diamond necklace.

"Like it?" Burgess asked.

Clarisse closed her eyes and clutched the necklace against her breast. She was sitting on the floor, her legs folded under her. A drop of blood formed where she had torn a bit of skin from a knuckle.

Burgess held out his hand. "Up you come." He pulled her to her feet. "Let me put it on for you."

Benjamin watched silently while Herbert Burgess hung the necklace about Clarisse's neck, the two of them amorously intimate, Clarisse shy and flushed as a bride lifting her veil for the kiss of her groom. "It's beautiful," she whispered. She went to a mirror and turned this way and that, breathing deeply, the stones flashing and coruscating upon her breasts.

Benjamin approached her and studied the necklace. "I say," he said, "that is a handsome piece of goods."

She looked at him with surprise. "Oh," she said. She had completely forgotten him.

Benjamin chuckled joylessly. "I had no idea you could rise to so ecstatic a state over such baubles."

"Dear Bunny, do you like it?" she asked, lifting it from her neck. "Isn't it beautiful, isn't it just gorgeous, gorgeous, gorgeous?"

"Oh, quite."

Clarisse returned to admiring her prize in the mirror, and for a while no one spoke.

"Oh, Clarisse, please," said Benjamin, finally losing patience. "Don't we have more important things to discuss than your diamonds?"

"Mr. Whipple is right, my dear," Burgess said.

"Yes," Clarisse agreed. "Yes, Bunny, you are right. You must talk things over."

"I just cannot understand," said Benjamin sulkily, "your, well, I can only say, highly exaggerated reaction to this gift of your husband's. Of course, it is quite valuable and beautiful, but really—"

"Forgive her," said Burgess. "The female of the species is really quite frivolous. Perhaps you have noticed."

"I like diamonds," said Clarisse flatly. "I like beautiful things very much; you must accept that, Bunny, because—"

"I do," said Benjamin quickly. "Of course, I do. Let's drop the subject, shall we?"

"And I told you before, our situation is for you two men to decide. You talk it out, the two of you." She returned to the mirror once again. Her voice softened as her eyes feasted upon her diamonds. "I just don't want to be bothered."

Burgess came to Benjamin and took his arm. "We can talk in the den."

Benjamin hesitated. "I don't—"

"Oh, Benjamin!" Clarisse said sharply. "Please!"

Burgess smiled at him. "Shall we get it over with, then?"

Benjamin went with Burgess to the den. His host came to a lion skin–covered door in a wall of the den, and opening it, motioned Benjamin through. "We'll be more private in here. The servants, you know."

Benjamin entered and Burgess followed. The door clicked shut behind them. The room was relatively small and lined with a thick, sound-absorbent corklike material. There was a work area of some sort at one end of the room with a long table covered with tools and vials and supplies of all sorts. There was a large freezer and, next to it, a furnace. The rest of the room, save for a few chairs, was bare, one strong bank of fluorescent lights overhead washing it to a somber blankness.

"My workroom, Mr. Whipple," said Burgess. "Our business will be safe from prying ears here."

Benjamin glanced back uneasily at the door through which he had entered. So fine was the crack of its outline that he could not find it in the wall. There was no knob.

"The gnu's head," Burgess was saying, "you will remember I brought with me from Africa, was taken to this room. And prepared here." He pointed to the worktable. "The excess flesh incinerated there." He pointed to the furnace door. "And is now there." He pointed to the freezer. "Waiting."

"Oh yes?"

"I have made myself an expert, Mr. Whipple, in preparing animals of all sorts for mounting." He leaned casually against the wall. "I began my study of taxidermy with rabbits. Small, helpless rabbits. But stuffed rabbits have a way of seeming to multiply. I graduated to larger animals. Because I am an ambitious man, Mr. Whipple, a hungry man. I have large appetites—"

"All this is quite interesting," Benjamin said nervously. "But, after all, it is not what we came here to discuss, is it?"

"Yes, Mr. Whipple, it is," said Burgess. He lifted a pistol from his pocket and pointed it at Benjamin.

"Wha-What?" stuttered Benjamin. "What are you doing?"

"Has it struck you, Mr. Whipple, how much this little room resembles an abattoir?" asked Burgess.

Benjamin backed up against the wall. "You're joking with me! You don't actually intend to murder me. No! Ridiculous!" Benjamin turned suddenly and scrabbled at the wall where there ought to have been a door, but nothing gave. He faced Burgess again.

"Very well, I'll leave. I shall go away and I'll never see Clarisse again. She was lonely. She doesn't really love me. Please, you must understand that. What difference can it make to you if I go away—it's all the same, isn't it?"

Burgess shook his head and raised the pistol.

"You are insane! Clarisse will hear—"

"Clarisse has her diamonds." Burgess shook his head at Benjamin again as one would at a dull-witted child. "Don't you understand?"

Quite suddenly, Benjamin did understand. He was staggering in the clear flame of revelation when Burgess pulled the trigger.

"You may come in now, dear."

For hours, while Herbert Burgess had worked in the little room adjoining his den, Clarisse had drifted in a diamond dream, casting light this way and that across her neck, holding small, twinkling mirrors in her palms, exploring all possible angles of reflection. She heard her husband calling to her through the half-opened door to the den finally, and she put away the lights and the mirrors and went to him, ravished by the weight of the cold stones upon her skin.

The gnu's head was mounted at the end of the room near the door. Burgess was standing before it, holding two glasses of champagne. When she entered. he held a glass out to her. "Our traditional toast, dear."

They stood solemnly, lifted their glasses toward the gnu's head for a moment, and then sipped at their drinks.

"I am afraid we are creatures of habit," Burgess said and sighed.

"Yes, we are."

"Do you want to see him?"

"All right."

Burgess put his drink down and pulled a small ladder so that it stood under the head of the gnu. He mounted the ladder and lifted the animal's head from the wall. "What do you think?"

"He looks almost alive."

Benjamin Whipple gazed down at them through his protective sphere of plastic, grinning, a small bead of saliva glistening in the gap between his teeth. "I thought that a realistic touch," Burgess remarked. "A bit of plastic."

"It looks very natural," said Clarisse. She turned away and sipped at her champagne.

Burgess replaced the gnu's head, and descended the ladder.

"When you described him to me in your letter, I thought a gnu, being an ugly fellow, and quite stupid, would be appropriate. And a rare white-tailed gnu—what other specimen could a sportsman mount without suspicion?"

They stood in silence, holding their champagne glasses. Their glances moved together down the row of African animals, past the white-tailed gnu, the giraffe, the Cape buffalo, past the warthog, past the two lion heads and the leopard head, past the waterbuck and the sable antelope, past the rhino and the nyala, past the kudu, the marsh buck, and the giant eland—and rested finally upon the last trophy at the end of the room: the small, mild head of a North American mule deer.

Clarisse sighed. "He was the best. So sweet." She sighed a longer sigh. "It seems so long ago—"

Burgess stroked her hair sentimentally. "Your first diamond brooch."

Suddenly she tensed and moved away from him. "Is it true, what you told Bunny? Are you giving up hunting?"

"I'm considering it quite seriously." He looked at her, studying her closely for the first time in a long while, seeing the marks of aging: the blotching, the wrinkles about her eyes and girding her throat, and the deep lines cut in the sides of her mouth. A few more years and the skin would be too loose to smooth into the appearance of youth.

"I still want my diamonds!" she said sharply, stroking the stones about her neck. "Besides, you have room on the wall." She pointed to the single space left on the wall opposite the gnu's head.

"Very well," Burgess agreed, "one more trophy." He took her into his arms and held her, and while her fingertips slid again and again across her diamond necklace, he commenced planning for the closing of the circle, the mounting of the last trophy.

Yes, the time was approaching for the slaughter of the Judas goat.

FALL INTO
THE SUN

AFTER the breakup with his wife, Grayson took the bus across the bridge into San Francisco. He thought he could stay in a cheap hotel, but he was broke. He ended up in Golden Gate Park. The park was flat and open. You could sleep almost anywhere. There were others, each with his own wound. They showed him how to live on the street—where to beg, which agencies would help, and which would not. Sometimes he would join them in their camps, drinking, laughing along with their end-of-the-line laughter, with the camaraderie that meant nothing. Day by day, his spirit weakened, freezing in the ice field of the hopeless. Still, he cherished hope. One day he would go north across the Bay and rebuild the life he had destroyed. So he settled into the life of the park while the weeks and months wasted themselves.

That all ended the night of the murder. It was drugs, of course. He wasn't into that life, but as the others said afterward, it could have been anyone. In the dark, they could think you were the one they wanted, and they'd get that knife to your throat before you could move. The man's desperate cries woke him. He lay, tense and frightened, listening to the gagging sounds of dying. Nearby, they were whispering: "We should help him!" "Stay here! They'll think you're with him!" "He'll die!" "Let him die!"

He lay awake until morning came. The thought of staying longer in the park sickened him. With the first light, he gathered his things and left, not looking toward the brush where the dead man lay.

He found a new place. He rode a bus up a hill through a quiet neighborhood. Where the bus stopped and turned to go back down the hill, there was a park crowning the hill. A few dirt paths wound through the eucalyptus and pine, sloping up or down, rarely level. Leaf–strewn paths amid much shrubbery, and thickets with slim tree trunks like rusted iron bars disappearing into thick greenery. Whatever grew was untended, except if a tree fell across a path it would be cut and shoved downhill. Off and on, a few others would come to live in the park, but soon the isolation of the place would bother them and they would leave. The park was too far from the streets where you could pick up some money and it took too long on the bus to get to The General Assistance office on Mission Street. But the loneliness suited him. He stayed several places in the park, moving usually for greater comfort but sometimes because of the cops.

They would find his place, gather his things, and trash them. Once, they caught him. A hiker had seen him through the trees and pointed him out. That time, they took him out of the park with all his goods.

"We don't want to see you here again," they told him.

Finally, he found a way to work himself into the deep shrubbery. From the street, all that could be seen was a twenty-foot rock face with knots of plants embedded in it; above the rock were high bushes. But he found that stepping through a crevice, down one ledge and then another, he could reach the street. Hearing the sounds of the living in the surrounding city, he didn't feel he was alone. He slept under the bushes in among the bugs, small animals, and birds; an animal himself. He defecated each day or so, choosing a different place each time: here a church restroom, there under a tree, then into a brown bag tossed into a dumpster, against a wall now and then, left there for the owner to find. And he drank cheap, sweet wine, killer of appetite, drinking by day and by night, carefully taking the empty bottles away from his lair.

And every few weeks, General Assistance. He would stand in line, do the things and take the shape the desks expected of you; sad and sick and mad at the exploiting elite; say the words the desks wanted to hear and then you'd be paid. And the free meals and the cheap meals and the dental school and the teaching hospital; the students, one after the other, peering at you, into you, and one day they'll slice and saw apart your body—see if they remember you. And the prayers of the holy, the tears of the tenderhearted, and all the rest of the useless gestures. Sometimes he wondered if his dying would not be the best for everyone. He would feel the pulse in his leg, the place that, once cut, would stay cut. Then laugh at himself and drink his wine. *Who am I kidding? I don't have the nerve.* And he would laugh again about his dying.

The day he had sworn to himself he would see his wife and his son finally came. It was a Saturday, early in June. He hadn't gone the year before, though he had sworn that he would. There had been the rain and the cold. And the drinking. He knew he had to be clean. Three years—too much life had been lived. People forget, even the only people you love. It would be walking back into life, to see her again. And his boy. How old would he be? Eleven? Certainly, it didn't have to be today. It could be tomorrow, Sunday. Or it could be next weekend. And what if they had gone, moved away?

What do you expect after all this time, they're going to stick around just in case you stop by? "She kicked you out, damn it!" He spoke the words aloud. He looked around, though he knew no one could hear. He shook his head. She was right. When his job moved out of state and he couldn't find another like it, he could have looked for something else or gone back to school or done a lot of things. He closed his eyes, grimacing, pressing a clenched fist against his forehead.

His biggest mistake had been bringing the bottles into the house, drinking when she was at her job and the boy was at school. He had wanted to keep his drinking in the bar, but it just cost too much. Once the unemployment ran out, he had to cut back. He hated drinking alone. It put it right in front of you, that you were there, alone in the house only to drink, only to get drunk and stay drunk. He fought it. I ought to be looking for a job, any job. I owe it to her and the boy, he would go on. I can't let this thing get away from me; I've got to control it. And he would try. One day, nothing. Then the next day, because he had drunk nothing the day before, he would allow himself a shot or two. The third day, it would all collapse, and he might finish the bottle and go out and get another.

Then one day she came home early.

He opened his eyes, blinking, pushing away the memories. He had drunk nothing since the middle of May, almost a month. It could go on and on. He wouldn't ever start again. He stood and pushed aside the branches that hid his place and stepped out onto the rock. First, he would have to clean up.

The Laundromat was at the bottom of the hill, where the bus turned. When he walked in, two Asian girls were working five tubs of dirty clothes. They pretended not to see him. A lanky kid sitting on a washer grinned at him. In a little alcove beside the last dryer, Grayson stripped his clothes off and wrapped a ragged towel around his middle. As he threw his clothes into a washer tub, an older woman with red hair and rimless glasses came into the Laundromat. She stopped, staring at him. She might have said something: he should wear a shirt, he shouldn't walk around with bare feet…but the long hair and the beard kept her quiet. You never know, he could be one of the crazy ones; the kind that would follow you down the street, yelling at you, with only a towel on. Not stopping to fold them, she pulled her clothes out of the dryer and pushed them into a sack. She left quickly, scowling once at him from the door.

Of course, the beard would have to go, and the hair would have to be trimmed back. It was a little tricky, but after you had done it a few times, and didn't confuse yourself looking into a mirror, you could do a fairly good job. He had brought scissors and razor, and he started in over the laundry tub.

The grin on the lanky kid's face grew bigger. "Why don't you go to the barber college?"

"No money."

"Hair like that, they'd do for free. For practice. You ought to go."

He brushed away some loose hair and looked up. "You ever cut hair?" The kid shook his head, still grinning. "You want to try?"

The kid haw-hawed a couple of times, looking away. He slid down from the machine he had been sitting on and sauntered out to the street.

Once Grayson got the hair off his shoulders, he trimmed it further with a few more cuts. It felt neat enough. He started on the beard. He finished by washing his head under the tap with laundry soap, then rubbing his soapy hands over his body, down his legs, between his toes. Flinging the towel onto the floor, he changed into his clothes, still warm from the dryer. He walked outside, where the kid was watching the traffic pass by.

Grayson gestured at his hair. "What do you think?"

The kid shrugged, not smiling. "My stuff's ready," he said and went back inside the Laundromat.

Down the street from the Laundromat, there was a mirror and picture frame store. In its window was a large, almost full-length, mirror. He had passed it many times, not looking, sometimes seeing from the edge of his vision an image, moving with him across the face of the mirror. He avoided mirrors. What did his face, the way he looked, matter? He didn't care what they saw, looking at him. Mirrors were for other people, people with jobs and careers. Anyway, what would he see? Himself, only different. The same face, only altered; what did it matter? You looked at yourself because other people did. When they stopped looking, or looked at you a certain way, then, hell, let them look.

Today, he walked to the store and stood in front of the mirror, his head down. He meant to look today. This was what she would see, and he wanted her to like it. He stared down at the tops of his shoes, seeing the traces of the scuffs he had rubbed at with the wet towel in the Laundromat, then closed his eyes. Almost shyly, he lifted his head and stared at his reflection. It was him and it wasn't him. He brushed at his hair with his hand. His skin had browned and coarsened. There were lines he didn't remember. His eyes were reddened, as if he had been crying. He laughed, but the laugh didn't make the look go away. *Well, so what? It's still me.* He studied his clothes, smoothed a wrinkle against his body. He looked again into his eyes and then turned away with a shrug.

He caught a Muni bus downtown, and at the Transbay Terminal waited for the Marin County bus. There were a few men holding out dirty cardboard cups. They looked at him, grinning. One of them offered his cup.

"Help yourself," he said.

Grayson smiled, shaking his head. In a clear plastic funnel, he held the dozen roses he had bought for her. He should have something for the boy, too, but he couldn't think what. Money would be best anyhow, so he had a fresh twenty dollar bill in his pocket. He wondered how they would greet him. Best to think they would embrace him, welcome him in, and offer him a cold drink. He and she would sit and talk, and he would tell her how he had changed. She would squeeze his hand and ask him why he hadn't come home sooner. She would tell him how they had missed him. It wouldn't be like the time before, when he had tried to tell her he had a disease, that alcoholism was a disease, and she wouldn't listen.

"It's a weakness, not a disease," she had said.

Now he would tell her she was right, and that it was everything that was wrong, not just the drinking, everything that he had done. And not done. He would tell her he was clean now, that he hadn't touched anything for almost four weeks. And so now they could start a new life together.

On the bus, he pressed back into his seat and let his muscles untense. Through the window, he watched the water of the bay sparkling through the breath of fog blowing under the bridge. Steadily and solemnly, the bus moved up the gentle arch of the bridge and down. On the far side of the bridge, looking down on Fort Baker, he saw his first view, after nearly three years, of Marin County. The bus moved uphill, through the tunnel, and down again, the wheels rolling close to the edge of the concrete. The roll of the bus reminding him of that other bus, the one that had taken him to the City after their long night of fighting, ending with the boy getting up in the middle of the night and walking, sleepy-eyed, into the kitchen, and she grabbing him and holding him close, not letting Grayson near either one of them. He had left them in the morning. He had told himself he'd straighten it all out in the City and go back to them in a week or so.

He closed his eyes, slowly rubbing his face. When he reopened them, he saw Mount Tamalpais through the windshield over the driver's shoulder. Green and serene. He smiled, remembering her say that, and remembering again, as he often did, that one special day with her on the mountainside, when walking up the path had seemed to be wading through an inversion layer; warm air on their faces, cool air chilling their bare legs, the demarcated temperature moving slowly up and down their bodies like ocean surf, until farther up the path they had stepped fully into the warmth. They had smiled, then laughed and squeezed each other. He was smiling now, trying to recall what they had said to each other.

He glanced at the driver and saw he was staring at him from the rearview mirror. For a moment, Grayson was confused. Had he said something out loud? Or had he laughed? He smiled and the driver looked back at the road. *It's all right*, he thought, *it's really going to be all right. All you need is the love of your family and you can do anything.* It didn't have to be a profession: all it had to be was a job. Anybody could get a job.

When the bus arrived at the station, he went into the restroom and sprinkled a few drops of water on the flowers he was carrying. It was warmer here than in the City. He smiled into the mirror over the basin, this time seeming more familiar to himself.

It was not a long walk from the station to the corner where he turned onto their street. It was the same leafy street with the fifty-year-old one-story bungalows, with seeds and leaves collected on the roofs, left there until the days of rain came again, and modest cars lined bumper to bumper against the curb. He hesitated and then walked until he was across from their house. He stared at it, trying to see through the blank stucco wall. He looked for movement inside and saw none. Probably she was in back, doing the laundry. He could feel himself breathing, his chest rising and falling.

All right. Go over. Ring the bell. He took a few steps and stopped. A woman was on the sidewalk across the street, walking toward the house. He watched her with a sudden fear. He remembered that hat and those sunglasses against the very white skin and the walk—the slow, pacing walk. She moved nearer, not looking at him. *Let her reach the house.* He stepped to the curb, about to call out to her, and then saw it was not her. *God, I'm crazy.* He wiped his lips and laughed. He went across the street and up the short walkway to the door. He pressed the bell and remembered the sound the chimes made. He waited a moment and then tried again. *She's in back. You can't hear the door when you're in back doing the laundry.* He went around the house to the sliding glass doors. He rapped on the door, looking inside. *Maybe she's not here.* He grinned, stepping back. *Yes, that's it. She's out. I could come back tomorrow. Or wait around here until—*

He caught the movement out of the corner of his eye, and then she was past him, up the few steps, sliding open the door and blocking the opening with her body before he could move; a compact Chinese woman.

"What you want?" Her voice was harsh and loud.

He blinked and shook his head. "You live here?"

"I say, what you want?"

"I want—" He stopped. "My name is James Grayson. My wife is here. I mean, not here, but—"

She shrank back through the door opening, staring at him. "You go!"

"I used to live here. My wife—" He held up the rose bouquet for her to see.

She slid the door shut and clicked the lock. "You go now!" she cried out from behind the glass.

He tried smiling at her. "I just want to know, because we lived here before—"

"You must go now! I call 911!" She glared at him threateningly. She made a quick movement with her arm toward a telephone.

"Okay, okay. I'm going." He waved his arms limply. He turned and walked back to the sidewalk. The woman was watching him from a window.

Why didn't I believe she could have moved? He took a few steps, then stopped, confused. He looked back at the house. The woman was still looking at him. *I've got to get out of here. She's going to call somebody.* Then he remembered the Reynolds. They lived just next door and they were friends. She would have told the Reynolds where she had moved to. He rang their bell, smiling. They had spent some good times together; they were good people. He heard movement behind the door.

The door opened and a man he had never seen before, dark and lean, stood looking at him. "Yes?"

"Hello. Are the Reynolds here? I'm looking for the Reynolds."

"Don't know them."

"They're friends of mine. And my wife's. They used to live here."

"No Reynolds here. It's Ruiz now."

"They lived here. Maybe you know—"

The man frowned, his eyes suddenly small and mean. "I tole you, man, I don't know those people, okay?"

Grayson smiled again. "Okay. But maybe you know—"

"Hey, man, what's your problem?" He waved an arm. "Get away from here! I don't know your people."

Grayson backed a few steps down the walk, trying to smile.

"Váyase! Go away! Okay?"

Grayson turned away. From the sidewalk, he saw the Asian woman still staring at him from her house. He didn't want to walk past that house again. He continued down the street.

What could he do next? How would he find her? His thoughts kept pulling him back to the woman behind the sliding glass door crying out at him, her eyes frightened and angry. He would have to replan everything. He would have to start from the beginning again.

He reached the street corner and remembered the two of them strolling together in the evening. He was walking now where he had walked with her. So little had really changed; the same trees, the same houses, the same cars. There was the alley between the open carports serving the double row of apartment houses, and in front of them, the line of mustard-blossomed trees. He walked to the next block, where the better homes began, and where they had once dreamed of living. He saw again through the trees the rise of the hill and on its crest the large house with its gleaming white balcony.

He heard her saying, "That's where we start from."

"That's right," he had said. "That's the real place we start from. Let's walk up there."

She shook her head. "No. Someday we'll pile all our furniture in a truck. That's how we'll go there."

He took her hand and started toward the hill. "Come on."

"No!" She pulled away from him. "I mean it. I don't want to see it any closer unless that's where we're going and not coming back." She was serious.

"You are crazy," he said, with a laugh.

Afterward, when they would walk that way, they would stop and look up the hill, not speaking. Grayson, looking up now at the house on the hill, forgot the roses he still held and let his arm fall to his side. The roses loosened in their plastic holder. He reached down to stop their fall and then shrugged, letting them spill to the ground, watching each stem as it slipped away. He stared at the pile of blossoms on the ground, not really thinking of anything. A drop gathered at the end of a stem and fell on a pink petal, beading it with moisture. He reached down to pick up the blossom, then straightened, shaking his head.

He waited at the station for the bus that would return him to the City. Stepping under a canopy, he wiped a film of perspiration from his face. The sky was clear blue and the sun nearly overhead. He liked the warmth, but his body wasn't used to it.

He noticed a skinny white cross rising through the shrubs at the top of a nearby hill, and thought of the massive cross at the top of his own hill. Under that heavy concrete cross, worshippers would gather at sunrise each Easter morning. His first year, he was there, too, standing apart from the others, trying to worship. Before the service was over, he had backed away, back into the trees, away from those people who seemed to be singing hymns in a strange language, speaking words that had lost meaning for him.

That night, he dreamed he was no longer sane, that he had joined the others in the streets, the schizophrenics and the other crazies, his mind invaded by the strange and the incomprehensible, staring back at a world that he had left. He woke in the dark with an agonized cry, his chest heaving.

On the bus he took the first seat, opposite the driver, next to the window. A gray-haired woman in a white T-shirt sat behind the driver, and with the movement of the bus, her eyes slowly closed. His eyes closed, too. He became aware of the rushing traffic noise and the driver shifting down and then down again, and the cars moving faster past the bus as it slowed going up the hill.

He dozed, then opened his eyes. Looking out the window, he saw Mount Tamalpais in full view, rising pyramidlike to its peak. The mountain meant nothing to him now; it was only an impassive monument of nature. He took a deep breath. The bus was descending the hill to the bridge and the City beyond it. Fog from the ocean was falling over the rough hillside, cold, white streamers reaching out toward him. Crossing the bridge, he looked toward the ocean, not the side people leaped from. That was on the other side, where people stood on the broad sidewalk looking inland over the Bay.

I'm sitting on the ocean side, not the side for suicide. He smiled to himself. *The ocean side, not the suicide.* He smiled again, repeating the phrase in his mind. Looking forward, he saw the bridge's far end washed away by the fog entering the Bay. Soon, the City would be a chill gray.

In the park, he approached his place cautiously, as always, looking and listening, walking past the hidden path, stopping and looking around once again before entering. He was tired. He slept, then woke, then slept again, and then was finally awake, unable to push the thoughts away any longer. He rolled onto his side.

The Asian woman's face came back to him. She wouldn't listen to him. She was frightened. What would his wife do when she saw him again? Perhaps she'd be frightened, too. And the boy. Again, he heard the sound of the glass door sliding in its track, the lock clicking, the woman's hard voice: "You go!" Perhaps if he had caught her, kept her from going inside, and made her listen, maybe now he'd know where his wife had gone. *I should have stopped her. I should have made her listen to me.* He shook his head. *No, there could have been real trouble.*

He sat up. He forced a smile and then a laugh. He thought again of slicing the artery pulsing in his leg. *Someday, people are going to see me, and there'll be blood all over.* He laughed. It was just a comedy. *I ought to have that mirror now and see what a dummy looks like.* He laughed again, this time a real laugh. He looked up through the trees toward the gray sky. It really was funny; just because today hadn't worked out, everything had to be over? No, he was going to keep looking. He wiped his lips. He had stopped drinking for her. He could stop drinking for her again. He knew he couldn't ever drink and be with her. But finding her could be weeks away. Months away. He needed a drink. He took the twenty dollar bill he had meant for his son from his pocket. Sherry. Two bottles. Enough for the rest of the day and the night. He stuffed the money back into his pocket.

He moved slowly toward the break in the cliff wall, stopping to look at the house tops through the trees. He heard a bus passing up the hill on the boulevard beyond. He was sick of the sound of buses. He walked faster down the trail, sliding on the dry eucalyptus leaves. Reaching the break in the cliff, he slipped again on the leaves and his feet went out from under him, pitching him forward over the cliff edge into the air.

When his eyes opened, it was nearly dark. He felt confused. His leg hurt. It was that pain in his leg that had pulled him up into consciousness. He rolled onto his back and moaned. He straightened out his leg slowly. It was swollen but didn't seem broken. Lying on his back, he remembered shouting, throwing his arms out, and dropping heavily, all in an instant. *What a damn fool! What more can happen today?* He cursed and laughed, rubbing his leg. He'd have to get help, probably end up in General Hospital. He pounded his fist on the ground. *Damn! Damn it all!*

He had fallen behind shrubbery, lit by streetlights not far from the edge of the pavement. He'd have to get to one of the houses across the street, ring the bell, and ask for help. He closed his eyes. He didn't want to move. Maybe somebody would come along and bring help. He looked up at the darkening sky, thinking again of the day now past and what he would have to do to find his wife. He pictured her as he had so many times before, her eyes condemning him, and then finally relenting. And the boy, almost a man now. James Edward Grayson Jr. As he repeated the name, he drifted into sleep.

Again the pain roused him, pounding at him insistently. Night had come. He grabbed the trunk of a tree and pulled himself up onto his good leg. He tried a step but he couldn't walk. Letting himself down on his knee, he found a fallen tree limb. Using it, he pushed himself up. Teetering, almost falling, holding the tree limb under his arm, he slowly worked his way around the shrubs to the street.

The nearest house was lit, its living room curtains flickering with bluish light cast by the television. A trim Spanish-style house, with an orange tile roof and white stucco walls. Crossing the street, Grayson stumbled and fell, wincing from the twist the fall gave his leg. He lay in the middle of the street and then pushed himself up again. Reaching the house, he rested, leaning against the door. A small light shone on the doorbell, and a plaque above it announced in gold letters on a black background, G. W. Lui.

Ming-Hwa, the wife of Gong Wei Lui, rose from her cushioned chair, stretching her body during the break in the drama on the television, a sad story in Cantonese. It was the time of day she enjoyed more than any other. She glanced at Gong Wei, nodding in his chair, tired from work or bored perhaps, ignoring her in his tiredness. She would prepare some tea later, once the play was over, and the two of them would sip tea through the first few minutes of the next drama in Mandarin, trying to follow the players. Then she would rinse the cups and they would retire. Perhaps he would want to make love. She felt that taking in his member would calm her, would transport her. Their lovemaking was becoming better, now that they were past the early awkwardness, now that they knew each other better in the marriage that had been arranged from across the Pacific Ocean. She stretched again and sighed, looking fondly at the television screen, where her attention would return once the merchants had hawked their goods.

The doorbell rang. It must be Tan Lee and her husband, she thought. They had told her that perhaps they would stop by so they could share the play together. Smiling, she opened the door.

There was a stranger, a man, a Caucasian, disheveled, leaning on their door, a club in his hand, speaking the rough, flat words the whites spoke. She stumbles back. She crys out softly and when he takes a shaky step forward into their house, she screams.

Behind her, Lui leaps to his feet. "Why did you open the door?" he shouts. "Stupid!"

Ming-Hwa steps back twice, three times, gasping frightened sobs.

Lui yells at her furiously, "Get out of the way! You fool! You made a terrible mistake!" He waves her away. "You dumb country woman! Get out of my way!"

Facing the intruder, forgetting his English, Lui yells, "Get out of my house! Get out!"

But the stranger moves forward, gripping the door, lifting the club from under his arm.

Quickly, Lui snatches his pistol from the hall cupboard. "Get out now!" he shouts.

The intruder, talking rapidly, lurches toward him, brandishing his stick.

Don't shoot to wound, they had told him, shoot to kill! Holding his weapon with both hands and crouching for greater stability, Lui takes the position they had shown him. Again the intruder violently pushes the club toward Lui, balancing crazily on his legs, crying out something. Lui, his hands not shaking as he had feared they might, fires twice into the white man's chest.

The first bullet cuts clean through, searing Grayson's flesh; the second strikes bone, knocking him backward onto the concrete walkway. Falling, Grayson wonders how he could tumble once again down the rock wall that he knew so well, falling farther than he remembered.

Lying dazed on the ground with warmth and aching cold pulsing through his body, he is with her again on the mountainside, the cold air and the warm air wrapping about their bodies and the two of them embracing, her eyes bright with love and forgiveness and a fierce blaze bursts out in his chest, a column of fire roars up into his throat, into his brain, and with sudden fury burns itself out into cinders and darkness.

DEBLIN

THERE IS DEBLIN; your and my Deblin fantastic ambitious wakeful hunted expression. A wood slab head dark with dirt and age old coveralls worn sometimes work day times; other days Sundays holidays baggy brown jacket gray trousers muddy brown shoes the big dangling hands pushed into coat pockets knuckles bulging through the cloth. His face long lank mournful, a dark moon. Work day workman work things work prepare for get ready mornings in the dark winter spooning stiff porridge from the cracked chipped bowl dark room hands arms moving about before the dawn silent lips sealed mind wandering among silent numb things. Strange heartbreaking morning awakening. Distillation of the others in distant homes rooms apartments ready to converge on the cold machinery the fetid buses streetcars the autos coughing and fuming the ripped-up unhappy slave aware surrendering to the other men still in bed warm rooms drowsy breakfast softly served the soft gentle awakening, the sweetness of indulgence and the laughing women. Deblin! An obscure bolt, a wood screw squeezed into a tight socket a number punch card Social Security draft card, fingerprints innocuous heavy work hand pressed into the black ink of bad check passers and murderers, innocent guileless servant pressed into dirty malleable ready heartsick life bleeding out in a thousand minutes the seconds each hour day year robbed first white hairs carious teeth forgotten sweetnesses senses closed brief angers, wakes solemn wakes shuddering with tears for a thousand other things trembling beside a corpse not yet his own.

Deblin's car, shattered wrecked transmission growling knocking cylinders greased soiled seat cushions. Working man's car. Transportation. Each day struggling, fighting the nameless tormented beast of steel. The hard cold machinery. Each day everywhere the machinery cold waiting numbered like Deblin manufactured with the name of Toledo Cleveland Chicago Philadelphia painted black hard grease coating everywhere.

Each day spent in winter the summer telescoped, a faraway view, winter all about, the cold thrust everywhere cold fingers gloves legs toes ears the heart pulsing helplessly somewhere the heart somewhere the soul caked over forgotten unnecessary nonmachine senses plugged-up forgotten.

Deblin in his car in the cold the starter throbbing. The car pock pock sputter die. And again. And again. And a roar and then the accelerator roar, another two miles and the heater heats the snow struggle the slip-slide of worn tires across the snow to the slushed street cold hands on the steering wheel cold feet Deblin hunched forward staring out the windshield on his way to work. Deblin inarticulate. Deblin dumb Deblin voiceless a solemn animal groan a groan moan from birth healthy freshness to death worn out old shucked off. Deblin in his car. Four steel walls and top and bottom; glass so the authorities can look in. And numbers stamped other numbers motor serial series driver's license registration the world reaching into Deblin's steel tomb stamping typing printing numbers. A highway number. Deblin's highway. His name, a number a hasty notation vital statistic employee garnishee taxpayer more numbers the money in his wallet in the bank in the hands of creditors all skimmed off the crust of existence the numbers of tomorrows mortgaged spent the interest payment gliding into already stuffed pockets. Deblin mortgaged to the mortician on the corner waiting patiently impassively for his payment. Fierce birds licking his skull clean sopping up the juices skimming gleaning sowing their contracts in Deblin's trusting nature. He will pay. How many years on the job? He will pay. How high the interest? Tax him. Higher tax. Bind him down poor dumb fool. The ancient profitable trust. Give as little as we can. Take as much as we can. Come on cream-filled hands dip in this is Deblin silent dumb Deblin.

Wake up in the sudden heartache morning Deblin. Fifty years. Ten years more, sixty. Tomorrow all the creatures that fall on your body will find bones. Cast away Deblin.

Deblin in his car, Deblin clammy cold eyes sealed ahead thoughts drifting moody in a sour light. Today yesterday. Yesterday today. Tomorrow. All days. From where flow the broad rivers the waters cold from where? A cold glacier shedding moisture in a northern day drooling out its body onto the wastelands. From the deep crushed ice under the body of the vast moving crushing grind of ice the glacial stream the echo of Deblin's soft moan the night moan the lonely awakening in the night moan the cars moving out in the street the streetlight the cold bed the heart's cry aching. Still he lives has lived. The great dumb mouth. The silent brain picking about among its tiny pangs.

Deblin remembers. In his car the sudden heat of remembrance biting into his cold skull the last night moan the crazy staring face staring down into his heavy-lidded eyes the face long moaning tiny smile sudden deep-down laugh the face hovering above his cold bed night wind in-blowing. Deblin's face.

"Wherefore? Where from? Where to?"

Deblin stares.

"Take my hand."

"What?"

The face blinks disappears bobs back disappears.

Deblin sleeps. And the hollow vast bobbing face question interrogation. Why this inquisition?

Deblin wakes.

"Take my hand."

"Where do we go?" Deblin wants to sleep.

"No matter. Find my hand."

Only a face. No hand. Deblin casts about in the darkness. No hand. "I cannot find your hand."

"I have no hand." The face smiles, disappears.

Deblin in his car. Bleak machinery. A face without hands, he wonders. And as he ponders the cold street bursts into Deblin's skidding car steel crushing bloodied steel with sudden agony. Devlin screams into the dark.

Silent waiting hands feel in his pockets a coin a bill a receipt a check anything more? Keep looking.

Deblin. Philbert D. 121-18-6655. 180 A21. 1305. All the numbers. Hands in the pockets faces overhead unfriendly only searching through. Businesslike. No compassion. Oh, I didn't know the man. Kept pretty much to himself. Didn't have much to say. Used to eat his lunch alone. Strange sort. Strange fellow.

Numbers, sheets of numbers. Floods of numbers…tell you everything. Name an anachronism. Obituary column the name. No good a name. The parents name father mother relatives children progeny contributions to the unending no name generations.

And the birds fly away the flesh-eating birds. The flesh gone plucked pulled bitten. The worn sagging limp flesh that had nutriment. Birds flocks of birds skies full of birds whirling and wheeling blackening the sun, testing their ever stronger wings, bringing into cozy aeries their fierce young, born with eyes rapacious flesh-bent. The thousand raptors banking wheeling overhead.

I, HARRISON SEABROOK...

I REMEMBER IT AS a rainy day in late spring when I found myself sitting in the parlor of Mrs. Anderson, looking into her solemn face across a cup of tepid tea. Mrs. Anderson was one of those inane persons who presume to foretell events. Who has not known one of her kind? Who has not a friend who is "psychic"? Surely, prophecy is a most ingenuous pastime. Still, there is a peculiar sort of person—not I—to whom a known future appeals.

She was saying, "Knowing the future, Mr. Seabrook, is truly a most basic talent of human beings. We have simply forgotten our heritage. The ancients knew. You know, Mr. Seabrook, the ancients were wonderful people."

"Very likely," I said.

"Oh yes, it is true. They were wonderful human beings."

She shook her head and a strand of sandy hair fell across her flushed forehead. "Did you know that I predict the future, Mr. Seabrook?"

I smiled and looked into the depths of my teacup.

"Oh, I do not tell you this to impress you. I very rarely tell anyone about my knowledge of the future. It is a sacred thing with me. Most sacred."

My mind wandered. She continued on about her Delphic abilities, but I thought how unlikely a nest Boston was to hatch the egg of prophecy. Here, we look back upon Boston's august past, and that is all that we hold to be valuable. For we know that the past extends with unbroken continuity to the present and to us, and thus we hold the past to be more than moribund. It is our responsibility, our joy, and our sustenance. Who among us looks forward without pain when feeling the change, the violation of all that has gone before? How well we know that the future must be less than the past. So while Mrs. Anderson prattled on, telling me of the nobility of her pursuit, I remarked to myself what short shrift her talent must receive on the banks of the Mystic. Poor Sally Anderson!

"Would you like to know your future?"

The soprano ring of Mrs. Anderson's voice hung in the air like an evening church bell.

After a pause, I smiled, wondering how I could contrive to depart. "I am not sure that I do."

"I can tell it to you, you know."

I found her confidence unsettling. I put my cup down upon the glass-topped table in front of me. Too late came the thought that she might well snatch the cup from its saucer and set about dredging up intimate revelations from its arrangement of tea leaves.

"Some claim they can read tea leaves," remarked Mrs. Anderson archly, reading my thought, "but they are only guessing. One either knows the future or one does not. One does not need tea leaves." She leaned forward, staring at me portentously. "There is violence in your future, Mr. Seabrook."

I stared at her a moment and then I rose. "It has been such a pleasure to chat with you, Mrs. Anderson. I trust you will find Boston to be more than even your pleasantest of expectations."

We walked into the hallway across a threadbare carpet and stood for a moment at the front door, chatting of inconsequential things. Her hand reached out and patted my wrist, as one would the head of a sick dog. "I don't wonder you wish to leave so suddenly, Mr. Seabrook," she said. "Oh no, I don't wonder." Her hand clasped mine, her face quite serious. "Do be careful."

"Good evening," I murmured.

I walked out into the street. The New England sun was glimmer-

moodily through the usual overcast. The rain had stopped. Everything seemed in place, all quite oblivious of my momentary panic. While I walked, I coaxed reason into jestingly reasserting itself. The whole situation was, of course, absurd—that I should be upset over the maundering of a dowdy Cassandra! Nevertheless, I found myself gingerly thinking of Mrs. Anderson's prediction. Odd it is that the most outrageous conviction of another can half convince oneself. It was absurd.

Violence and Harrison Seabrook had always been quite contradictory propositions. During the war, when bombs were crashing into London streets, I was stationed in the quiet north of England, far, even, from most of my own compatriots in the south. On but one occasion, when a crippled Atlantic patrol plane burst unannounced over that somber little army village, did I hear an air raid siren squawk out in real fear. Those halcyon days while empire struggled with empire, and democrat and fascist descended together into the furnace of oblivion, I passed secure as a nut in its shell, far from the thunder of conflict. And now, here in Boston, the most nonviolent of American cities (my Boston, at any rate), any sort of threat to my person seemed absurdly farfetched.

Mrs. Anderson was a friend of a friend of mine. Betty Johnson is a most dear friend. I had known Betty eight years, since she had come to work for Lodge, Jones and Company from some obscure Midwest town. Betty has embraced some strange enthusiasms in the time I have known her, but then she is not a native Bostonian; to recall her background is to be charitable. She is a dear, dear soul, and I have often told myself that if I should ever seriously contemplate marriage, Betty's would be the first name that would occur to me.

It was on a warm evening two days earlier that Betty had introduced me to the idea of visiting the prophetess.

"Even if you don't accept the idea, Harrison, that one can predict the future—and Sally can, you know, she's very good at it—you must find it an experience quite different from anything else you've ever known." Betty's face was serious.

"Dear Betty," I said and patted her hand affectionately. We were sitting in a quiet café on a side street. The door was open and the gentlest warm summer air brushed through the room. I felt tolerant toward the most outrageous of subjects, and even fortune-telling was well within my bland sphere of amity.

"Are you afraid of the future?" The question was a most unlikely one to pass Betty's lips, and she frowned as soon as she had said it. "I am sorry. That was a stupid thing to say."

"No. No." I brought my coffee cup to my lips and sipped. "Very well, then, if you feel so strongly about her, I shall see your prophetess."

Betty's frown cut a bit deeper into her forehead. "I'm so sorry. I know you, Harrison. You'll go to meet Mrs. Anderson only to show you don't blame me for saying such a silly thing. Who isn't afraid of the future just a little?"

"Not I. Not of the future I shall hear from your Mrs. Anderson, at any rate. By the by, how did you happen to meet her?"

Betty smiled, her eyes twinkling. "You shouldn't have asked me."

"Oh? But for that very reason I shall have to ask again."

"It's going to sound ridiculous; I actually met her in a séance. She was telling fortunes all over the place, so, of course, I insisted upon her telling mine."

With a smile I said, "Typical Betty."

"It turned out, she was too accurate for comfort. Afterward, I went to her home and we became friends."

"If you can't beat 'em, join 'em. Seriously, Betty, now I insist you introduce me to Mrs. Anderson."

I received my introduction to Mrs. Anderson. Walking now from my interview, I thought Betty might have been too obliging. Violence! So vague. I would not have minded a specific prophecy. For instance, a prediction that I would stumble and fall into an open sewer on my way home. I could at least prepare myself to fall with some grace. But this broad reference to violence opened up multitudinous avenues, down any one of which, figuratively speaking, a juggernaut could rush upon me. The early part of our interview, I recalled, was devoted to chatting of trivialities, as if I meant to keep the purpose of my visit a secret from her. Perhaps she only felt an obligation to blurt out some shred of the supposed future, as it appeared I was about to leave and take nothing of her art away with me. If that was all it was—simply her professional character asserting itself, offering whatever came most easily to mind—then I would allow myself to be consoled and let this absurd uneasiness disappear into the darkness of my subconscious.

I lay on my bed that evening in my darkened apartment, a bare bone, my heart shriveled by a sense of isolation that had reached into me from nowhere. It was utter nonsense, yet truth there must be even in utter nonsense, for how could I allow myself to be gored by the horn of so remote a dilemma as Mrs. Anderson had presented to me? It was perhaps nine in the evening. I lay on my bed still clothed, my bedcovers not turned back. I listened to the idle sounds of the night, the clack of heels on the pavement outside my half open window, the whish of tires, and a voice raised querulously in the distance, quieted by the mollifying bleat of another's voice. Lying on my bed, my mind drifting, anchorless, in the darkness, I recognized that presence which had slipped into my consciousness, dissipating that too secure life around which my soul had huddled for so many years. Yes, terror had come, a blind and unreasoning terror, shrieking in the wind.

I do not remember how many days it was after my interview with Mrs. Anderson that I lost my right leg. The mind is reluctant in unpleasant things, adamant in refusing to recall which day, which month of the year an unpleasant event occurred. Well, now that I badger my mind, I do remember the month. July. Summer had at last broken through a wet, chill Boston spring, and each day was fuller in air and light and the odor of growing things than the one before. Oh, why must any harsh thing happen in the month of July? Save pain and hellish things for the months of winter, and leave July to that time when life is, at long last, thoroughly re-established, not to be wilted by the late frost of a bitter winter, nor blown away by the frantic winds of autumn.

Betty visited me in the hospital. It was dear of her, of course; still, is it only a ritual affirmation of our own wholeness when we extend our sympathy to one upon whom calamity has fallen, be it blindness, amputation, failure? Her hand was unnaturally warm on mine, for it seemed to me that the blood had crept out of my extremities in horror, leaving all my remaining limbs ice cold. The flowers she had brought with her were clustered in a vase—bluebells and lilacs, which, I expect, she had taken from her own tiny backyard garden. Those poor, amputated flowers! While I watched through the clear glass of the vase the sap gently ooze from their torn stems, Betty talked to me.

"The whole office is so happy you are better. We're so glad you're improving so fast, so quickly." She gripped my hand. "Poor, darling Harrison,

we are all so sorry for you." Her face flushed, as if the thought had just occurred to her that she had broken the vow she had made to herself not to
acknowledge my calamity. She dropped my hand and took up a pendant
that hung about her neck. "Look, isn't it sweet? I saw it only a week ago
and I grabbed it up. I'm so proud of it. Hand-crafted silver."

"Indian, isn't it?"

"Yes, American Indian, a tribe somewhere in the Southwest with
such a difficult name I put it out of my mind immediately. I feel so selfish
about owning it."

I admired her pendant with a smile. "You are not selfish, Betty, not a
bit of it. It is a lovely thing and you deserve to own it."

Betty dangled the pendant from her fingers and we both stared at it.
It was an embarrassing moment. I could almost see in her moist eyes the
reflection of my form, lying on my back on the hospital bed, and on the
lower part of the bed under the crisp, dehumanizing hospital sheet, the
outline of one leg where two should be. Poor Betty, she must have found
it as if talking to a person with an enormous, flushed, wart-spangled nose;
the more one wanted to ignore it, the more obvious one's distraction.

"We can talk about my leg," I said, point-blank.

"Oh, Harrison!" Her hand shot out and nestled under mine. "Harrison…" Tears filled up her eyes. She blinked and wetted her lashes. "It's
all so rotten."

"Yes. It is rotten."

"Of all the people on earth, dear Harrison." She shook her head, with
a hurt, exasperated smile. "It was so sudden, and so…so…" She could not
finish.

"I will tell you what else it was," I said. "It was quite ridiculous. All
quite ridiculous."

My injury had swooped down upon me in the flattest, most ordinary,
pointless way of mayhem possible. I was driving my little Fiat on a Boston
street—even now, I don't recall the errand on which I was bound—and
with the casualness and swiftness of a pair of shears snipping through
cloth, a huge truck materialized out of limbo and crashed through my
car. All this was told to me after the event. I can only remember lying
on the pavement, with gushing scarlet blood I knew so horribly was my
own blood flowing past my face in rivulets through the dirt of the street,
while above me the green trees danced around in a dizzy swirl. In the next

moment of consciousness, a surgeon appeared on the blurred edges of my eyesight, his cheery, plump face poised above me like an objective moon.

"Coming around?"

I nodded my head weakly. My misfortune was explained to me in a few moments, the healer talking in that vigorous, healthy way surgeons have. "It was simply a matter then of splinting the leg; dressing the stump a bit more neatly," he ended clinically. He patted my hand and asked me the names of a few friends. Among other names, I murmured Betty's. He rose. "Chin up!" he said with a hearty smile and left me to myself.

My surroundings were spotless, immaculate: the white walls, the scrubbed ceiling, the white enameled metal table beside my bed, and the clean, coarse white bedsheets. Only I was marred. I looked into the space where my right leg once had been, oddly at that moment thinking not of my real future, but of the future that had been predicted for me. I thought of Mrs. Anderson, her high, thin voice squeaking, "Violence. Violence," again and again. I hated her then. I hated her as men hate powers beyond themselves, powers oblivious to human welfare. I hated her as one hates the sea that drowns one's child, as one hates the war that destroys one's comrades. And I knew that, as soon as I was able, I would return to her.

Betty was still speaking warmly to me, her sympathetic hand thumping mine, telling me that my accident was not ridiculous at all. Not at all. She finished her story of pity with a few more sentences and then stood.

"Whatever else has changed," she said, "our relationship, dear Harrison, has not. We shall continue our little tête-à-têtes, our sharings—I'm so looking forward to that, Harrison."

"As am I."

"Dear Harrison, do cheer up. I know—oh, how well I know—what you feel. But please always remember that you are not alone—you do have your friends. Whenever you feel low, whenever you feel too alone, call me. Please." She leaned toward me. "Will you do that, Harrison?"

Looking up into her round, white face, I said, "Sweet Betty." Her head slowly withdrew from my steady gaze, and my sight settled on the stainless ceiling. She stood by the door.

"Harrison..."

I turned to her.

"I will be back to see you very soon. Please try to look on the good side of things."

"The left side."

"No, dear. Try to be—optimistic."

"Yes. All right. Yes, of course."

She half opened the door. She turned back to me, her forehead corrugated by a violent frown. "That terrible woman!" she said fiercely. And she left.

Betty's last thought hung like a miasma by the door where it had been uttered, dissipating slowly, like vapor from an atrocious brew. And I knew our relationship could no longer be as it had been, would never again be as it had been. Nor would anything else in life be as it once had been. Life, perhaps regretting its previous neglect, had taken me up, and I felt held in its teeth, helpless as a mouse in the jaws of a cat.

I lay on my bed in Saint Alban's Hospital, two blocks from the narrow Boston street where I had lived so many years of my life, so many safe, secure years, and my lost leg hung from my mind like the weight of a great clock, a pendulum tick-tocking through space, sweeping back and forth, back and forth in the darkness, where time hatches its plots and conspiracies are whispered through locked fingers. I heard words uttered by metallic voices. I crept closer to the veil of darkness, kneeling under the white and shining leg that swung its giant arc overhead. I heard between the swooshes of its passage through the closeted air a name whispered. My name. Coupled with it was a word I dared not hear. I shrank away. Support crumbled beneath me and I stumbled backward over a soft precipice and into darkness.

Of course, I knew that I would see Mrs. Anderson as soon as I was able. The woman fascinated like a cobra's distended hood. History says the ancients fancied wisdom in the form of a snake; in just such a shape I fancied prosaic Mrs. Anderson. For I knew now that the bite of her knowledge was not without venom.

But I did not, I could not, call upon her immediately. Upon my removal from the hospital, Betty visited me in my apartment. Her awe of the prophetess had changed to hate. Sitting upon an armchair, her legs folded under her, her eyes blazing, she said, "A person just does not have the right to predict the future of another human being. Why can anyone presume that they have such a right?"

"By earning it," I answered. "By hitting the nail on the head." I stroked my tender and itchy stump. The pant leg had been folded under and pinned to my clothing by an efficient and sympathetic nurse before I left the hospital. Strangely, I found the sensation of sitting on the folds of clothing more irritating than the amputation.

"She is a detestable creature," Betty continued. "She should be prevented from doing what she does. Isn't fortune-telling illegal?"

"No, no, she should practice her—profession; she has a certain gift." I glanced at my crutches, leaning like two fresh-cut cornstalks in a corner of my little apartment. "I'll confess I was quite skeptical, but I have been converted." I nodded my head. Betty's frown grew more pronounced. "Yes, my dear, quite converted. In fact, one of the very first things I am going to do once my new leg is fitted is to go around and see Mrs. Anderson. I shall ask, 'What now, Mrs. Anderson?'"

"You can't be serious!" Betty's eyes bobbed like corks.

"Oh yes, I am quite serious. Mrs. Anderson ought to pay her respects to the dead, to the Harrison Seabrook who is no more. And I must pay my respects to a sovereign predictor. Oh, Betty, please don't pull such a very long face. Anyhow, the worst has happened." Luxuriously, I stretched my right leg out to its fullest extent, before remembering I no longer had a right leg.

Betty rose from her seat, quietly padded over to me, and knelt beside my chair. Her hand gripped my arm. "Harrison, you are becoming quite morbid."

Inexplicably, the magnificent old grandfather clock I owned, which had been meticulously carved out of rich, dark mahogany many years before, came into my mind at that moment. I heard its brass weights sweeping back and forth with muffled clicks inside its coffinlike enclosure, and thought that in the many years I, and my family before me, had possessed the great clock, its sound had never once been out of accord with the progressions of time. As Betty and I stared at each other in silence, she with so obstinate a will for my welfare, I heard the tock, tock, tock of my grandfather clock marching into my consciousness, solemnly marching out of the dream-filled past, out of the days and the years that had now become abstractions, marching into the present, slaying a moment with each slice of its pendulum, marching on and on beyond me into the future, taking me in its wake, pulling me up and up the mathematically spaced ledges of an endless space of gray rocks, hauling me up until I was too worn to follow, and there releasing me and continuing upward into endless tomorrows while I tottered and strained on the heights and darkness snapped at my heels.

"Morbid?" I smiled a quick smile. "Well, I am thinking of my contretemps, so if that be morbidity—"

Her grip on my arm tightened, I could feel her nails making red impressions on my skin. "Harrison, I am not going to let you see that woman!"

"Betty—"

"I am going to be health and sanity for you. I am going to be today, now, this moment. I am not going to let this experience twist and change you." Tears washed her eyes. "Oh, Harrison, how could such a thing happen to someone so dear?" Her face pushed against my chest, and I felt the wet of her tears through my thin shirt. I stroked her hair.

"Betty, do you think, after all, that Mrs. Anderson might really be a prophetess? I mean, it is coincidence, isn't it? After all, it cannot be possible to know the future. Her prediction must have been only a guess. It was so vague."

Betty's head jammed tighter against my chest, then suddenly pulled away. She rose, smoothing her dress with her hands without looking at me. She walked to her purse and slipped out a compact and a gauzy handkerchief. She dabbed at her eyes and her cheeks and blew her nose. "Promise me, Harrison," she said, "promise me you will never, never return to that woman."

I shrugged my shoulders. "If there really is no such thing as fortune-telling, what does it matter?"

"Harrison, please give me your word!"

"Why should you insist upon my giving you my word unless you believe—ah yes, but of course you do believe."

Betty dabbed her eyes again. "Please, Harrison—"

"Betty, I'll see Mrs. Anderson once more. And then no more."

Betty was silent.

"Can you see? It's as if I am in a dark room, and someone had the power to turn the light on and off. I will ask Mrs. Anderson, 'Give me light.' Don't you believe she will?"

Betty turned from me, still silent.

I pulled at a fold of clothing under my stump. "You see, if the future can be known, then it must be known. What has happened, has happened; I accept that, but what of tomorrow? I must know. I must see her."

"Yes. You must." Betty's voice was as colorless as mud. She nodded in my direction once, and without another word, walked out of my apartment.

In the silence I heard the banal tick-tock, tick-tocking of my grandfather clock.

"No, you haven't got it fastened just right. That strap goes around under the leg." The broad, cheerful face swooped down and blood pumped redly under its skin. "Here. And here." Big, square hands yanked expertly, and my new limb dangled from my stump as it should dangle. "Try it now."

I stood, rocking back and forth.

"Didn't fall that time, eh?" The prosthetist grinned. "Now you realize how important all those exercises were. The muscles must be strong because they must support half the weight of the body."

I grinned back at him. "I really don't believe I can walk with this thing."

"Certainly you can."

"I don't think I want to walk with it."

"Oh, now, now." He backed up a few paces. "Come on, walk over to me."

I inched my new possession under me a few tiny paces, balancing on my left leg.

"No, no! Walk! Pick it up and walk!"

I lifted the thing up, my left leg moved to follow, and the whole apparatus collapsed under me. I sprawled on the floor.

"Well, it's a knack," said the prosthetist, lifting me up by my armpits. "No doubt about it, it's a knack. But you'll get it. Everyone does."

I stood erect once more, wobbling and smiling.

"Anyhow, we've made our first step, haven't we? We've made our first little step." He backed away from me, smiling nicely. "Now, let's try again. Walk over to me."

By that afternoon, I had learned my new trick.

Two weeks after, I was walking—still a trifle inexpertly—to an appointment with Mrs. Anderson. She had been most contrite when I phoned, assuring me that were the future hers to make, her clients would know naught but pleasant experiences.

Welcomed into her house, I balanced in her living room, noticing for the first time the tentative arrangement of the furniture, as if it waited for the direction of a more orderly mind than hers. Mrs. Anderson stood before me, her uncombed hair and her broad, common face, untouched by make-up, giving her the appearance of a nineteenth-century cockney maid.

"Sit down, Mr. Seabrook. Please sit down," she said.

I tottered to a great, threadbare armchair.

"Would you like help?" she asked.

I shook my head and plunged backward into the chair, bouncing for an instant on the enormous springs.

"How can I tell you how sorry I am?" she said. "Still, I knew it that day, the moment you walked into this room. Disaster was written all over you." And she frowned.

"I realize you are not to blame, Mrs. Anderson." I pulled a pack of cigarettes from my pocket. "May I smoke?"

"I do wish you wouldn't." She scraped a kitchen chair to my side and perched on it like a barnyard fowl. "Smoking and drinking interfere with the spirits."

"I see." I replaced the cigarette.

"I understand you would like another prediction."

"Quite so. I will say frankly that in spite of what has happened to me, I am not convinced of your powers. True, you did predict an accident—or violence, I think it was, —which is a great deal more than anyone else had foreseen for me. But 'violence'—I felt at the time that you were being awfully vague."

"You want to know if perhaps it wasn't just a lucky hit."

"I wouldn't say lucky…"

"I'm sorry but I never fail, Mr. Seabrook."

"Indeed?"

"Well, now—" She stared at me with that same frown of a moment ago. She rose. She looked down on me. "The same thing," she said.

"I beg your pardon?"

"The same thing. It hasn't ended. More violence, Mr. Seabrook."

In spite of all the mental shrugging I could manage, ice gathered about my heart. I struggled against an impulse to cry out. Mrs. Anderson hovered over me, her eyes exuding sympathy.

"Oh, come," I said weakly.

"Yes. Violence. It is written on your aura in capital letters."

"Well," my voice trembled. "Only violence? If you could tell me what was coming, perhaps I might avoid it. Can't you be more specific?"

She shook her head.

I pushed myself out of the chair. "At least, tell me what part of my body—"

"All I see is violence. Violence that might even come from you."

"You mean I might become violent?" I nearly laughed in her face. I, who had lived so remarkably quiet a life, at least before my leg was lost; I, to whom violence had always been so strange, so alien? I turned about and made for the door. "Ridiculous," I muttered.

Mrs. Anderson came up behind me and clutched my sleeve. "You must pay me my money."

I paid her. "Thank you for everything," I said dourly.

Outside, though it was the blandest of summer days, I was not calmed by such ordinariness. I tightened between a pull of similarities, remembering that other day when I had stepped from Mrs. Anderson's house into a prosaic world, smiling at primitive superstition. The irony was, now I had become a primitive, a believer. Reality had slit its way into my body and sliced my little world apart with the rudest of cuts. I took a taxi home and sat in my apartment through the gathering twilight, sucking at a pipe held with whitened knuckles, going over and over again all the possible rationalizations. I came finally to the end of a long thread of intellectualizing, seeing that there was but one thing I could do. I could wait.

"Terrible!" cried Betty. "Terrible! Terrible!"

It was the next day, another lovely day, a Sunday, and she had entered my room and was standing in the center of it, her arms folded about a vase of near-violet carnations, her pale blue dress slightly rumpled.

Betty's concern drowned my own. I patted her arm. "Perhaps she is wrong. She very well could be, you know. After all, the future is still the future. How can anyone guess the unknown twice in a row?"

"Horrible, awful woman! Why don't the authorities put a stop to her fortune-telling?"

I took the vase of flowers, a get-well present, from Betty's hands and set it down upon an end table. "Thank you so much, they're just beautiful. But Betty, even if she does predict the future, can we blame her for how the future comes out? Is she the cause of tomorrow? I think not."

Yet this very thought crouched in a dark mental crevice, whispering that Mrs. Anderson was not a mere prophetess, a seer into tomorrow, but that she and the future melted into one, producing events that those who must suffer them were powerless to avoid. The thought lashed at my reason. I sank backward into the divan.

"Disgusting, hateful woman!" cried Betty. "Hateful!"

"Betty," I murmured, "there is a favor I would like you to do for me."

Betty sat down beside me. "Of course, Harrison."

"I would like you to visit Mrs. Anderson—"

Betty wagged her head violently. "Never!"

"No, please listen to me. Listen! I want you to ask Mrs. Anderson if her prediction for me has not some alternative. I-I'll double her fee."

A sob bubbled in Betty's throat. "I can't, Harrison. I just can't." Her gloved hand half-muffled her voice. "I cannot speak to her. I swore I would never see that woman again."

"Please, Betty—please. See her. You might—save me."

Betty stared at me a long moment and then said, "Very well. Yes." She leaned forward intensely, clutching my hands. "Harrison—please— you must not believe what she says. You must not expect violence. You must believe only in peace and love and that you are protected from evil." She shook my arms nervously. "Oh, Harrison, believe only the best can happen. Believe!"

"Yes!" I said, caught up in her emotion. "Yes, I will!"

She left me for her interview with Mrs. Anderson.

I loosened the straps on my right stump. I felt a horrid suspension of tranquility, a breath caught in the throat, waiting for Betty's return. Logic was no use to me. Terror had neatly peeled away the comforting ratiocinations of civilized man. I was a cold primitive, crouching in a rainstorm, cowering ignorantly under the searing tongues of lightning, the hound-bayings of thunder. Had I ever lived? No, I knew now I had not. I had only held a mirror before me and, with waxen fingers, traced

the pale reflection of life. And now life, the primal usurer, demanded payment. What use were the years of cultivation, the years of pursuing the
elusive subtleties of civilization? Trumpets had sounded and my destiny
had run out onto the marching field to hear reveille.

The phone rang and I struggled over to it. "Harrison?" I heard.

"Yes, Betty—"

"I'm so terribly sorry, Harrison, but I had to phone you instead of—I
couldn't see you again, the way you looked—"

"It's all right. You saw Mrs. Anderson?"

"Oh, Harrison, yes—that monster, she will do nothing."

"Oh." My voice was calmer than I thought it could be. "No, of course
not."

"Harrison, if I had the courage, I would kill her!"

"No, you mustn't think that. Anyway, thanks for talking to her. Thank
you, Betty, so much." I gently settled the receiver in its cradle.

I must wait. Horror chipped at me, flaking away bits of reason. No!
It must not happen! I would protect myself. I would be very cautious, not
even step from my apartment. I would wait....

During those three or so weeks, now scattered in oblivion, Betty neither phoned nor stopped by my apartment, yet I could feel her presence,
holding her breath, pressing her fingers against her strained mouth. My
pity for her was almost as great as hers for me. I did not go to the office
and neither did she, being sympathetically ill perhaps. I suppose I could
have continued my life, could have bumbled through the streets and the
traffic, could have worked the apparatus that I had come to call privately,
"the parasite"—my false limb—under my office desk and then out again
for lunch, or coffee break, or day's end. But I was terrified. For the first
time in my life, I knew what men in the combat zone, or men split by
disease, or men interdicted by furious suppression of the subconscious
knew: the gigantic presence of fear as unending pressure on the mind.
Fear, skin-crawling fear, wasting the body and the soul like fever, like
naked skin drawing taut over throbbing bones. And I would curse myself
for succumbing to it.

I took to strange ways alone in my apartment, slipping from one
room to another in the darkness of night, protected, I thought, from the
luminous cat's eyes of fate by its velvet veil. I would sit silently in the

blackness, perhaps sipping an iced tea, whilst staggering blindly among my thoughts for a beam of light. I would stare at the streetlights outside my rooms glowing faintly upon my drawn shades, painting slender bars of light through the interstices at the casement limits, the while reflecting dumbly upon their symbolism. And tock-tock-tock, both as memory and reality, the grandfather clock, stiff in its corner, let drop each last moment as dew dripping in the dawn.

Dawn? I would ask myself. And there would come the answer: I wait for the daylight. Yet each day, when it came, no matter how bright, was the night also, for I had drawn my window shades across the face of reality.

During rare impulses, I had fancied myself a handyman, and here and there about the apartment were nearly completed or partly completed projects that had attracted my energy. There was a double-latched lock, a folding hat-and-coat rack, a combination shoe scraper and polisher. And a holder for my ties made by fastening two lengths of steel in a block of varnished wood. It had never occurred to me when I constructed this piece that the twin lengths were set at eye's height and at eyes' distance apart.

As Mrs. Anderson had predicted, the inevitable happened. It was night and in the dark I stumbled forward violently. The two prongs of the tie holder, sharp as knives, crashed into my eyes and with a terrible flare of pain tore apart my optic nerves.

"Don't go to her again!" said Betty, a voice in a sea of blackness. "Don't, please, please, don't!" Her hand, warm and sweaty, clutched mine passionately.

It was after the hospital. I sat in my apartment, Betty beside me, reflecting that time, for me, had become only the measure of blank monotony. "What can Mrs. Anderson tell me about tomorrow?" I asked Betty. "To a blind man, what is time?"

I felt her lift my hand and hold it against her tear-dampened cheek. For a moment she sobbed. "My God—oh, my God—she pulled you down into hell!"

"Do you think so?" I pulled my hand from her grasp, quite without emotion.

"Dear Harrison, what has happened to you?" cried Betty.

What has happened? I am a man no more. "My appointment with Mrs. Anderson is definitely made. Tomorrow at two in the afternoon. A taxi will pick me up and take me to her. It would be bad manners to delay."

Betty was silent.

"Betty," I said, a bit impatiently, "I am not at all sure of myself when other people in the room are silent. Anyhow, I really do not want you here. Please—would you please leave?"

I heard her rise very slowly, and move stealthily away from me. One cry escaped her and I heard the door opening. "Good-bye, Harrison."

Tomorrow thundered like Stentor bellowing across the Styx. Tomorrow at two shrieked like a chorus of bugles in a military camp. It was my only thought.

Mrs. Anderson's soft, meaty hand tugged me through the void to a chair. "Well, Mr. Seabrook, back again."

I inclined an ear in the direction of her voice. "Yes, back again."

"We are having a terrible time, are we not?" she said. "I am so sorry. I think the loss of one's sight is the most awful thing that can happen to one. Yes. If I were blinded, I just do not know what I would do."

"No?"

"Did you know my vision is perfect? A perfect twenty-twenty."

"Indeed?"

I heard her shuffling about the room and then stopping, probably looking down upon me. "You came to me for another prediction, Mr. Seabrook."

"Yes." My throat was dry as bone. Emotions that I had thought long since gutted out of me cut into my soul.

"You just felt you must look into the future once more." Her voice was cold, almost severe, and for a frantic instant I wondered if my fancy that she and time had coupled to issue forth violence were only fancy. I hunched, almost cringed, in my chair, my head thrust forward intently beyond the axis of my spine. I listened to her walking about, first sitting and then rising.

"Would you care for some tea, Mr. Seabrook?"

"Tea?" But how could she think of tea? "No. No tea. I must know my future!"

"Well, I should like some tea, if you don't mind." I heard her walking away from me. "I'll be only a minute."

I suddenly realized that she was frightened, and I understood her at that moment not as the female Jeremiah I had imaged with prophecies gathered like thunderbolts in her arms, but as only a vague, frumpish, middle-aged female used by forces beyond her comprehension. Mrs. Anderson knew my future, and with a cup of tea was putting off the telling of it.

I relaxed in my chair, hating her all the more, hating her as a fly might hate a spider that waited, fat and half-conscious, in the center of her web for the violent buzzing to end so that she could, without malice, in simple response to instinct, consume him. I hated her as men hate most those grand powers of nature oblivious to our comfort and our destinies that nonetheless reign over us. Let God save us from this hatred, for what use is God himself if he cannot be called upon to attend this extremity of human misery?

The violence of my hate almost disarmed me. I was not certain I could contain myself when finally she told me her prophecy.

She was back in the room. I heard the tea tray rattling in her hands. "Please take some tea, Mr. Seabrook. There are some nice, fresh biscuits, too."

"Very well."

I felt a napkin flutter to my lap, a warm saucer thrust into my hand.

"The biscuit is on the saucer," said Mrs. Anderson.

"Thank you." I sipped the tea. A shadow of silence lengthened between us. I was not used to my blindness, and with silence I felt myself drifting from reality, an abandoned ship slipping from loose moorings. I grabbed at the present, wide-awake, terrified as if I had dozed off in the heart of a jungle. "I don't care for tea. Please—" I held my cup out to her. I heard her as she set her cup down, padded over to me, and lifted my cup from my hand—listening so intently that the sounds drew contours in my mind. I heard my voice grate, "Don't put me off. Do your predicting."

Silence.

"Mrs. Anderson!" I roared. I searched the room with my hearing, scraping over the dull, low noises that always are present: the outdoor sounds, the clocks, the blood in the ears....I came to her suppressed breathing. I stared at the sound from my shrunken eye sockets.

"Yes," she whispered. "Yes, I'll tell you."

"It's the same, isn't it?" I shouted at her. "Isn't it the same?"

"Yes, oh yes. More violence!"

I struggled up, balancing on my remaining leg. I wavered a moment, searching my memory for the position of her front door. I sidled forward into the darkness. I brushed irritably against her warm, lax body and stopped. Violently, I turned and fell upon her, and we were on the floor and I was throttling her.

"Violence!" I cried at her sardonically.

She did not struggle. Even gasping for breath, she did not struggle. Her throat was limp and her body passive, yet even after minutes I knew she was still conscious.

This passivity of hers maddened me. "Don't you want life? Don't you want to be saved?" I screamed into her ear. I imagined her eyes, bulging with pain, staring in my own dead ones. I shook her with all my strength. "Scream, damn you! Scream! Scream!"

I felt a hand, limp and warm, rest on my forearm. No, the prophetess would not war with destiny. She was alive and thought of herself as already dead, in transit to oblivion, bundled up in a shroud and rushed to an invisible depot that reverberated with the noise of distant engines.

"Farewell, then!" I spat at her. I squeezed till my fingers went dead.

The cold night air swept against my ankle, my exposed shank. My arms were quite numb. Then it was Betty, squatting on her thick thighs beside me, her voice calling my name, her finger tapping on my shoulder, but no longer did I dwell in her world. Mrs. Anderson was prophetess and priestess, too, bringing to full circle her membership in the occult, initiating me into her universe. I followed where she led, descending to the shores of her ocean, and there cleansed myself of the conceits of the past. Tugging me by her wrecked throat, she entered the endless waves. Naked and teeth chattering, I followed.

BROWN
DAYS

THERE ARE BROWN DAYS, blue days, gray days, black days—as many days as there are colors. This day was a brown day, a brown New England autumn day. Old Jack Frost had not rioted with his color brush, as was his wont. On his first tripping, tra-la-lee swing through the forest, he had slammed smack into winter. Everything had been killed quickly, and the autumn was all over brown. Besides this natural brown, there is a certain human mood that is brown. It is wasted, uninspired, and half-paralyzed. This day, and Dan Lenton, were both colored brown, a lengthy crayon scrawl of a Saturday brown. And the house and the furniture in it and the wallpaper and floors were quite brown, an exhausted, ancient dusty brown. Dan's sister and mother and father had left to see a motion picture (in bright Technicolor), and Dan was alone in the house. The cat, Even Steven, a sybaritic tiger that had never liked Dan and that Dan had never liked, had disappeared into the cold brown outside even though the cat detested cold more than rain. Dan was alone, deserted, and hours more would pass before he could expect the return of anyone.

He stood in the kitchen in brown, snapping kitchen matches at the stove. Either the stove had lost its harsh surface or the match phosphorus was soggy, for not one burst into flame.

Dan sighed and, hearing his sigh, sighed again.

"Frig, frosh, fruit, fram—jam," he muttered monotonously. "Damn."
He picked up a match from the floor and scraped it across the stovetop
and watched the match flame. It seemed to him that even the flame was
brown. And in the match's light he saw he had scratched the stovetop
with the match. "Brown damn."

Why couldn't he think of anything to do? When everyone was here,
he wished they would leave so he could execute some project or other that
really needed doing. Now, not even masturbation had any appeal. It was
a brown autumn day, and there was no getting around how very brown
every damn thing was.

He walked into the living room and stood in the middle of the room,
breathing heavily. "I'm sick of this house and every damn lousy brown
thing in it!" He could go over to Frieda's and watch television with her,
but nothing was on television Saturdays worth anything—and if there
were anything good, it wouldn't, after all, be anything. Besides, Frieda's
grandmother did nothing all day but sit in front of their television, cack-
ling and exuding body odor. What was more, she had mouse hair on her
face, and it was a sacrifice to look at her. He wished he could call Frieda
and ask her over, but no dice that kind of deal since that business with
Lucy. Christ, don't people ever forget those things? Jesus, what a foolish,
stupid thing, catching his stupid spaceman cuff link on her brassiere strap
just as her dad walked in! And him pulling and Lucy protesting, "Don't,
don't, you'll rip my brassiere," and they both look up, and there's Old
Dad taking it all in, his face getting redder and redder. And that was bad
enough, but Dan's hand gave a reflex tug and Lucy's brassiere did break
and Dan's hand came out still holding what the Lord knew every guy in
senior class had got to cup and squeeze at one time or another. That was
the unjust thing in the whole situation. Why did so ridiculous a thing
have to happen to Dan Lenton and no one else? And the fathers and
mothers and the rumors growing until everyone looked at him as if he
were a sex manic caught in the act of forcing Lucy's maidenhead.

"God, how I hate this jerk town!"

He stared out the window. The sun was hidden and even the clouds,
which should have been white, seemed to have a brown cast.

"New York. Just as soon as I graduate, off I go to New York, never to return. These Turnerville folk are, without a doubt, the world's prize bumpkins, provincial and lowbrow, to a man. It just can't be love that ties people to the misery of living in this asshole of creation. It's just that they are all too dull, too slow, too old, too damn dumb *brown* to get out!"

He slammed his tailbone into the easy chair and held his chin in his hand.

"But I'll get out! Like a stag at sunrise!"

He looked at the chafing his watchband was giving his wrist. Time had become a physical irritant.

"Why, oh why, was I born in this dumb town? The mystery of the ages. My family can't be too bright, or else why did they stay here?"

Dan stood up suddenly.

"I'm going to turn the dial of my tie match color chart to brown. I'm going to swipe a handful of brown crayons from Kresge's and check off every item in this damn brown town! Jesus, to think it's actually true there's a whole continent of small brown towns. Brown towns, town brown—Christ, I'm babbling like a kid!"

Dan jumped across the room. His shank slammed against the leg of a small table and sent the lamp that was on top of it bouncing across the threshold into the dining room. Dan yowled.

"Oh, Jesus, Jesus," he said, rubbing his shin, "Jesus. Goddamn!" He sank into a rocking chair, rubbing until the pain softened and his anger cooled. "What am I doing? Can't I even get across the bugging room? I even forgot where I was going. Oh yeah, the basement. And if I don't stop this chattering, people are going to start forming a ring around me." He set the lamp back on the table, smoothing out a crease in the shade, and went down the dark brown wooden stairs to the basement. He stopped in front of a bare, dim bulb caked with brown dirt.

"What am I doing down here?"

He switched the light on over the workbench. His dad had not cleaned up since he was down here last. A long time ago. Bits of wood, sawdust, and cut ends littered the table. Dan turned on the saw and listened to it hum for a few seconds.

"Wood is brown. Why couldn't trees grow lilac color? Or shocking pink?"

He took a bit of wood and split it with the saw.

"Or ivory. Instead of hunting elephants, you just chop a tree down.

And as she falls you yell, *Ivory!* Another giant tusk bites the dust." He turned off the saw and the work light. "Balls." He walked back to the small bulb hanging from a beam on its long, frayed cord and stared at it. A bulb, burning juice cooked out of a stack of coal forty miles away, a brown, dim trickle from the last tiny capillary. A light too faded even to print its image on his retina. A light was lit in the great darkness, and when the light was turned off, there was the darkness again. He mounted the wooden steps to the kitchen and looked back down into the base- ment. The darkness hadn't really disappeared at all. He turned the light off and waited, looking down the steps, but the darkness did not turn portentous or ominous. It was only black. At least, it was not brown.

"I should make plans. I am going to leave—what a heady thought! Just as soon as I graduate. The hell with what they want! The big city. The big, bad city. Who's afraid of the big, bad boo-boo? Hell, there I go, babbling again."

Why is it that on certain days you can't think? Thoughts stay frozen in the brain, like fish in a frozen lake. And windows have a hypnotic at- traction, any window, any view, and any day, be it black, blue, or brown. You stand in front of the window and stare dazedly into the day—noth- ing you see, you remember. Parades, bombs, baseball games, seduction, and murder; all sink into the blank, white unconscious. Looking out the window now and it is a cold brown November Saturday—

I remember when I was fourteen. Christ, what a lousy age! Forever unzipping your pants and squeezing your sex or squeezing your pimples or squeezing your muscles; the age of the big squeeze.

Anyhow, that whole brown week. It began with old man Burgess sitting down with his shotgun between his legs and the muzzle in his mouth and pulling the trigger. Lucky he did it in his own house; other- wise, they would not have known for sure who it was that had commit- ted suicide. So they say. I hope I never see anything that bad. And his mother in the next room, stone deaf, lying in the same bed she'd crawled into seven years earlier. When I was seven—I wonder what color that day was. Green? And she didn't know it happened, doesn't to this day, know her son blew his brains out with a shotgun. And the Samuels and the Gales and Archie Harris—what a skinny creep he is; whatever lousy thing happens in this town, Archie Harris's eyes are glued on it—the neighbors crowding into the room after they heard the shot. They say Mrs. Gale swept up the brains and poured them back into what was left of the skull—who else would tell such a story but Archie Harris?

I wonder why I think about that week. That whole brown week. Autumn brown, but it was March. New England spring looks so like New England autumn. The difference you know only by smelling the air. Autumn is burning leaves and clean air. Spring is perfumed by all the sweet, dead grass rotting all winter under the snow; that sweet, sweet odor that the snow and the cold had frozen into the earth. What was that something in English Lit? April is the cruelest month. Yes, early spring is when all the brains get blown out.

That week, I began to think about dying. That's really funny, thinking about death when you are only fourteen. Nobody takes anything you say seriously at that age. Dad was telling Mom the details of the killing, and she was saying, "Oh, now, don't, don't."

I just said right out, like a fool (I guess at that age everyone is a natural fool), "I wonder where old Burgess is now?"

"Danny! Don't be facetious!" Mom was frowning.

But I kept right on. "I mean, he's not here anymore but he's still alive. Only now he's either in heaven or hell, isn't he?"

"That's the belief," Dad said.

"Then why did he shoot himself? He was going to get old and die, anyway. Why didn't he just wait?"

"Yes. Why not?"

"Danny—" Mom began, still frowning.

"Let him talk," Dad said. I amuse him sometimes. He was looking at me and smiling. I know now he does that not for me, but for Mom.

I felt a little embarrassed. "I guess that's all I wanted to say."

"That was a whole lot," said Dad.

Mom looked at him with that Please-dear-not-another-lecture look.

"Men used to believe that the unexamined life is not worth living," Dad said. "Is it possible Mr. Burgess examined his life this morning for the first time and concluded that neither the examined nor the unexamined life is worth living?"

"William," Mom said, "you know they were poor as church mice."

"That reason is reason enough. However, dear, before we consign Mr.

Burgess's death to rejection by Mammon, we should consider the point Danny brought up. What about Mr. Burgess's immortal soul?"

I don't know why Mom just sat there. Almost always, when Dad starts talking like that, she just gets up and starts doing the dishes or the sewing or polishing the furniture or something. And then Dad shuts up and wanders into the living room and pulls a book from the bookcase. But she sat there, even looking ready to break in if Dad should say something too far out. Maybe it was because of me.

"Why do men do these things?" Dad said. "Religion says the reason is original sin. Perhaps that only means the human is prone to error, no doubt as a result of having lost the touch of certainty with Eve's embrace—"

"William! Please don't say things like that!"

Dad winked at me. "Some people are very devout. This means they believe whatever they've been told. In that sense of 'devout,' if we may put aside the subject of death for a moment, most men are devout in most ways. We live in a world that has been spoken to by authority. Men believe and so find security. And now we have returned to Mr. Burgess—possibly the shell of security just rubbed thin and broke."

"William, how can you say those things about him?"

Dad wasn't smiling. "Bess, I feel rotten about this thing, the same as you. But let me mourn in my own way. Have you forgotten I knew old Red all my life?"

Mom said nothing. Neither did Dad. I sat there feeling younger and younger.

"It doesn't mean anything—growing up together, doing the same things, going to the same schools, knowing the same people," Dad said finally. "No matter how close you are to another human being you will never know him. So he's gone. And that's that. We will never know who left us."

Mom touched Dad and he took her hand. Dad had big, square hands, tanned and heavy, and Mom's small hand seemed to disappear inside it up to the wrist. It's funny, the things we sometimes remember.

The next thing was that same day or the next day or the next and it was evening, and Dad was standing in a doorway smiling down on me and asking, "How's your thinking going?"

"What do you mean?"

"About death. Mr. Burgess and his immortal soul. And so forth. Reach any conclusions?"

Uncomfortable and a little angry, "No. I mean I wasn't really thinking about that."

"No? Baseball, then? It's the season. I don't know why I haven't heard any baseball talk so far this season."

"What about the funeral? Mr. Burgess's funeral, I mean. He has to be buried and everything. Why haven't they had the funeral yet?"

"Mr. Burgess is already interred in the cold, cold ground."

He turned abruptly and disappeared from the doorway.

Brown with scarlet splashes. I guess it's the wild, terrible scarlet that makes the brown so damn brown. Two very vivid scarlet questions. Number one, How was it a man could die by his own hand? Number two, How was it a man could die and not have a funeral? Another mystery, why was Rachel Burgess walking in the street five or six times a day, passing our house walking as stiff and rigid as a steel duck in a shooting gallery? Where was she going, from where had she come? The very next time she walked past, Mom happened to be in the front room and she said, "Poor woman, I don't believe she has but that one dress."

"Why does she keep walking around like that, Mom?"

Mom looked speculatively at me, and then walked out of the room without saying anything.

A fourteen-year-old just can't stop asking questions.

I don't know how old that brown week was by then. Maybe it was that week no longer but the next, and not brown, but tan (because it was sicklied through with the pale cast of thought). It is painful to walk around with a lot of big questions inside. You feel distended and pushed out of shape. It is something like the few minutes before birth, I suppose; something that was growing inside, gathering itself up to push out, heels last, into a new world, with everyone praying the mother lives. Only in this case, nothing is born, nothing can be born. These questions aren't going to be answered. They haven't been answered during all the ages past; perhaps they never will be. But at fourteen, you believe they will be. Your dad is going to tell you; he will, once he conquers his embarrassment and talks to you seriously.

It is something like sex, you suppose. You have to flush the facts out like you would a covey of partridges from under a bush. The secret is to press upon the parent, but not too strongly. Firmly but gently.

Dad looked back at me from the window. "This is the first real spring day. Come, let's go for a walk."

We were walking together. There is a moment in remembering when the consciousness gathers all the light of reality, inside and out, and there is a click like a camera and there you have a color picture inside for life. A point of reference. Forever afterward, you remember either forward or back from that moment. Only in that one moment can you smell the air (yes, Spring filled with Spring) and feel the very shape of the clouds moving toward the sun, feel even the corner of your shoe pinching your toe. My father and I walked so rarely together. Why should he ask me to walk with him this day? It was the promise of revelations to come, of questions to be answered, that made that moment then and forever so keen. Yes, it was this moment when he took me outside, and we stood together on the sidewalk, his hand on my shoulder, feeling the warmth of that first spring day that I always first remember. And an instant later, Rachel Burgess marching toward us, her head up, her eyes staring at us or through us. My father dropped his hand. I looked up at his face and saw that he had not wanted to meet her. That he feared her, hated her, pitied her, agonized over her. I remember that heartbreaking moment. For it was the first time I had ever looked at my father and he was no longer only my father; something had put aside the frame I had always seen him through, and he was no longer only my father, but another human being.

"Good morning, Rachel."

She had not been looking at us, after all, because she started, and her eyes got all tangled up with focusing and unfocusing. I thought she would say nothing, but finally she nodded her head and said, "Good morning. What a beautiful morning."

"Spring has arrived."

"Yes, yes, it is Spring."

Father had come around to Rachel's side, and now he picked up her hand and he lifted it almost as if he were going to lift it to his lips and kiss it.

"May we walk with you?'"

She did not seem to know what to say. Dad pulled at her gently, and the three of us were walking down the sidewalk. I see the leaf shadows of the great maple that had long grown beside our house, the leaves still

little more than buds, spread out on the walk before us, the groups of
light and shadow lifting up to our faces as we pass. But my memory of
the very next instant goes shimmering and vague, and voices move about,
disembodied, like the words heard in dreams, and I no longer remember
who said what or why it was said.

How could he have done it?—You, how can you absolve yourself?—
My heart aches so—Because—Yes, there is always because—But I cannot, I cannot—He did suffer, yes, I know he suffered—Everyone knows,
everyone—But why do you torture yourself?

And the images and the sounds all melt into a brown memory.

Funeral or no, Burgess must have been buried. Something had to
have been done with his body. It stood to reason, what with that ancient mother of his, lying in her hard, smelly bed, deaf as a park bench.
But with a keen sense of smell. I remember a baby squirrel I had, and it
caught a mortal case of pneumonia, I guess, or of fright and it died. After
just a day, my mother took him out of my jacket pocket where I was keep-
ing him because of his soft fur and she made me bury him.

I went down to the town cemetery and looked for a rectangle of
fresh-cut sod. There at the main entrance, sitting in the new, pale green
grass before the vaults where the Perrys bury themselves because they are
the only ones who can afford to, was Archie Harris. I tried to walk past. I
had always hated that guy, and especially then, as he was sitting, leaning
against the dark stone vault, his mouth open and his tongue scraping his
yellow teeth.

"What you want, Danny Lenton?"

"Nothing." I moved but he threw a leg across the warped macadam
walk.

"I know what you want. You wanna throw a posy on Burgess's grave."

I shook my head.

"Yes, you do. You wanna tear up a handful of grass from the grave
and press it in some book you got home."

I jumped suddenly and was past him. He was laughing. "You ain't
gonna find no grave."

I took a few more steps and then turned back. He was crouched
against the vault, his face wrinkled like an old man's, his fingers straining and closing on the air like a hawk's talons. "No grave here, boy." He

scrabbled in his shirt pocket and brought out a book of matches. "Look, boy," and he struck a match and held it, staring and chuckling at me, until it had burned down to pure carbon. "Look! Look at this!" He struck another match. "Looky here, boy!" His hand shook so with laughter that the match bounced to the pavement, sputtered, and burned out. "Damn it, boy, look at what I'm trying to show you!" He got to his feet and set the whole book of matches to blazing with one stroke and, holding it up like a torch, came toward me at a pyromaniacal trot. I ran around the vault and up the tiny hill it was burrowed into, wondering what that damn fool Archie was talking about. It was a cinch that if Burgess had been buried in the cemetery, Archie Harris would have been there at the burial, hidden behind a tree probably, but there watching and remembering all the mean details. If the coffin had slipped going down, he would have told everyone he saw the top open and a cold, white finger poke out.

What did all this match business mean?

It wasn't until I was standing at the Burgess's plot, hidden down in the slump of ground that ended at the grist mill and the railroad track beyond, that I finally caught on to Archie. Cremation. I hated him—an easy thing to do. Mothers in this town almost specify hatred toward Archie Harris. My dad says that's probably why he's so mean. "We wonder which came first, the hateful character or the mothers' injunctions to hate. Do you notice, the hate gushes forth only in one's first encounter with him, and that it fades to contempt and regret in retrospect?"

This was in the evening after supper when we were still sitting at the table. I don't remember Mom sitting with us. Maybe she had left, as she so often did when Dad started talking.

He was pushing his palms against the white tablecloth, and I saw his tanned hands, brown against the white cloth (only lightly dappled with spilled food). I remembered dreamily, a day or two before, Mom's white hand resting in his.

"Possibly, it was done on the spur of the moment," Dad said, speaking of Burgess. "A wild desire to finish with death before his mother should rise from her bed and search for her son."

"But she's paralyzed....She can't walk. Can she?"

"For reasons of emphasis and irony, I have exaggerated the effect of fear and hatred. No, she cannot walk. Not even such evil can cause such a miracle. She lies on her bed still, staring at the cracked ceiling, listening to whatever sounds deaf persons listen to, obliged to ask for whatever she desires, wondering why her son never visits with her. She brings to mind a mounted butterfly. Or moth. Or cricket. Consider this, son: the old lady was once thought to be the most intoxicating beauty this town of Turnerville had ever known."

I was lost. A conversation with my dad was not the easiest thing for me while I was growing up. Sometimes, he would streak off in an unexpected way and leave me wondering what we had been talking about. It made me impatient. It made Mom worse than impatient. She would just walk away when he began that sort of talk. I couldn't see what old lady Burgess being an ex-beauty had to do with her son being cremated.

"In such indecent haste," Dad was saying, "as folks say. Well, I say, if a wife can't cremate her own husband, who can? Do you understand that it's solely a matter of taste?"

I nodded my head.

"Some folks actually believe they will feel the oppressive weight of their gravestone, but nevertheless expect their survivors to obtain for them the largest and most ostentatious block of granite possible, because that form of immortality, at least, is forbidden to paupers....But what was I saying? Ah yes—I think that they will not. Earth, grass, gravestones, and cemeteries—these belong to the living. What is likely to press its oppressive weight upon the departed in the afterlife—if there be such an animal—is not a burden of stone, but of guilt."

Listening absently, I pictured in my mind an urn, gray, figured with flowers and angels and filled to brimming with the ashes of old Burgess. It had a cover, of course, so the ashes wouldn't blow about the living room with a sudden puff of spring breeze; a heavy cover, embossed with tangled vines blooming with thorns and roses. I thought of the urn sitting on the mantelpiece over the old fireplace, which had been bricked up when Burgess put in the oil stove, between the gold-framed wedding picture and the German cuckoo clock. The centerpiece, the focus of the lines in a cat's cradle. People would enter the living room, sit down, say how sorry they were and, without looking directly at it once, stare out of the corners of their eyes at the fat gray urn, from the time of their coming to the time of their going.

"Dad." It was embarrassing, but I could not rein in my curiosity. "Have you gone over to see his ashes?" Lifting off that heavy cover and looking into the urn was something like having a grave and headstone, after all. Perhaps better, being more convenient.

"Ah, dear me, no," said Dad. "No. There are no ashes to be seen. No, son, not as much as are to be found on the end of a cigarette."

My urn vision shattered into bits.

"Some folks say they were flushed down the toilet. I should imagine three or four pullings of the chain would do the trick. Other folks say they were thrown onto the ground for the wind to tend to. My suspicion is that the ashes drifted through Rachel's fingers during her frequent walks through our quiet little town. Her way of returning Red to the soil that bore him, to his fellow man, that we might breathe him in and tread upon him; to all humanity, that we may consider in how many ways a man might be wronged. Alas, all these audiences are imaginary. Everyone runs from the dog that broke its spine."

What dog was that? It can be exasperating trying to talk to Dad. When I ask questions, sometimes he answers me (and gets me more confused), and sometimes he only shakes his head and says, "You are your mother's son." So I forgot the dog (a little brown dog yelping off into eternity, his tail between his legs).

But I asked, "Why did Mr. Burgess kill himself?"

"Didn't you ask that question the other day? Have we come full circle? Or are you spiraling—the same question on a different level?"

"I mean Mr. Burgess. You talked about people dying and all that, but I want to know, why did *he* die? Why did he shoot himself?"

"Oh, I see. You want the particular, not the general. Well, then, let what I have said, or not said, float about in your mind as background, and let shine in center stage Red Burgess. 'Front and center, Red! Why did you do it?' And Red answers my question with a mumble, 'I don't know.' 'Don't what?' the inquisitor cries out. 'Speak up, Red. Tell us why you did it. Give us a reason. The world demands a reason. Life demands a reason. The instinct of self-preservation demands a reason. Why, Red, why?'"

Dad got up from the table and asked again, "Why?" He squeezed his hands until the knuckles whitened.

"There are some questions," he said eventually, "that I think may never be answered. They come wrapped in their own mystery; the questioner must be prepared to depart empty-handed."

"He really did kill himself—it wasn't an accident, the way some people say?"

"Who are they who say this? The kind-hearted? The self-deceiving? The euphemizers? There are those—and I have nothing to say against them—who would prefer not to face ugly facts. Death is an ugly fact; self-inflicted death, uglier still. The world is ugly beneath its beauty; the footing is treacherous. Therefore certain bland, well-meaning folks would prefer the harsh truths be coated over with a sugary glaze. I hadn't heard of the accident hypothesis. Who told you this?"

"Well, Mrs.—"

Dad held up his hand. "Stop. I believe I know the name. I have lived in this town all my life. I know the names. The same who are so unkind to the living." He shook his head in an exaggerated way. "Is it not a noble thing to consider—the act of suicide? A man says, Look, life has driven me to this. Beware, all you who yet live."

"Why didn't God save Mr. Burgess from killing himself?"

"What?"

"Why didn't God save Mr. Burgess?"

Dad looked as if he were about to ask again, What? He smiled then, and looked away. "What man knows what happens in the mind of God?"

We both listened to Mom crossing the kitchen floor from the sink to the cupboard and back again. Dad lowered his voice, knowing that Mom wouldn't allow him to say disrespectful things about the Lord to me. "Hasn't it occurred to you there may not be a God?"

I whispered, too, coming closer as he bent toward me; a pair of absurd conspirators. "Yes. I thought of that. But if it's true, why should anybody go to church?"

Dad smiled and said nothing.

I continued. "When Reverend Filkins says, 'Have you been saved?' does he mean really saved? Wouldn't God have saved Mr. Burgess if he had asked him?"

Dad still smiled, the ends of his lips tired and thin. "Perhaps."

"Then why didn't he?"

Dad sighed. "Youth is a bladder full of questions. I remember the first question you ever asked me. It was not unlike those I am being asked still. You asked, 'Daddy, why do you breathe so hard when you lift me up?' How shall I, I thought, explain human physiology to a child? But at least I knew the details of the human physique; they were there to be explained. Your question now, I suppose, is, God, why do I breathe so hard when you don't lift me? To cut short a circumlocution, I imagine Red Burgess did pray; not the solemn, hand-folding kind approved by preachers and other uplifters, but the screeching and wailing prayer of a mortal soul in extremis. All evidence suggests the more desperate the need, the more distant the god. The Almighty wanders through a heady environment of roses and cello sonatas. He avoids the naked concrete passageways that terminate in abattoirs or dungeons or catatonic trances. It is the frail mortal who has learned to scream; Godhead is silence."

Dad was staring off into space, the same as he did whenever he quoted some poet or other. I always got the feeling during those moments that he was reading from the page of some book inside his head and that he had completely forgotten me. I really knew better than to ask him all those questions. I knew whatever answers I would get would either have to wait until I grew old enough to understand or would go round and round, like a snake swallowing itself until there was no snake left. But it was at those times that we were closest. And once we had finished talking, my questions answered or unanswered, he would look at me, amusement in his eyes, the same as had been there throughout the conversation, but now, added to it, glowing and warm, would be love.

Still, he hadn't brought light to the darkness. The mystery to me, then, was only Mr. Burgess, who had put himself so violently beyond the pale of the average experience. I supposed if Dad would only settle down and tell me how old Red Burgess had thought and acted, especially the week or two before that morning, I would be satisfied. I sensed that Dad knew more than he had told me. For example, he knew Rachel Burgess, but he had come to know her better on that walk through our first spring day. I remember now waiting on her porch after we had taken her home until I became bored and walked away, a little mad because they had gone inside the house and were talking so long with words I could not hear. I hated Rachel a little for taking Dad from me. That day, we had walked side by side, father and son still, but also for the first time as equals, too. For a time, I had lived in the adult world. Then Rachel had come and with her arrival the world had suddenly turned turbid and dark, stalked by enormous beasts melting in and out of darknesses I had never noticed before.

"Chemistry teaches us that every action leaves a residue," Dad said at last, "and so poor Rachel is the residue of her husband's action. Ah

Rachel, poor Rachel; she must go to her grave bound to adjectives that diminish her humanity. Not pretty Rachel, not lucky Rachel, but poor, brave, lonely Rachel, emptying the slops of a deaf paralytic, living on charity, survivor of a selfish, furious madman, who dragged death out of its hiding place and spilled it all over the living room floor."

The brown gradually did fade away. That spring helped a lot. Mr. Burgess really should have lived to see that spring. It was exceptional; that was what everybody said. I returned to boyhood because it was spring and everything was racing, racing toward the sky, and I put back into the Pandora's box I had opened those questions having to do with life, death, and so forth. The brown gradually faded.

Still looking out the window and it was brown everywhere. Dan began to hear his breathing once again, coming up out of the past, his chest aching. They would be getting back from the movies soon. For a moment, he hoped they would never return; better to be buried here in privacy, looking out the window, wondering what the brown in life meant. He walked out to the kitchen and poked his hand into the bread box.

Nibbling on a piece of buttered bread, he returned to the living room and stared outside again. The past would not return. Tomorrow would be tomorrow, and now was only the raw present. The present moved into the past nevertheless, moving silently under his feet like flowing oil.

He finished the piece of bread, rubbing his buttery fingertips against his pants, still searching the brown out-of-doors. Car tires crunched into the loose gravel of the drive and crunched again, answering the unsteady foot on the brake. Of course, Mom was driving. Dan held his breath, listening for the car doors to open and the humans to step out onto the gravel of the driveway and to talk. A bundle of running cat, Even Steven, darted across Dan's field of vision toward the people in the car, the people he cared for.

"Damn cat, disappears all afternoon, and then the instant they get back, there he is. Damn dumb cat!"

The motor died. He heard their footsteps, but no one was talking. He knew they had not been talking in the car either. Dan closed his eyes and tightened his jaw muscles until they ached.

He turned and watched Sis through the kitchen door window as she twisted the back door knob and slowly pushed open the door.

"How is he?"

She put her tiny, seven-year-old finger to her lips. "Ssh. Mummy says talking tires him out."

She came to Dan's side and took hold of his hand, and the two of them stood quietly watching as they entered.

"Danny, please," Mom said. "Help us."

Dan stood quite still, helplessly watching his dad's face, more pale and drained of vitality than he had ever seen it.

"Danny, please—"

Together, they helped him to his room. He was smiling and mumbling and trying to assist them with his cane, using it with self-conscious inexperience. They took him to the edge of his bed and eased him down.

"Shame you didn't see the movie with us, Danny," he was saying softly. "Shame. Dandy movie. Lots of action. Pirate picture. Kind of picture makes you proud if you have buccaneer ancestors. "

Dan realized he was still holding his father's arm. He dropped it as if it had suddenly blazed with fire. Shocking—bone, nothing but bone.

"Rest, William, now please rest," Mom whispered.

"Well, yes…rest…rest.…I am so god-awful tired. Silly. Movie had a Spanish grandee." He slowly lay down on his bed. "'Punctuated' by a sword, ha! As with a horizontal exclamation point, falling down the grand staircase. Why do Hollywood Spaniards so rarely die with dignity?" And then he was mumbling to himself, gazing at the ceiling.

Dan slowly backed away, watching Mom pull off his shoes and wrap a blanket around him. He waited for her—it was late, after all, and time for supper—but instead she sat on the bed and stroked her husband's face as tenderly as if her fingers were slipping across a page of braille. Dan left the room and closed the door, though there was no reason why it should be closed. When he turned from the door, Cathy was standing at the end of the hall.

"How was the movie, Cathy?"

"Okay." She took a step or two toward him and stopped. "It was a pirate picture."

"I know."

"I don't like pictures about pirates too much."

Smiling, he walked to her and put his hand on her shoulder.

"Why didn't you come see the movie with us?" she asked. "What did you do all day?"

"Stared at the brown everything."

She looked up at him. "You should have come. It was so hard—" Her face was soft and flushed from earlier tears.

He took her with him into the living room. "I don't know why anyone would want to go to a movie. I don't know why anyone does anything anymore. I want to be a million miles away. I wish I were in New York City and I were about five years older than I am and making lots of money."

"Are you going to leave?" she asked with a surprised face, eyes screwed up and glistening with fresh, hot tears.

"Just as soon as I can get out of this damn brown town." He moved to the window once more and glared out into the darkening world, the brown trees and sky and the weathered brown house across the street.

"Please don't go away, Danny, please—" She came crying to his side and pushed her child's face against his shirt. "If you leave, there'll just be me and Mummy."

His breath caught in his lungs, almost a sob. But of course, it was not a sob. He had sworn to himself long ago that he would not cry. He had made many pacts with himself since his mother had first told him about his father. The first pact had been that, being a man, or very nearly a man, he would look at what would happen without shaming himself. He had prayed many times since that his emotions would not betray him. He had prayed, not knowing to whom.

Cathy pulled on his arm and whispered again, "Don't leave home, Danny, please. Please…"

He turned to her, smiling. "I've got to graduate first anyway, haven't I? That'll be a good year after—" He stopped, his brown mood draining him of all brighter colors. With a tiny shock, he saw that all the brown was not part of the world, but part of himself. At the same time, he had known all along this was true. Dad had once told him that all his moods he could control. It was his duty, in fact, to conquer those sad moods, inspired by tragedy. He felt helpless nonetheless, nailed down to a certain thing that must be.

"If you go, take me with you," Cathy insisted. "I don't want to stay here alone."

He squeezed her and, trying to think of an answer, saw Mom in the doorway, crying.

"Mom?"

She waved her hand weakly. "No. It's nothing. It was such a long day." She walked slowly into the room. "This time is the last time," she said. "The last time." She shook her head. "Supper will be late."

"Mom, I want to go to New York when I graduate from school."

"Yes, if you want, Danny."

"It's all right, isn't it?" Hesitant, harboring a downward-spinning spirit.

"Yes. It's all right." Her face seemed soft, almost translucent. They looked into each other's eyes quietly. There was a message she took from him, but he had given none. He could not have said what that message was. She went into the kitchen.

Cathy was still clinging to him. He pulled her down onto the sofa beside him and softly stroked her hair. He stared bleakly at the deepening brown outside until Mom called out to them in a loud whisper, "Supper's ready."

MY CHICAGO FRIEND

I REMEMBER THOSE WINTER DAYS in Chicago. Cold, frosty clouds drifting across the sky from Lake Michigan. Icy days, reflecting a piece of my life that grew sour from my finding the hardship of life through the soul of a friend. I bore my own pain, succumbing only occasionally to an uprush of self-pity; it was the pain of Chapin, my friend, that awakened me to the cry of universal distress, the moaning that drones on and on in all hearts.

In those days, Chapin was my only real friend; and I don't wonder that he was. I pity him, looking back and remembering me as I was then, a lank, morose, brooding fool; don't ask me why. He lived in a two-room apartment on Superior Avenue, scrabbling up each morning out of sleep and gulping down a pint of cold milk for his breakfast. Sometimes, when I was up early enough in the morning—a rare event, because I didn't have a job to go to—I would see Chapin from my window, half trotting across the dead cold street among the other automatons, toward the Station on Chicago Avenue. He wore an oversize brown coat throughout the winter, wrapping it around his skinny body because most of the buttons were missing. A great length of artificial fur held together in the middle by a belt the width of a cummerbund. This garment fascinated me. I would picture it as it might have been when first bought on Michigan Avenue by some debonair gentleman, a society leader, bound for a winter week in Montreal. And upon his return, the coat having suffered its first stain—a dash of French claret—being given by him to a servant who, out of respect for the superior emanations the coat had absorbed from its owner during its week in Canada, sold it, not to a stranger but to a friend. And so the coat had descended the social orders, coming to rest finally upon Chapin's shoulders. Of course, I never knew how the coat had happened to come to him, so I fell back on my imagination, picturing Chapin poking through the push-carts on Maxwell Avenue and stopping, his eye caught by a great brown thing draped over the side of a cart that was half devoured by its enormity.

"You like that coat?" From the pushcart, "That garment's the finest material from Michigan Avenue—feel it—only a first-class society man would have such a coat. Try it on, try it on! See! It fits perfect. This coat cost many times what I ask for it, but I got to sacrifice it. Such a coat, it'll last a lifetime. You'll never have to buy another coat as long as you live. Here, here, feel the material. Feel it!" And so on and so on until Chapin succumbed.

Chapin had a butter-soft heart. He could not resist for long anyone who seemed to depend on him. The merchant needed Chapin's money and he got it. Everyone received from Chapin whatever was Chapin's to give. The brown coat had been worn by Chapin many winters by the time my winter arrived, when I would watch him from my dingy window disappear down the street on his way to work. The coat sagged from his body, obviously never cleaned, disreputably stained, but still Chapin's pride in it never waned. He saw it still at its best, as he saw the people about him, whose faces never aged and whose hearts never grew callous.

I never knew where Chapin worked, an odd thing. I never thought to ask, and he never mentioned it. That was a really odd thing, for the second or third question Americans ask a new person is, What do you do? I wonder why I never asked. Now I am curious; what sort of work would a man like Chapin do? Had I asked him, what would he have answered? Probably, he would have shrugged his shoulders: Does it matter?

One winter night, my spirit was sucked up about my heart. Picture the cold room in which this shriveling up happened: nine feet long by seven feet wide; for sleeping, a sagging cot with a clumsy set of drawers against the wall, the space between them barely two feet. A large mirror over the set of drawers pitched at an angle so the image in it continually stared at the person in bed. And if it would stare at me, I would stare back, stare and wonder and drift into an ever-descending circle of gray thoughts. Isn't there a certain point in the soul's descent when it stops, exhausted? Yes, that time when thought tires and one sleeps. But there are times when sleep also is the enemy. So it was this night. I threw on my coat and hurried out of my room and down the cold, silent street to Chapin's apartment house. I ran up the four flights to his rooms and banged on the door. His radio was playing some silken dance music. And I heard voices, his voice and a woman's voice.

"Hello?" Chapin called from inside.

I felt betrayed. He had never called out before. Always he had come to the door, no matter how he might have been dressed or how inconvenient it might have been for him, always he had opened the door and welcomed inside whoever was at his door. So there I was, burdened with a fresh stack of miseries and bitter opinions, and Chapin was bouncing around on his great, ugly iron bed, I supposed, with some broad from Rose's, the sleazy bar down at the corner.

"Never mind!" I shouted through the door. "Never mind!" I blundered back down the stairs. "I won't bother you!" Do your screwing! Do your screwing! I said silently. And when I burst into my room, I tore off my coat in a rage and threw it in a heap in the corner. At that moment, I hoped to never see Chapin again.

A day or two later, I found out that Chapin had a daughter, and it was she I had heard talking. Alma, the waitress at Harrison's Café, the one other person I was friendly with in Chicago that winter, knew Chapin and knew his daughter and while I huddled in despair and self-pity over a cup of black coffee after the noon rush, she told me about her.

"I didn't know that he had been married."

"Sure. Sure, he was married. And he has a daughter."

"What's she like?

Alma poured herself a cup of coffee and walked around the end of the counter. She sat on the stool beside me.

"Wow, what a morning rush!" She reached down and rubbed an instep. "I see I got to change back to my old shoes. You wouldn't believe how long my dumb feet take to break in a pair of shoes."

Alma was not anything like the waitresses in Hollywood movies, who are always flippant and blonde and, if not pretty, were once pretty. She had a big, round behind, but the rest of her was stringy and sinewy. The skin on her face was wrinkled, her blonde hair aged to the color of dust. The left side of her face twitched constantly, squeezing one eye up to a fleshy slit.

"Yeah, Chapin's got a daughter. She's a cripple, poor kid. She don't have crutches or have to sit in a wheelchair or anything like that, but she's got a big hunchback on one side of her and it kind of twists her around. And she's real short."

I shook my head. "Where's she been all this time?"

"Somewhere in Wisconsin, I think. Relatives up there been looking after her." She sipped her coffee. "She's a funny kid. Real bright. Her eyes are real pretty, like they're always laughing. Funny, a cripple like her."

A fat woman entered the café, dragged in by two small children. Alma slipped off her stool and limped behind the counter. "Damn shoes. Can you imagine that, a kid that looks like that laughing? If I looked like that, I don't think I could do nothing but cry."

I put the money down beside my cup and walked out into the windy, slushy weather. That night, I went to visit Chapin, for the first time not carrying any particular problem of my own in my cold hands. He had been sitting alone in a big, tattered armchair directly beneath the bleak light of a 40-watt ceiling lamp. It was as chilly in the room as it was out in the hall. I turned on a burner on his hot plate.

"You're not cold?" I asked. "It's like an icebox in here."

"Yes, I guess it is." He reached over, dragged his enormous brown coat from the foot of his bed, and tucked it around his legs. "Yeah. Sure a cold night. How you been, buddy?"

"You know me." I hunched over the hot plate, warming my chest. "I heard some news today. I heard about your daughter."

Chapin grinned. He looked lively for the first time since I had walked in. "Yes! My girl! Her name is Phoebe. Phoebe May. May for the month of May, because May was when she was born." He was gazing at some sweet picture in his mind. "May, that was my idea, but we named her Phoebe after my wife. She was a lovely girl, my wife was."

"Alma told me. You could have knocked me over with a straw. I can't picture you being married."

"Sure. Sure, I was married." He stared at me solemnly. "I was married sixteen years ago—let's see, August 14, 3 o'clock in the afternoon. We had a real wing-ding church wedding, her people and my people up in Wisconsin. Sixteen years ago last August."

"Where's your wife now?"

Chapin's gaze moved away from me, his mind drifting into a wilderness where dumb animals receive their wounds and steel traps clip off furred legs. "My wife, Phoebe, was on her way out to California the last I heard. Twelve years ago that was. Twelve years ago." A spasm shook his head. He smiled wryly. "Maybe Phoebe May and me will go out there one day and look her up."

The next moment, the door banged open and a heavy-set, tanned woman in a blue cloth coat barged into the apartment, pulling a small, misshapen creature after her: Phoebe May.

"How was the movie?" Chapin's voice was high and strained, almost childlike.

"Wonderful, Daddy." Phoebe made a move toward him, but the woman held her close to her side, staring at me in an ugly way.

"This is Mr. Will Willoughby," Chapin said, smiling at the woman.

"How do you do?" I said.

She screwed up her nose and turned away.

"Phoebe May, this is Will," said Chapin. "Remember? I told you about him."

"Hi, Phoebe May. Good to meet you." Alma had been right about Phoebe May: her smile was lovely.

The woman broke in. "Phoebe May and I will be at the bus terminal tomorrow morning. The bus leaves at exactly 9:04 on the dot. Remember that!"

Chapin smiled shyly. "Can't you wait, Mrs. Modesta? I hate to ask you again, but it's just one more day. I can't miss work. Can you stay over until Saturday, and then I can go down to see you off?"

"Tomorrow. I ain't got the money to stay."

Chapin flushed and looked away from her. "All right. I'll give you the money."

"No! I don't want your money."

Chapin knelt and held his arms out to Phoebe May.

"Phoebe, honey...say good-bye to your dad."

Phoebe came to her father and rested against his shoulder. He kissed her cheek. The big woman granted them a moment more and then pulled the girl away.

"We're leaving when I said," she told Chapin. Without another look at us, she pulled Phoebe May after her out the door.

Chapin stared at the floor and then looked up at me with a hound face and hound eyes.

"Will, can you do me a favor? Can you get down to the bus station tomorrow? I want you to give Phoebe May a note from me, but don't let Mrs. Modesta see you."

"Who the hell is that old monster, anyhow?"

"My sister-in-law. I'm sorry she didn't act friendly. She's just that way."

"She's got a whale of a personality."

"Will you give Phoebe the note for me?"

"Anything that old satchel wouldn't want me to do, I'll do."

Chapin found a stub of a pencil, and on a piece of lined notepaper slowly wrote to Phoebe May. "Phoebe May is almost sixteen," he said between the slow words. "When she's sixteen, the court said, she can come live with me. My wife's folks don't want to let her go. They ain't bad people. I think they just believe Phoebe, my wife, she's going to come back home." He finished the note, folded it around some money, and pressed it shut between the palms of his hands. "Money's for her bus trip down here when she turns sixteen. Next May."

In the morning, I skulked around in the bus terminal until Mrs. Modesta went to buy a magazine and I could give Phoebe May the letter. "From your father," I whispered. She took the note out of my hand like a soft fawn nuzzling for a piece of sugar.

Exactly when a Chicago winter finally turns into a Chicago spring I don't know, but the day comes and a hand that had been pressing against your heart for too long lifts. The hand may come again for a few final, dismal squeezes, but this isn't anything to feel bitter about. I had a job at last, helping to lift pinball machines onto quarter-ton trucks and wrestling jukeboxes around a huge, drafty shipping room. I was desperate and morbid still, of course, and seeing Chapin and talking with Alma in Harrison's Café after work eased a little the carrying around of that heavy sack that was me. I had forgotten all about Phoebe May.

On a warm May evening, with a soft wind that had been loading itself all day with an incredible weight of sweetness, the sweet push of God's breath upon that lump of trash that had become man, I walked the four flights of stairs up to Chapin's apartment and opened his door. Phoebe May was there and he was holding her to him with his huge, knobby hands. She started when I walked in, frightened, trembling like a small animal. The first thought that came to my mind was, She's run away. I stood, clutching the doorknob, not knowing whether to go in or leave. Chapin said, "It's May, Will. It's my Phoebe May."

Phoebe May had run into Chapin's apartment only a few minutes before me. Her thin jacket was still clumsily pulled over her warped back, and her cheap suitcase had fallen on its side on the floor. I stared at her. I couldn't help staring. I had never really noticed her before. I had never before seen eyes so clear. Alma had told me that Phoebe had remarkable eyes. "Real pretty eyes, like they're always laughing." They were more than that. I know now that a person sees once, perhaps twice, in a lifetime a human being whose gaze draws upon something within that was once called the soul. When it happens, you feel a quickening, a yea-saying, a sudden come-and-go glimpse of truth. And this being, trapped in the tiny, twisted body of a hunchback!

"I'll come back later," I said. "I'll come back later." I stumbled back through the door and closed it and ran down the stairs. I don't know why.

I saw Phoebe May and her father only two or three times after that, before I left Chicago. I had not wanted it to be that way, but too much was astir with Chapin. A great battle was going on with Wisconsin. Mrs. Modesta rolling down like a cannon. Chapin fighting the fight of the weak, hiding Phoebe May, playing dumb, pleading to be left alone. Mrs. Modesta rolling away, back to Wisconsin, only to roll down once more on Chicago, driven by fresh fury.

That summer, my own destiny was doing some rolling around, too.

I have a picture in my mind of the Ancient Mariner watching the ghost ship sliding past, hearing the click of dice on her deck. My ship was as aimless as his, bound for no better destiny. I left Chicago. I drove an auto dealer's black Oldsmobile into Houston, Texas, seduced by some vacant Texas dream of millionaires splashing through petroleum, tossing unneeded dollars to the wind. I felt the time had come for me to take my share. I discovered the truth about Texas soon enough, but out of pride I stuck it out. I lived through summer and into fall in Houston, and then I left. On a dusty day in November, I was sitting again in Harrison's Café, watching Alma serve apple pie and coffee to a Southern kid in a faded Army fatigue jacket who might have run away from the same Texas I had.

Alma came over and we exchanged hellos and how-have-you-beens. I asked her about Chapin and Phoebe May. With a smile, "Has Wisconsin given up on Phoebe May?"

Alma's face twitched two or three times. "Chapin! That damn fool! He made the kid get an operation on her back! She's dying up there in his rooms."

"Alma! No!" I couldn't believe it.

I ran outside.

"That stupid fool doesn't even have money for a hospital!" Alma called after me.

The Chicago wind was whipping the fresh, blustery clouds of on-rushing winter across the sky. Entering Chicago the night before, I had glowered out from the Greyhound bus window at the first snow of the season shaken down out of the dark sky. Winter again. Winter sweeping over the opulence of autumn, sweeping away the sweetness.

My mood changed and I decided not to see Chapin at once. I walked instead to the shabby hotel on Ohio Street I had stalked into the night before, made my way up to my room, and flopped on the bed, gasping with rebellion. I hated all life and I cursed life, cursed the approaching winter, cursed Texas and Chicago, and cursed the girl dying in Chapin's rooms. Who, I cried, will accept responsibility for all this? I got up from the bed and kicked at my luggage, still unopened in the middle of the room. I was waiting, talking to myself, crying to myself, waiting for Chapin to come home from work. I dug my alarm clock out from a suitcase I had stained that summer with watermelon juice, and set it on the dresser. Fifteen minutes to five. Five minutes to five. I threw on my coat and ran to Superior Street and up the stairway to Chapin's rooms. I leaned against the stair railing and stared at his door, panting. Chapin was talking and a soft, invalid voice was answering him.

I banged on the door. "Chapin!"

"Hello? Who is it?"

"Open the door, Chapin. It's Will! I just got back."

"Will! How are you?" Chapin yanked open his door and grasped my hand. The same Chapin, but more bowed, more humble, a spirit half slain from numb confusion.

Phoebe May was lying on his bed, her tiny head turned to me.

"Phoebe May?" I said. "How are you?"

"Hello, Mr. Willoughby. I'm fine."

"Oh, call him Will," Chapin said gently. He pushed the door shut behind me. He folded and unfolded his hands, looking at me, looking at Phoebe May, wanting to speak, wanting to explain the complete, full, valid explanation that was turning in his mind like his anxious hands, folding and unfolding.

I went to the side of Phoebe May's bed and asked again, "How are you?"

"Phoebe May had an operation," Chapin said finally.

There came to my mind that sentence in the New Testament, that simple and clear and definite phrase after all the ceremony, the scourging, and the cross-bearing was done, those heart-shattering words: "And they crucified him."

Chapin sat down beside Phoebe May. "I guess an operation wasn't the best thing."

Phoebe May caught her father's hand. "I wanted my operation," she said.

Chapin shook his head. He turned away from her and stared down on the worn, frayed carpet. He shook his head again.

"I didn't want to be like I was anymore," Phoebe May told me. "I didn't want to be a hunchback. I made Daddy get me the operation. I just kept after him."

Chapin gently, weakly shook his head.

Who is there to be blamed in such matters? Perhaps it was then that one of life's secrets revealed itself to me as I, briefly ascended from my own morosity, stood to one side and watched fate, or whatever it was, squeeze its talons into one of its victims.

I discovered later that Chapin had spent all his savings on Phoebe's operation. The surgeon had promised nothing, only that Phoebe May had a good chance. Phoebe May had pleaded for the operation and Chapin had finally given in. As the old saying goes, The operation was a success but the patient died. And after the operation, the relatives from Wisconsin—especially Mrs. Modesta, who hadn't, for a moment, given up—swooped down and came to stare at Phoebe May, shrunken and doomed on the great iron bed, and turned to tear at Chapin with their eyes and their tongues. Alma told me all this after it was over, me sitting with my chin in my hands on a stool in Harrison's Café, Alma with tears in her eyes. All those years ago, and I still remember that moment with the same cold rebellion.

There were not many more days that I went up to Chapin's apartment to see Phoebe May. But I went every day, sometimes taking flowers. I stayed as long as I was able. Phoebe May was weak and getting weaker quickly. We would talk and Chapin would sit in a chair watching us, his knees primly together, saying nothing.

The last day came. That day, at my usual time, 5 o'clock, I softly opened the door, holding roses still glistening with the florist's spray of water. I saw Chapin, fallen on his knees before Phoebe May, his head down at her side, resting on her one upturned palm. Her eyes were closed and I knew it was over. I stood there, I don't know how long, wondering whether I should go in or not. Chapin had not heard me. I decided finally to back out, closing the door as softly as I could. I fumbled and the roses fell from my hands onto the dingy hall floor. Very appropriate, I thought bitterly. I kicked them away and went down the stairs.

It is because I truly hate Chicago in the winter that I decided then to leave for California. That terrible Chicago winter, reaching into summer hearts, breaking summer dreams. That brutal demarcation of the seasons so you could never forget when a season goes and that another year has passed. California seasons change gently, year blending into year, and it is with surprise that you discover that it was not two years or five since such and such a thing happened, but much longer.

I had moved out of the hotel on Ohio Street and back into the same old, musty room I had occupied the previous winter, so I could be closer to Phoebe May and Chapin. So my life habits had been much like those of the winter before, the only exception being that it was not about myself that I brooded. From the window of my room I could once more see Chapin's comings and goings. On occasional mornings, when exceptional cold would force me out of bed, I would wrap a blanket about myself and stumble to the window and watch Chapin leave for work. And in the evenings, my chin sunk into my hand, I would see him return, hurrying along the street, his brown coat flapping open on the few warm days, wrapped tightly about him like a shroud on cold days. From my window, I saw Chapin leave for the last time.

He left, smothered in his great brown coat, clutching an old suitcase bulging with clothes, walking slowly away. I did not rush out into the street to say good-bye or wish him good luck. I watched stolidly from my room, watched his slow figure move down the street, bumped by people hurrying to and fro on their errands. I watched him leave Chicago forever, without an impulse to rush out, grab him by the arm, and cry out for him not to go. I hated him then. I hated his helplessness. I hated him because life had no more use for him.

That day, Chapin's last day in Chicago, the sun shone with winter's prickly brightness, a metallic sun glaring from windows and shiny automobile bodies. It was early afternoon when he left, and it was only chance that I noticed his figure crossing the street. After he had vanished around a corner, I stared out that cold window another hour or so, my mind as frozen as the ice on the street. Finally, I put on my coat and walked to Harrison's Café. I told Alma that Chapin had gone.

"That old fool!" She wiped the counter viciously with a greasy cloth. "Just an old fool!"

"Alma, I'm going, too," I said. "I'm going to California."

"No kidding?" She stopped her counter-wiping.

"I'm going to leave this damn town for good. I'm leaving bright and early tomorrow morning. Bright and early."

Alma drew a cup of coffee from the big silver coffee urn and put it down in front of me. "You don't have to pay for that." Her eye twitched a few times. "I don't like to see you go, Will. I like you. Chicago ain't so bad."

"Oh no? I hate the winters. That damn snow and the wind blowing and blowing on you until you feel like a Popsicle. I'm not going through another winter here."

"You know, I went out to LA once. About five years ago."

"Oh yes? I didn't know that." We stared at each other, dreams teetering on the brink of a precipice. "Why did you come back?"

"LA isn't anything. It's all the same for people like you and me." She shook her head and stared down the long, vacant counter of Harrison's

Café, pulling at a strand of hair.

The next morning, I left on a Greyhound bus for California. For all I know, I was following Chapin in his search for the wife he had lost there twelve years earlier. I tried not to think about that. I meant to put all those days in Chicago out of my mind. A new place, a new life. And I really did try to live a new life. But now and then, I would find myself looking into the faces of the people that walked past me. Sometimes I would think I saw Chapin and I would raise my hand and start to call out. It wouldn't be him and I'd pass by, wondering why his memory kept coming back to me.

Still, I thought that one day I would really see him. I would clutch his hand. "It's okay," I would say. "You're okay."

He would be surprised to see me. "You're here, too," he'd say.

And we would talk about Chicago a bit. But then his face would blur like a reflection in a dark mirror, and I would see then that it wasn't Chapin's face at all, but it was my face and there were tears in my eyes.

Why would there be tears in my eyes? Why would I cry?

MERCY KILLING

"**M**RS. TAYLOR! Next!" said the nurse.

Mrs. Agatha Taylor rose slowly. The several women sitting in the room had formed a circle of hostility against her while she waited to enter the Population Control director's office, staring at her with hatred. She understood them. How often in the past had she, too, hated and envied women like her: pregnant women.

One of them, an angular, stiff woman with a hard, embittered face spoke: "Pig!" her lips snapping shut like a turtle's beak. Mrs. Taylor hung her head, and her face flushed with guilt.

The nurse jabbed a stiff card at her. "Your report!" The report stated that Mrs. Taylor was nearly full-term pregnant. She took the report and placed her damp hand upon the cold metal of the doorknob. She prayed.

"Please go inside!" The testy voice of the nurse was like a whip. Mrs. Taylor pushed open the door of the director's office and closed it behind her.

"Mrs. Taylor?" The voice caught her and pulled her into the room. The director was white and neatly, antiseptically dressed. His lips were thin and tight and bloodless. "Sit down, please." He looked at her distastefully. "Your chart, please."

She gave him the chart. He only glanced at it. "How did this happen?" he asked.

"I did not go to the monthly examinations when I discovered I...I was..."

"There is a penalty. You know that. A fine."

"I know."

"You knew and still you—" He waved his arm impatiently. What did it matter what she knew? The director said, "I have made an appointment for you—"

"Please." Her voice was trembling violently, but she forced herself to speak. He must understand. "Please...please, let my baby live. Please. Do what you want with me, but let my baby live."

"Mrs."—he glanced at the chart—"Mrs. Taylor, you know the law. If I made an exception in your case, I would have to make an exception in all the cases. And where would our Population Control be then?" A joyless smile came and went. "I can do nothing. You know that."

She sobbed.

Tears. The director's face reddened. Much better to have a woman for this job. Where such things were concerned—pregnancy and the rest—women were ruthless with one another. "It is a matter of statistics, madam. Statistics. The computers predict..."

It was inevitable there would be some Mrs. Taylors, women who found they were pregnant and simply did not come for the monthly exam. And inevitable that months would lapse before they were caught. With an overworked, inadequate staff, there had to be some sloppiness. That did not remove the necessity, however. Only authorities would ever know how close humanity had come this past winter to catastrophe. Only the most meticulous, detailed analysis of the crisis by computers and only the strictest rationing, the most adroit shifting to here and to there of available supplies, had averted mass starvation. Each slice of bread was accounted for.

She was sobbing, ignorant of all this. The director tried reasoning with her: "You know the law. All unlicensed pregnancies must be aborted. In your case, abortion being medically unsound, you will wait the week or so until the birth, and then your issue will be disposed of."

"No!" she cried. "God in heaven, no!"

The director fought down his impatience. Silly woman, couldn't she see that nothing she could say would change things? "You have broken the law, madam! Had you obeyed the law and appeared for your regular examination, you would not be in this situation now."

Her face was white. "It is only one child. One mouth, one tiny mouth, such a little difference—"

"We cannot make an exception. Surely, that is fair." It was absurd, and he really didn't have the time, but he continued to explain. "The arithmetic of the situation is this, Mrs. Taylor. As of my most recent report, dated April 10, 2095, at 12 noon, 23,664,231,410 human beings lived on this earth. The number of births permitted this year is 15,135,305, at the assigned birth rate of .6423 per thousand."

Her face was turned from him, and he knew she was not listening. He did not care. Numbers were his life. All his daily frustrations were dissolved in the exactitude of mathematics.

"There being some 150,000 inhabitants of this village of ours, the World Population Control Council allows us 96.34 births this year. Drop the fraction and it becomes 96. When you consider, Mrs. Taylor, that in the old days, when there were no restrictions on population, a year's births in a town of this size might run to 4,000, you can see with simple calculation that but 2.4 percent of fertile women can be blessed with motherhood this year. Now, these are the facts, madam."

Of course, he would not tell her all the facts: how there had been an error in calculation—a human error, naturally, some such utterly foolish thing as a misplaced decimal point, a wrong digit; simple carelessness. It was a moot point, how it had happened and who was responsible. Did it really matter? There had been an overestimate of the permitted increase in population. But now the error had been found and corrected, and the computers demanded the birthrate be cut back drastically.

Her chart was in front of him. He picked it up and studied it with more care. "Look here, Mrs. Taylor, the records say you have a son of eleven years."

"Yes—"

"Then you have a family. Do you see how selfish this is? There are many childless young women of good physique, emotionally and mentally stable, whose right to pregnancy is of the first priority, but who are not permitted to become pregnant."

"And they are not pregnant," Mrs. Taylor said with woman's logic, "but I am. You cannot murder my child!"

The director shrugged. With 23 billion people weighting the earth, murder was a public service. He jotted something down on a pad of paper. "Now I am making you an appointment for tomorrow. You will report at 2:30 p.m. to the admittance desk of General Hospital. There you will remain until you are ready to give birth." He stood and rubbed the excess perspiration from his hands. "I am sorry, Mrs. Taylor. Perhaps you will have another chance. In seven years, an excess of births over deaths will be permissible. Perhaps then…" He walked from behind his desk to guide her to the door. She got up slowly and he looked at her body with some surprise. A pregnant woman was so rare a sight these days, he had forgotten how big the bellies became.

She grasped his arm suddenly. "Please—"

Her eyes had that savage, hysterical look he dreaded so much. "Compose yourself, madam—"

"Please," she said, her fingernails digging into his arm, "please, my baby wants to live, let it live—"

"Do you want me to call security?" He gritted his teeth. The situation was impossible.

"Please, please, please—"

He pulled at the fingers gripping his arm. "It is hopeless, madam. Prepare yourself."

Abruptly, she went limp. He pulled away from her grasp and pushed a button. "I will see that you have transportation home. You must still pay the fine, of course."

The door opened.

"Please see Mrs. Taylor out. Take her home."

As the evening hardened into night, Agatha Taylor walked about her bedroom, packing a valise with pajamas and underclothing. It was a confused sort of packing; dirty shoes on top of white blouses and boxes of powder with their lids askew. She said to her husband, "You don't want the baby. You never wanted the baby."

Her husband, Benjamin, leaned against a wall, watching her. He did not speak.

"You did not want it, you don't—" Her arms fell. She might have cried, but she was too weary. She went to her husband and he embraced her. "I'm sorry," she murmured. "I'm sorry—"

"I blame myself," he said. "I should have insisted you go for your examination. All those months, I stood aside. I did nothing. Now look where we have come to!"

She pressed her lips against his chest. She whispered, "Don't you want the baby?"

"We mustn't think about what we want. Don't think at all. Go to the hospital, come home, and forget. Don't think." Gently, he pushed her from him. Her swollen belly embarrassed him. He thought of the swelling only as a growth that must be removed. "Why do we talk of it?"

She moved from him and sat on their bed. "If it is not this one, then I must wait seven years. I will be too old." She closed her eyes. "Help me, Benjamin, help me, help me."

He looked out of the window into the night. Argument was futile. The law said what the law said. He, too, would like things he could not have: a meal such as he had enjoyed when he was a boy, his stomach stuffed with food and enough left on the plate to throw away. But such things could not be. They ought not to be thought of.

A growing uneasiness had been drifting about his mind. David, his son, was still outside, alone in the night. "Where is David?" he asked.

"I don't know."

"It is late. He should be home. It is dark."

She rose from the bed, closed the valise, and set it on the floor. She stood, half dazed, in the center of the room and stroked, slowly stroked, her midriff.

They heard the noises outside at the same time: several people hitting and running, angry voices, and the sound of a boy's scream. Together, they ran to the front room.

"What is it?" Agatha cried. "Who is it?"

Her husband flung open the door.

A crowd of people, mostly women, were dancing around, picking and scratching at some object crumpled on the ground. In the dim light from the street lamp, Benjamin could not see what it was. Then it moved.

David!

Benjamin shouted and rushed into the crowd. He swept David out of his circle of enemies and carried him to the house. With a cry of agony, the mob leaped after him. David's arm was bloody and slick; Benjamin's hand slipped, he lost his grip, and David tumbled to the ground, moaning, half-conscious. Then Agatha was there. She pulled David to his feet and, moving clumsily, dragged him to the door. Benjamin turned on the crowd.

"What are you doing? Are you crazy?"

They ignored him and, looking beyond him, cried out, "There she is!"

"Get her!"

Benjamin pushed the first woman away and backed to the door. "What do you want? What did you do to my son?"

"Nothin' next to what we're goin' to do to her!"

"Kick her!"

"Kick her belly!"

Benjamin shouted at Agatha, "Get inside!"

But David fell again. A slim blonde girl grabbed his leg, pulling him back across the threshold. Agatha held his shoulders, braced against the door, her eyes closed, panting with exertion. Benjamin shoved the blonde girl back into the crowd. "What are you people doing? What do you want?"

"She's pregnant!" a woman screamed, her face ugly with frustration. "Pregnant!"

"Leave us alone!" A sudden black veil of pain dropped over Benjamin—someone had struck him. He staggered back, fighting unconsciousness, fighting to stay on his feet.

Benjamin recognized the faces of neighbors. Mrs. Brown and her teenage daughter, Edna Grout, and Mr. and Mrs. Atcheson—they were pulling at him, scrabbling to get at his wife, heaving and shouting, eyes blazing with hate.

"Please!" Benjamin cried. "Please!"

A moment of jostling, of frantic struggle, and they had hold of Agatha, pulling her outside—

"Wait! Stop!" A rough hand yanked Agatha free of her neighbors and pushed her, weak and trembling, back into Benjamin's arms. The sheriff had come. "Stop! You people can't do this!"

"She's pregnant!"

"She has no right—"

The sheriff lifted his hand and the crowd quieted before Authority. "You folks let me handle this!" He turned to Agatha and Benjamin. The crowd pressed into a phalanx behind him. "I've known for a long time that you were pregnant. I also know you went to the Director. What did they tell you?"

The authorization for the hospital was folded in Benjamin's pocket. He took it out and handed it to the sheriff.

The sheriff read the authorization. He turned to the crowd and held up a hand for silence. "All right. Now, this says Mrs. Agatha Taylor must go to General Hospital tomorrow afternoon. Says she's to stay there until the baby's born—"

"How did they let her be pregnant?" yelled an angry voice.

"My wife's young!" cried out another. "How come she can't be pregnant?"

The sheriff held his hand up again. "This woman is going to the hospital tomorrow, and they're getting rid of it. That's enough. That's the end of it. Now go home, all of you!"

The people moved away from each other, slowly dispersing. They were silent, their wrathful eyes speaking for them.

"Thank you, Sheriff. Thank God you came!" Benjamin said.

The sheriff brushed the comment aside and pulled David to his feet. "Go inside there, Sonny!"

They went inside. Benjamin steered Agatha gently to a chair. The sheriff stared at her. "These people aren't bad. You've been sneaking around, trying to hide that big belly of yours. I don't blame them."

"How can you say that? They would have harmed her!"

"Yeah? My wife wants a kid, too. What makes your wife better than mine?"

Benjamin wiped the blood from his son with a handkerchief. The boy's shock had faded, and now he sobbed uncontrollably.

"And my son?"

The sheriff moved to the door. "Make out a report," he said. "Come down to the station." He opened the door and turned back to them. "You want to make out a complaint against any of those people, that's your affair. My advice to you is, forget it. It is your fault, all of it. I wouldn't care if they beat up all of you and burned down your house!" He left, slamming the door.

Agatha's face slowly sank forward into her open hands. Her chest heaved in spasms. She was unable to cry.

Benjamin put David to bed and came back to Agatha and knelt beside her, putting his arms around her. He kissed her. "Darling," he said and was silent. He had meant to comfort her, to tell her to forgive the people, for they could not help themselves. That it was the terrible frustration of instinct, and that they envied her and hated her. After she gave birth and came back alone from the hospital, they would come, one and then another, to beg her forgiveness. And then she must forgive and be content to forget. But he found he could say nothing.

Agatha was moaning in his arms, rocking back and forth, and the moans formed words: "I want my child, I want my child, I want my child!"

At precisely 2:30 in the afternoon of the following day, Mrs. Agatha Taylor reported to the admissions desk of General Hospital. The necessary information was taken, and a young nurse escorted her to her room. It was thought best by the authorities to assign Agatha to one of the few private rooms. Benjamin had come with her, and he stood now beside the bed.

"You'll have to leave, Mr. Taylor," said the nurse impatiently.

"But can't I stay a moment with my wife? I—"

"You have to leave. If you want to see her again before she goes home, make an appointment at the desk."

He kissed Agatha tenderly. "I'll come again as soon as I can."

"Yes," she said. She clung to him.

The nurse pulled her arm away. "I have to do my tests now. I have other patients."

Benjamin kissed his wife again. "Good-bye." And he left.

The nurse took her samples from Agatha's body. "How is it they let you get pregnant?"

Agatha said nothing.

"I want a baby, but they say I can't have one for years. Maybe never." She jabbed a needle into Agatha's arm roughly.

Agatha still said nothing.

"You didn't go for your exam, did you? But they caught you. They always catch you." She put the blood sample on a tray. "And they're going to take the baby, aren't they? Good. Who are you to have a baby and I can't have one?" She paused at the door. "I even feel a little sorry for you. You're just stupid, that's all." The door closed after her.

Agatha had changed to pajamas, and when the nurse left, she got into bed and pulled the covers up about her. Yes, she had acted stupidly. Who but a fool would believe that pregnancy could be hidden? Or a baby be born and its cries be muffled when eyes and ears were everywhere? It was wise of the authorities to announce the candidates for conception before they had conceived and then hide the women away in a Control colony while they had their children. Population Control selected mothers-to-be by lot once the eugenic qualifications had been met. Everyone said that was just. Sitting on her bed in the pale, cold hospital room, Agatha cursed her foolishness. What had she believed? What had she dared believe? That she could hide? That she could escape the consequences of her folly? But that first month when she found she was pregnant and did not go to her examination, she knew she had surrendered reason. A subterranean part of her had thrust itself into consciousness and had claimed her and so savage, so irresistible was it that even Benjamin had been silenced, permitting himself to hope with her, giving to her, out of his and David's, the extra rations of food she needed.

Agatha's hands dragged slowly down her flesh to the risen, quickened mound of her abdomen and, clutching tightly, her eyes closed, she breathed out in jagged breaths. "No, no. God, no." Hope was shattered, the chalice broken, the sparkling crystal dashed into the mire. The child must die.

One day passed. Then three days. Agatha had grown numb, eating, sleeping, and exercising within the routine of the hospital. But her mind drifted over vacant canyons, and she forgot where she was or why she had come there. On the fourth day, walking in the corridor of the hospital back to her room, she awoke.

The door to the room opposite her own was open, and its light was on. In the center of the room was an airtight chamber, with its glass mouth open, tubes connecting it to a small tank. In a red-painted section, black letters were printed on the tank: Danger—Cyanide Gas.

Agatha went closer and on a card by the machine saw her name and beneath it these words: "Issue of A. Taylor. Dispose of immediately upon birth. By authority of the district director."

She stumbled backward. A scream rushed to her mouth, but she pressed it back, hands to her mouth. She ran into her room and closed the door, looking for a lock to turn. But there was no lock. She fell back on her bed, trembling and screaming noiselessly.

Time passed and she caught control of herself once again, her emotions firming into resolution. She dressed. She had seen a stairway at the base of the hospital wing and, knowing so bold a move would not be expected, walked out of her room, down the stairway, and out of the hospital. Pregnancy was not easy to conceal but she wore her coat draped loosely in front of her. Home was many blocks away. She began slowly walking through the crowds of strangers. People ignored her. She was only another woman. They brushed past her with the indrawn, anxious, excluding face that had, within the past few generations, become the human expression. As she walked and rested, and walked again, she remembered how it had been with David. Though she was very near and the pains had already come, she swore she would not allow it to happen until she was home.

While the day darkened into twilight, Agatha walked a dozen steps toward home. Then after resting by leaning against a building, she walked another dozen steps. When she turned the last dark block, the writhing was crushing her body. Before her home she tripped and fell and could not rise. Her body was splitting. She could not strangle a cry of pain, and it burst past her teeth and hung in the naked air. She drifted then into a dazed blankness. A moment more and she felt arms lifting her from the ground and carrying her into the house.

"Benjamin," she whispered.

He lay her down upon their bed and there, bucking and twisting, drowning in an ocean of blood and water and pain, she gave birth.

The pain ebbing, Agatha forced her spirit back to awareness, terrified of unconsciousness. Benjamin's lips were against her cheek, and were whispering upon the tear and sweat dampened skin, "It is a boy, a beautiful, healthy boy." She heard it cry. Her lips moved. Benjamin put his ear close and heard the weak whisper, "Quiet. Make it be quiet." Unable to fight the weariness any longer, Agatha fell back into blackness.

She awoke and her tiny son was lying beside her, moving gently, lips sucking. Benjamin and David sat facing her. They were smiling. The night was quiet and the pain was gone.

Benjamin whispered, "We named him while you slept, David and I. We chose the name Edward. Do you like that name?"

She smiled, assenting, filled with so deep and upwelling a love for humanity that she could not speak. As a glass disappears when light shines through it, evil had vanished, as a dream before the morning sun. She believed at last that mankind was good and life was good.

"How long have I slept?"

"Hours."

David leaned close to his mother. He drew his soft, boy's fingers across her brow and across the red and wrinkled forehead of his young brother. David's face was still bruised and the scratches on his cheeks still healing, but he smiled. "I never saw a baby before. He's funny, he's so tiny."

Benjamin said, "He is beautiful, the most beautiful thing in the universe." He put his hand upon his wife's hand. "Forgive me. We will find a way. You'll see. While you slept, I prayed."

"I pray always," Agatha said. "Even while I sleep." Her gaze turned down to the small being beside her, and her heart engorged with love. "Edward....Yes, I like his name."

It was David, his ears made sensitive to terror, who first heard the noises outside in the night. He jumped to his feet, trembling violently.

"David! What is it?" his father cried.

Then they all heard: people milling about and talking and shouting, in front of the house.

The window exploded in a geyser of splintering glass, a rock bouncing and banging across the floor, and a deep, angry, masculine voice shouting, "We know you're in there! We know you got that kid!"

The voice was drowned out by a female squeal. It squealed again, "Come out! Come out!"

Agatha moaned piteously, inhumanly. She clutched the soft, whimpering burden beside her. Benjamin had leaped up and now he cried, "Don't be afraid! I'll talk to them! They must listen!"

He ran to the front door and threw it open. Savage cries eddied in the air. "Listen to me! Listen!" Benjamin shouted.

A twisted female face, vaguely familiar from the neighborhood, danced in front of him. "She had the baby! It's in there! She had the baby!"

"Listen! Listen to me! It is different now! Listen!" A momentary calm, like the intaking of breath, spread before him. He talked. "You came before, you injured my son, and you frightened my wife. Never mind. We forgive you. But now it is different—"

"The baby is alive in there!" a female voice screamed. The mob noise surged up.

"Listen to me! Wait! Yes, the child is born, a boy, a son. Listen! There is a new life in there! Have respect for this new life! Respect!"

"No!"

"I ask you all—be our allies! Don't tell the authorities! Let our son live! We will raise him together—all of us!"

"No! No! Kill it!"

Violent hands yanked Benjamin down from the doorway and into the mob. Fists and sticks chopped at him. "Kill it!" He fought them, all strangers now, a raging, blood red organism, hot, battering anger closing in upon him, throttling and absorbing him. The organism jammed into the house, found David, and threw him into a corner.

Then it fell upon the shuddering Madonna. "No! Don't touch him! Don't touch him!" she said, clutching and scrabbling. "Be careful with him! No!" He was torn from her. "No!"

The mother pushed herself up from her bed, shrieking, and staggered to the door. She saw her naked, squalling child bouncing from hand to hand. Dropped. Swept up. The little body motionless and hands in a wild frenzy, grabbing and pulling. An arm torn off. Blood spurting. Nails ripping into flesh—

The mother sank to the threshold of her home, screaming.

"Please! Please!" David's mouth pressed against his mother's ear. Her screams emptied into vacant air. A small boy, running too late to the sacrifice, stopped, seeing the small pink head, swollen and eyeless. He kicked it with all his strength and it rolled, slowly and softly, into the gutter, stopping in a sewer grating.

Satiated, the organism divided into its several parts and melted back into the night. As it receded, it gave up Benjamin, lying unconscious on the ground, an arm folded unnaturally under his body.

"Please! Please!" David knelt beside his mother, pressing his mouth against her ear, wetting his knees in the warm pool of blood forming beneath her buttocks while her screams turned to moans. "Please!" The mother, suddenly quiet, tried to raise herself and tumbled back across the doorway, David holding her, falling with her, whispering in her ear, praying, and trembling in a black insanity. He lay beside her in her cooling blood until the authorities came and pulled him to his feet.

LIVE &
LEARN

Duke County Sheriff's Department
Louisburg, Iowa

Dr. Forrest Benjamin
Medical Director
Victor Luce Psychiatric Hospital
Greenlawn, Iowa

Dear Dr. Benjamin:

Pursuant to Court order, what follows is a copy of the transcript of the voice tapes found in the recorder attached to the machine in Dr. Halleck's laboratory.

I am trapped inside Dr. Halleck's machine and I cannot escape. I have become a tiny, wandering homunculus in a dim wilderness of sudden horrors; shapes condensing from twilight dark, hands grasping, forms startling—

You must rescue me!

Complete blame for this contretemps must rest at the laboratory door of Dr. Halleck. I exonerate myself. Neither I nor anyone could have foreseen how unbearable this experiment would become. I have the highest regard for science, understand; yet how could I, a layman, have been expected to discriminate between the respectable, academic, somewhat stodgy science that devises new forms for water faucets, auto transmissions, and such practical things, and its kooky, far-out stepchild?

Yes! Mad scientist! It is this detestable breed about which I speak! Too late, I realize my tolerant, live-and-let-live attitude toward them to be abysmally misinformed. How contemptible are these fussbudget busybodies, poking about the rubbish of mankind with the andirons of pseudo-science!

I earnestly pray that you—or someone you might know more versed in these things (if there is anyone other than Halleck)—will find some method of extracting me from Halleck's machine.

Hold everything! Here comes another one—

A stream of water…another stream…and another.…I am surrounded by many streams of water…no, not streams but brooks.…Yes, that's it, brooks, many brooks.…There is a sound—what is it?—ripping cloth…tearing…ripping, tearing…spoiled…spoiled cloth—Ah, what a smell! Halleck knows I hate the smell of corned beef and cabbage. Of course, *because* I hate it so! Horrible! And to do this to me when I have not yet recovered from that sewing machine chittering and chattering in my bones for hours on end, stitching round and round and round the rim of that great, limp clock face—a stitch in time, indeed! Ah, that sadist! What a horrible smell! Worse than cooking food; the smell of rotten food…spoiled food. First, there were many brooks and then spoiled cloth. Too many brooks spoil the cloth—oh, the absurdity of it! Too many cooks spoil the broth!

Everything disappears and once again, all about me is wilderness. Give me a moment to recover.…

Please have patience with me if I seem, on occasion, to surrender to illogic. It is not easy concentrating amid such insane goings-on as I have been obliged to endure.

I know that my captor is a mad scientist. It is even possible that he would not object to this description, but would instead merely smile an inscrutable Mona Lisa smile, modestly accepting "mad" as a synonym for "brilliant." The colossal ego of the man!

It was during the course of my professional duties that I first met Augustus J. Halleck, BS, MA, PhD (plus the initials of countless domestic and foreign honors, awards, fellowships, etcetera, etcetera—the hell with eggheads!). I am a professional writer and specialize in the personalities of modern scientists, semiscientists, and technicians. Perhaps I should say I *was* a professional writer, for I am certain I cannot return to the world of words. Once Halleck finally releases me from his machine, I shall become a butler at some quiet, refined rural mansion. Or a sheet metal worker. At any rate, it was this weakness we all share, a weakness that distinguishes writers from the commonalty perhaps—this dangerous interest in new experiences—that made me so amenable to Halleck's proposition. Human beings can be such trusting fools; "yea-saying to life," as some idiot once put it. Humani nihil alienum—rubbish! In plain talk, all it means is we haven't the wit to come in out of the rain. (A cliché! Please forget I said it!)

This human failing was half the cause of my present circumstances. The other half—the half that sold me—was the very modus operandi of Halleck's Deconditioner, as he called his machine. It sounded so splendid as he explained the machine to me; how I especially, being a writer, would benefit from its operation. I actually was brought to the conviction that Halleck's creation would be the greatest boon to scribblers since Gutenberg. Halleck really missed his calling. He ought to be on a car lot, hawking Edsels. And caveat emptor, everybody! Anyway, combine these two halves of foolishness, and you will understand how it was I came to be Halleck's first victim, or "subject," as he euphemistically put it.

But I am getting ahead of myself. I must not confuse you. I myself am so confused, you understand. I have simply no idea what horror is going to leap out of this darkness at me next. But in spite of everything, I am still sane, and I beg you to excuse me when I go off on what seems to be a tangent. Bear with me, for I am depending upon you to save me. Don't fail me.

My name is Rolf Tibbett. I am thirty-two, in good health, and considered a reliable man by the editors of numerous national publications. As for my once-rich home life, it was given the quietus that black day when Helen abandoned herself to impulse and fled to Las Vegas with an

Italian bartender whose one talent was concocting well-chilled martinis. In six weeks, the breach was final, and I settled into a dark funk, which has lasted up to the present. It was this most devastating experience of my life that led me to shrug off the risks that I must, in all honesty, record that Halleck pointed out to me. I was, at that moment, a fatalist with ears open to the weirdest plots, the most dangerous enterprises. I will say this for my experience: the memory of Helen's base betrayal has not tantalized me since the moment I entered Halleck's machine. One small point in its favor.

It was a crisp autumn day. Dead leaves clattered about in the wind. Puffy white clouds brushed across a blue sky. I stood before 3315 Hillside Drive, Canton, Iowa, using my attaché case to shield my ankles from the needle-sharp teeth of a toy poodle. The pleasant, colonial-style house at this address was Dr. Halleck's. My interview with him would complete the exhaustive article I was preparing, tentatively titled "Twenty Prominent Scientists in the Field of Mind Research."

"Yap! Yap!" yapped the poodle.

A hearty, bluff middle-aged man, his brownish-gray hair in a brush cut, threw open the front door and yelled at the poodle.

"Chatter! Chatter, come away!" His blue eyes twinkled.

"Dr. Halleck?" I asked.

He nodded his head, grinning agreeably.

"My name is Rolf Tibbett. I phoned you."

"Yes, yes, of course. Come away, Chatter! Her full name is Lady Chatterley, for she possesses an inordinate interest in the opposite sex, poor creature. Please come in, Mr. Tibbett." His grin was toothy and sincere.

I followed Halleck into his home, swinging my attaché case unobtrusively at Chatter, who was trying to nuzzle at my pant cuff.

I liked the man at once. I expect Halleck makes a good first impression on everyone. It is only human, after all, to be taken in by superficialities. I emphasize this point because, as far as Halleck is concerned, first impressions are most untrustworthy. When you meet him, do not be taken in by his heartiness. Go directly to his laboratory and rescue me from his machine.

"Let us go to my study, shall we, Mr. Tibbett? Chatter!" He gathered his yapping poodle into his arms and returned her to the out-of-doors.

Halleck's overstuffed sofa was the only convenient sitting place in his study, so I sat on it, though I would have preferred desk and straight-back chair.

Halleck reentered his studio, empty-handed and smiling brightly. "I suppose I am taking a chance putting her outside—there is a wirehaired terrier in the neighborhood who fancies her greatly. Now then, Mr. Tibbett, where shall we start? Would you care for a cigar?"

"No, thank you."

"A drink? A martini, perhaps?"

"No! Thank you!"

I firmly pushed aside the associations the martini conjured up and began the interview. "Dr. Halleck, you suggested in your most recent paper that it might soon become practical to change human beings' present habits—"

"Decondition them."

"Oh yes, decondition them and recondition them to better habits."

"Yes."

"Mechanically. A certain popular periodical has called your suggestion 'mind molding by machine.'"

Halleck frowned. "In their ignorance."

"Of course. That paper was published three years ago. I would like to know if the past three years have been profitable ones?"

"To a degree. To a degree." He coyly slanted his head to one side. "You realize all this depends upon how precisely the experimenter can identify specific thoughts with specific brain wave patterns. And don't forget reciprocity, Mr. Tibbett. Can the experimenter introduce certain electrical patterns into the subject's brain with the certainty that definite thoughts will result? Why don't you ask me that question?"

"Very well, Dr. Halleck, I will ask you that question. In your experiments, how closely do you find brain wave patterns corresponding to specific—"

Surely, it is one of the pleasant things in the world, lying upon a deep, soft, yielding bed of moss. Just sort of lazing time away. The mattress makers of the world certainly have a great deal to learn from a bed of moss. Truly comfortable—

Look out! That giant stone! It's coming right at me! This moss is so deep I can't move quickly. Missed me! Big as a house! Look out! Here it comes again! Rolling…a rolling stone—A rolling stone gathers no moss! The stone has trapped me! It's pushing me toward a cliff! I'm going over! There's water down there! I'm falling—

Splash! Drowning…can't swim…drowning…save me (cough, cough)…drowning in still, deep water—Somebody has my arm (cough)… pulling me up—

Oh! Horrible! A monster has my arm! Horrible! Horrible! Let me go! It has my head in its paws…squeezing…my head shrinking…smaller and smaller…and the water…and the rolling stone—Caught between the rolling stone that gathers no moss…and the deep, still water…still waters run deep—Of course! They contradict! An inconsistency! And if the monster squeezing my head smaller and smaller is a hobgoblin— A foolish consistency is the hobgoblin of little minds! Who said that? Ralph Waldo Emerson!

Everything disappears. I can't stand much more of this—

The devil with the rest of Halleck's interview. I am going to tell you precisely where I am, so you can rescue me as soon as possible. I am in Halleck's laboratory. But whether I am inside Halleck's machine or the machine is inside me, I cannot say. You'll just have to decide that for yourself when you enter the laboratory. You'll either see me there or you won't. Halleck could even have pushed me into another dimension. I do not recall the process of arriving here. Suddenly here I was. Wherever "here" is.

But I am alive, as alive and conscious as I ever was, save that my body is plastic. That monster—the hobgoblin—that yanked me out of the water just now and squeezed my head between his huge paws, reducing my skull to the size of an orange, was real. And the feeling that my head had shrunk was not merely subjective. When I put my hand to my head, my fingers actually wrapped all the way around. But my head has since returned to its normal size. It follows then that my body is as plastic as taffy candy.

I wander around in what I can only describe as a void. But wander with the alertness of a stag in hunting season. I know not what fresh terror will pop out of nothingness. I realize this description sounds as if I may be drugged or dreaming, but I am not. I walk about inside something. Or outside everything.

Dr. Halleck is a widower and lives alone. A pity, for I have known few men who could benefit more from the moderating influence of a good woman. As it is, with Mrs. Halleck some ten years in her tomb, solitude has eroded what restraints curbed his innate tendencies, and he has deviated from the scientific community in a spectacular way. No one else knows of these unorthodox experiments of his. Least of all did I know, the innocent scribe wandering with my attaché case among the double-domes. It was not until the end of our interview, having asked the usual questions and jotted down the usual answers, that I began to sense something more prowling around behind those smiling blue eyes. What he told me was conventional enough, but he told it with the care of a man slowly peeling an orange, careful not to bruise the fruit. I got the impression that he would hand me the rind and keep the fruit for himself.

I decided to do some probing. "Dr. Halleck, have your experiments with the brain uncovered anything truly revolutionary?"

My impression had been correct. For a moment, he seemed tempted to tell all, but then he said, "No, Mr. Tibbett, nothing of any great moment."

"Perhaps something you would prefer to discuss off the record?"

He was the image of a man bursting with a delicious secret. He had lived alone too long. Too much solitude will loosen the closest of tongues.

A bit more would do it. "Trust me as your confidant."

That tipped the scales. For the next hour, Halleck swamped me with words. Starting on a far-out limb of science, he slipped from shoot to shoot until, to change the metaphor, he appeared to have climbed up onto the laps of wizards and warlocks. When I protested, he insisted energetically, "I can demonstrate it, Mr. Tibbett. Everything I have told you, I can demonstrate."

"But why haven't you written a paper," I asked, "and informed your colleagues of your discoveries?"

He waved an impatient hand. "They are not ready. They are too far behind. They would not understand."

His eyes were bright. "Mr. Tibbett, do you grasp the significance of what I have told you?"

"I'm not sure—"

"Let me tell you." He grabbed my knee enthusiastically. "The benefit to humanity will be incalculable!"

In my stupidity, I was thinking of the benefits, not to humanity, but to myself. What an ass I was! I wanted to convince Dr. Halleck to accept me as his first subject. If only I'd known that the selfsame thought was caroming around inside his brain!

I thought he was only being the good host when he invited me to stay for dinner, and then—when I happened to mention I had not yet gotten a room in town—insisted that I stay overnight as his guest. The next morning, while he fried us some eggs, breaking the yolks, I voiced the thought that had kept sleep from me all night.

"Dr. Halleck, you say your machine is perfected, that you need only a human subject to prove its worth." I took a deep breath. "Dr. Halleck, I would like to be that first subject!"

He placed the eggs on the table in front of me. "Sorry I broke the yolks."

"How about it, Doctor: could I be your guinea pig?"

He only said, "Perhaps you would like to see my laboratory. It is in the basement. Let us go there after breakfast, shall we?"

I gulped down my meal. When I had finished, I was surprised to note that Halleck, too, had gobbled his breakfast down.

Everyone has seen dozens of those Hollywood horror films that revolve about the doings of a mad scientist. There is always that scene when the scientist, having pulled open a couple of creaking doors and descended a dark staircase, steps into his laboratory and the camera makes a slow pan of the room. In the center of the lab we see what appears to be a surgical table, ominous straps dangling from its sides. Over it hangs a gigantic machine. Lining the walls are large panels with dials and darting lights. Test tubes, Bunsen burners, and other scientific whatnot clutter long tables. The atmosphere hangs heavy with the ozone from crackling electricity. Halleck's lab fit the bill to a fare-thee-well. It lacked only Bela Lugosi in a peasant's smock, limping out of a dusty corner, croaking, "Yes, master?"

I should have yelled to high heaven and bolted for the door. If I had, I expect I would have found it locked. I forced an airy laugh, making an inane comparison with the film capital of the world.

"Yes, Mr. Tibbett, perhaps it does look Hollywood," Halleck answered tartly, not too taken with my analogy. "However, I require all of this 'paraphernalia,' as you call it, for my work."

We made a quick tour of the lab while Halleck explained things with the tired exasperation of the specialist reducing complexities to layman's terms. For some reason, possibly a sense of doom, I was drawn to the huge machine hovering over the surgical cot. It was into this machine that I believe I was sucked, body and all, as a bit of lint is sucked into a vacuum cleaner. And in which I am now incarcerated, a tiny being wandering in a nightmarish wilderness. When you come for me, go directly to this machine and feel around inside it for me.

That very day, Halleck programmed the computer that controlled his machine. He had accepted me as his first subject. Undoubtedly, he had been waiting, like a spider in a dusty corner, for just such a dim-witted fly to come blundering into his web.

After dinner, tasteless not only for my anxiety, but because Halleck was such an inadequate cook (imagine: a TV dinner!), we went outside to his patio and sat in lounge chairs. He sucked on a dead pipe, looking for all the world like a kindly old country doctor, while Chatter, the poodle, nipped at my ankle. After a few minutes silently watching the sunset, he filled his pipe and lit it.

"Mr. Tibbett." Puff. "The Deconditioner is ready." He removed the pipe from between his teeth. "Your affairs are in order?" He smiled, patting my arm reassuringly. "I trust I don't sound too portentous."

I smiled back. "Shoot the works!"

With a warmer smile yet, he shoved a piece of paper at me. "Please sign this, if you will. It is a release. Just a formality."

I signed. It was a legal form absolving Halleck of all responsibility. I doubt if it will stand up in court. I returned the paper to him. He folded it and tucked it away into an inside pocket. A fat, heavy volume bound in blue was resting on his lap. He picked it up and held it aloft. "We shall begin with this book, Mr. Tibbett...."

Animals. Crazy, crazy animals. A dog walking around on his hind legs, licking my face, insisting I shake hands with him. I wonder what it can mean? And a tortoise shell cat come to brush herself against my leg. Meow! But the dog won't let her near me.

He growls and pushes her away. The situation is not unpleasant, save

for the lap, lap, lapping of the dog's tongue on my face. I never particularly cared for overfriendly dogs. He just will not allow that cat to approach
me. But then, it is the dog that is man's best friend. The dog disappears....But the poor cat! Hands materialize from nowhere and grab her!
Cruel! Cruel! The hands tear off her fur and pull off her skin! They are
flaying her alive! Yeoow! She screams with pain! Now the hands skin her
with a knife! They throw her into a boiling pot! Her skin peels from her
flesh! She is shoved into an oven to bake! Horrible...but there is more
than one way to skin a cat! So ridiculous! The cat vanishes....Why must
I see these things?

It is raining....Thump! Thump! Thump! I am knee deep in cats and
dogs—It is raining cats and dogs! More animals: an overloaded camel,
its back broken with a straw...sleeping dogs with Do Not Disturb signs
pinned to them—Let sleeping dogs lie...thousands of birds of a feather
flocking together...a curious cat killed...a goose laying golden eggs—an
ax chops off her head! Idiots!

The farrago of yowling, squealing animals disappears....

Where was I? Oh yes, Halleck holding that book—
"...Bartlett's Familiar Quotations."

As I stared at the formidably bulky volume, a shadow—as the Ro-
mantics used to put it—crossed my soul. He opened the book. "I doubt if
we shall find it necessary to work our way through the entire volume. For
an example," he said, turning a few pages, "I don't feel the proverb 'Wash
your hands often, your feet seldom, and your face never' is quite threadbare enough for our purpose. On the other hand, and on the same subject, 'Cleanliness is next to godliness' may well be." He closed the book.
"Besides Bartlett's, we have those advertising slogans so common as to
have entered the language. The cigarette that 'tastes good like a cigarette
should' comes to mind. Not only trite but ungrammatical. Advertising,
in fact, would appear to be a fertile source of the sort of stuff we want
weeded out, would it not, Mr. Tibbett?"

"Yes," I replied, a little distractedly. Doubt was beginning to enter my
mind. The thing began to appear endless.

Halleck tapped his pipe ash out on the green-painted cement of the
patio. "Are we ready?"

We went down to the basement and into Halleck's lab.

"Just get up on this table, Mr. Tibbett."

He indicated the cot over which was hung the Deconditioner. A bit nervously, I got on it and stretched out.

"Relax, Mr. Tibbett, please relax. I assure you, there will be no pain whatever. You will merely fall asleep. Gently…quietly…"

He slid a strap over my ankles and pulled it tight. I started up, suddenly badly frightened.

"Relax, Mr. Tibbett. Really, you must relax. My securing you to the table is only a precaution, a mere precaution."

He strapped down my wrists and hurried over to a console crammed with dials, excited as a kid on Christmas morn. The Deconditioner slowly lowered toward me from the ceiling. From where I lay, it looked like a huge vacuum cleaner funnel. I was terrified. I wanted to leap up and run like a thief. But Halleck was right. I was getting drowsy. In another moment, I fell asleep.

The next thing I knew, I was wandering in this void.

What an asinine scheme to which I agreed to submit myself! I am so ashamed of my stupidity. Anyway, this is Halleck's project: I am being declichéd.

Ridiculous, isn't it? Now that it is too late, I see what an absurd fool I was. Halleck must know how I am suffering inside this machine, but he is like a boy with a toy train. He just won't stop. Like all mad scientists, he is completely insensitive to human feelings.

Certainly, you can see how attractive the prospect of becoming declichéd would be to a professional writer. Imagine being rid, once and for all, of those hackneyed phrases, those tired old chestnuts that enter and dam up the stream of consciousness, which is the author's bloodstream, like deposits of cholesterol. With infectious enthusiasm, Halleck assured me I could look forward to my writing flowing on and on, fresh and new, each sentence sparkling as the morning dew. Henceforth (said Halleck) I would be unable to think of a cliché, for each one in the language would have been driven from my head by the Deconditioner. To illustrate, that episode some time back of the running water, the ripping cloth, and the stench of spoiled food, which wrung the phrase 'Too many cooks spoil the broth' out of my anguish; and the sewing machine beating away in my bones, 'A stitch in time saves nine'—now I can think of neither of these proverbs without flinching inwardly, for with them I recall the painful experiences with which Halleck associated them. The mind always skirts painful things. Yet more and more lately, the terrible, nagging fear whispers in my mind, What if Halleck's machine has the opposite effect—what if it does not repel triteness, but so drums triteness into my being that I can think in no other way? For I can think of these clichés even now: A stitch in time saves nine—you see? Ah no.…It must be that in the future my unconscious will grab these phrases and tear them to shreds before they have a chance to drift up into consciousness.

But I had no idea how unbearable it would become. I cannot guess how long I have been a prisoner of Halleck's machine. A day. Two days. A week. A month—I am completely disoriented and I feel that I am on the brink of madness.

Please come immediately to 3315 Hillside Drive, Canton, Iowa. Bring the police. I am convinced that Halleck will not give me up without a struggle.

But hurry! Consider how I dread the coming of the anatomical monstrosities! What horror when I shall have to witness the long arm of the law putting its foot down! Or a nose to the grindstone toeing the mark! What terror to be eyed askance and fingered gingerly!

Hurry! For Bartlett's Familiar Quotations is but Halleck's first book. There is politics to come yet—the whole subject is a cliché—and diplomacy. Show biz and advertising and—Lord, there's no end to it!

The fat is in the fire because I went the whole hog. Halleck made me sign on the dotted line, adding insult to—

Wait a minute! What is happening?

—injury. I am eating my heart out, more sinned against than sinning, and now there's the devil to pay. Put your shoulder to the wheel and take the bull by the horns. Go straight as the crow flies to—

No! It can't be! Halleck, you bungling nincompoop!

—Halleck's home sweet home and give it the once-over. Don't be a fair weather friend. Bear in mind, nothing ventured, nothing—

I am lost! Lost!

—gained. More in sorrow than in anger, tell Halleck the game is not worth the candle and handsome is as handsome does. But make haste slowly, for—

Truly…

—no man can tell what the future will bring.

Live and learn.

The transcript does not include the barking of the poodle that jumped on the table and disappeared into the device when it was inadvertently switched on by Officer Chedney. There is still no trace of the animal. Nor, as yet, of this Mr. Tibbett, self-identified as the narrator on the tapes.

Dr. Halleck will continue to be held in your high-security facility during our investigation. And, so I understand, afterward.

Following the order of the Court, the machine has been destroyed.

Very sincerely yours,
Detective Stephen R. Davison
DUKE COUNTY SHERIFF'S DEPARTMENT
Louisburg, Iowa

THE DOUMBRI

I

T WAS A SMALL, round marblelike object made of glass and magic. You held it in your hand—held it tight and waited—and all the wisdom of the past would come back, all the knowledge, the secrets, and the towering theories, one by one, tumbling one after another, all would come back. With it—and only with it—could mankind lift its belly from the earth and face and defeat the Krok, and then build again, theorizing and educating by listening to the voices of their ancestors. And soon, very soon, all would be as before. The yoke of the Krok would be pushed aside, as if mere thread, and human civilization would rise to the imperial structure that it once had been, before the cunning of the Krok had tricked and then despoiled man, taking all that had been gained in the age-old magnificence.

They called the small object the Doumbri, and it had long been lost—somewhere still on the earth but lost. Perhaps resting on the bottom of the ocean or perhaps buried in a crevice of barren rock high on some distant mountain. Yet still here on earth. The Krok knew nothing of the Doumbri. Only man knew. Man, who whispered its name from old lips into young ears down the many, many generations since the Krok first came drifting down from space, smiling with humanoid mouths and talking of peace.

The search for the Doumbri would never end. All day and every day, even by night in the patches of light dripped down from a pale, cold moon, there were humans searching, pushing aside blades of grass, reaching into holes burrowed into the earth, and sifting absently through beach sand. Brown hands, white hands, young hands and old, ever eager to close greedily about that round, hard, cold key to lost knowledge.

Of course, there were some who scoffed. Some who claimed there was not a Doumbri, that there had never been a Doumbri. Others said the Krok had stolen it long ago.

The boy lies on his back in the warm grass, listening to the chittering and fretting of the birds, the grackles and sparrows, in the shrubbery. The golden sun. The breeze flipping the dark leaves on their sides. The sweet smell of hay and flowers. He thinks again, as he often does, of the Doumbri. Was it real or was it not. Would it affect his life, as he grew to be a man, were it found. Staring up into the blue sky as his hand moves without thought through the deep grass.

And the miracle happens!

A round, cool sphere, a globe that trembles as his hand grasps it. His body shivers in the warm air as he lifts the object into sight.

"The Doumbri!" he cries out. "This must be the Doumbri!"

Holding it, soon strange thoughts come to his mind as the veils of the past fall away.

Since its first years, mankind was ever turning and steaming and cooking in the cauldron of nature. Until finally stepping out, separate, alone in the universe, challenging, seeking, probing, experimenting, and creating cauldrons of his own, man turning nature to his use, bending no longer to her will. And those first tentative steps, the first objects hurling about the earth, the first men orbiting in the awful loneliness, the first spaceships, the moon landing, and the planets after. Each jostling against the other, greedy to dominate space.

But when the Krok came, it was over. Finis. A period placed at the end of an age. Of all ages. The rollicking plant thrust back into the ground. The clock turned back and stopped. Man set thereafter to running about in his own tiny birdcage, hankering, discontented, yearning for what he knew not.

Holding the Doumbri, the boy sees airplanes and knows what they were meant to do. The ailerons, the tail, the fuselage, and the propellers. He sees every detail of the motor and how it was put together. And how the curve of the wing made the difference in air pressure so the whole great body would go up and up, till there was no air to sustain it. And the rocket motors thrusting their fierce heat outward and thrusting forward whatever vehicle man attached to them. The ramjet and the atomic pile. The fluids and the fissions. He sees into the heart of bombs brighter than the sun. And with sudden insight, he knows that matter has disintegrated itself into this fury at the speed of light. Does light move? Yes, at precisely 186,281.7 miles per second.

The visions grow. He is sucked into the vortex of a great war. Moans from a million twisted, tortured throats tear at his heart. He sees a woman running with her screeching child through a fiery street and then scorched into a sudden cinder by a white, blazing blotch of magnesium. He sees fingernails yanked out, ribs cracked with heavy blows and eyes dangling like swollen grapes from their sockets. Then old men bent and whitened with age and children whimpering, looking with wide, astonished eyes at their naked mothers walking into gas chambers. Bodies shoveled into furnaces. The crack of a mallet on a tooth and a tiny sliver of gold lifted from the dead mouth. Soldiers suffocating in earth-blocked caves. Walls slowly collapsing and popping open the living bodies caught under their weight. Bombs dropping and shells exploding. Shrapnel and grenades. Fire and torture.

The Doumbri trembles in his hand. He wants to cry out; he wants to throw up. Pain tears at his chest, but the visions will not stop. Other wars. Rockets arcing up. Mini-suns exploding and polluting life. Whole cities collapsing with one hammer blow. No time left for prayers, fears, or farewells. From under the sea or from far-away satellites, swift rockets streak up, hover in brief apogee in the black silence of space, and then down and down. And after the rockets, the robots. The swift electronic minds programmed to do what most men care not to do. Grasping human bodies, ripping open the soft flesh with jagged metal teeth, bludgeoning—

No! No! No!

The Doumbri skitters from his hand. He snatches it from the earth, where it had fallen, and throws it from him with all his strength down onto the rocks.

Ping! Ping-ping—pingpingping—and it cracks open on a rock edge. A graphitelike powder spills out, and with a sudden flash of white flame, disappears. He clambers down onto the rocks. The clear shell of the Doumbri had split in two, scorched from the heat of the burning material inside. He feels hot, angry tears on his cheeks. He sobs, pressing his heel against the shell of the Doumbri and grinds it deep into the earth. (Curse them! Damn them! Damn them!) And with fierce shame, knowing that he, too, is human, he grinds the fragments deeper into the earth. He sinks down and kneels, pressing his head against cold rock, seeing still the cruelty, the agony. Thank God, he whispers. Thank God the Krok came. Oh, thank God they came!

It is nearly night when he returns home, walking slowly up the steps to the porch. A cricket scrapes its legs with a chirp just in front of him. And he steps aside in time to miss crushing the ugly black shape. He watches tenderly as the creature scuttles across the warm wood and down into the tall, damp grass beyond.

He finds his father reading in the front room. But his book is on his lap and he is staring toward the wall, his eyes blank and far away, and when he turns to his son, almost hostile.

"Do you know what happened? I found—" The boy stops short. I cannot tell him, he thought. I cannot tell anyone, ever. He goes quickly to his father and presses his head against his shoulder.

His father shrugs. "Been away a long time." His voice is hollow, the warmth carved out, emptied out. He could no longer give comfort to anyone.

The boy pulls away and sees his father as he is, without hope and alone, achingly, incredibly alone. And in the fading memory of the Doumbri's flame, he sees in his father humanity's doom in its futile search for the forever-lost Doumbri.

THE WOODCARVER'S TALE

A TALE TOLD by a Woodcarver, a messenger of the Most High (or so he said).

Gather about me, said he, sitting, and I will tell you of the day when the lusty winds of August brought to the womb of a lady, sperm and egg and sexual congress, a struggling together of male and female bodies, which in time expelled the shiny shape, hairless as gut, of a boy child. An infant brought to full term, continued the Carver, whittling and chipping and forming his piece of wood, in less time than the usual nine months, perhaps in three months, as finger-wide strips of striae slashed across the mother's expanding belly, forming nearly as quickly as an hour hand takes to slide around the face of a clock. The day of delivery arriving, the infant drops down, dilating his mother's vagina with trembling fingers, so eager is he to be born.

The Woodcarver stared at the sky. A day like this day, he said, blue and golden, cloudless, windless, the sun at meridian. Men and their animals shrinking into the shrinking shadows. A day for truth, a day when all might be revealed, when the liar, the man of deceit, falls down upon the baked earth, and truths issue from his mouth like placenta, swollen and unfamiliar.

The infant, the Carver went on, grew to become a healthy boy with a quizzical smile and questioning eyes. In a clear soprano voice, he sang hymns in his church with the others of his age.

One day, the Junior Choir were taken out to a vacant field, where they gaped as the seeds of forty aspen trees were planted by their minister, shepherd of his flock, who ceremoniously, ritualistically, pushed the forty seeds into the ground, forty and not more, so each should grow and grow equally; so each should crack its shell, pop! In unison with the other thirty-nine, it would unwreath its twigs, unfurl its leaves, all as one, the forty as one. "For in this fashion," said their pastor, "did God create the universe. Thus a minute demonstration of innumerable galaxies striking light in the deep. And God did as I now do! He did plant the seed of creation in the fertile void. Did thrust in his spade thus: Whop! Dropped in his seed, covered it: Whisk! Whisk! Watered it: Splash! And moved thus far and no farther to thrust in—Whomp!—the next seed."

The Reverend grew silent, working in the vacant field. The Junior Choir, soon seeing there was no more to be said, left, one by one, for their homes.

In the days that followed, the lad asked his elders for the meaning of what he had witnessed. Some laughed and twirled a finger around one ear: "Cuckoo!" Others frowned, irritated at the Reverend for planting so many trees: "Fool!"

The memory faded for everyone, washed away by fresh events, except in the boy's mind, where it grew ever more vivid. He would stand at the edge of the field watching. He was standing there alone, wondering still, on the warm, wet evening when the aspens broke through the soil in unison, a chorus of forty.

Becoming a youth old enough to leave his home, he set out to search for someone who could explain to him what the Pastor had done. He had learned that there was a Sage living by himself, remote in the high desert, a Wise Man rich with knowledge. "If anyone can answer you, he can," he was told. In the silence of a desert afternoon the Youth found the home of the Wise One. He introduced himself and stood in the doorway, waiting.

The Sage

Creaky, bone-dry turning of wrinkled, crumbling pages. Overgrown nails scraping across misunderstood language. A musty room lit with mote-filled sunlight. The air still. Desert desiccation, brain juices sucked out, mental dehydration. Waiting for the incendiary burst of inspiration, which would not come. Tinder and oxidation browning the edges of rice paper. Time-knurled joints growling in wasted flesh. Bugging, pickled eyes, unblinking and slow moving in their sockets. Thin nerves, piebald skin, rigid veins.

In a desert dry voice, the Sage asked, "Who are you?" Immediately, he waved a hand. "Never mind. What do you want?"

Beginning slowly, the Youth told him of his Pastor, of the forty trees and God and the void and mankind and finally, that no one could explain any of it to him.

Slowly, the Sage looked away, staring out the window at the desert.

"Man and God," he said finally, speaking in a low voice. "God and man." He looked again at the Youth. His voice strengthened. "The journey of the ancients, is it not? The metaphysical journey." He paused and then continued. "Is there no magic? Then man would invent magic. And wizardry, jinns, gargoyles, and Medusa. While the peasant sweated in the field, the alchemist concocted gold-adoring potions. No magic? Then werewolves, ogres, vampires, and demons came tumbling out of the human imagination. And while the putative evil called up devils, drawing hexagons on the floor and circles in the dust, the stolid, solid alchemists, now physicists, were formulating formulae, inventing out of the smallest bits of earth, man's first real hell. No imagining about this hell. There, always waiting for man to discover them, were these fires of hell, waiting in the stones. Now man, as if he were God, may will his own destruction; no demon, no devil to invent it. Man invents himself, yet has only begun unraveling his own mystery. Consciousness, unconsciousness, ultraconsciousness..."

The Sage halted, slow blinking his rheumy eyes.

"But God," the Youth ventured. "What of God?"

"God?" A pause. "Man owns a God too small for the universe, his speculations are buried under mountains of muck shoveled up by his fellows. Too solemn, too naive, too new to the world, man then enslaves the machine and becomes slave to his slave. Son of the Egyptian, the Etruscan, and the Sogdian nomad, fellow of ten thousand dead races; a plain, ordinary animal, trained and clever, who has everywhere built a wall of ritual about him, masking the darkness. Man—you and I—crying, swaggering, bullying, cowering, vomiting, and fucking, all within that dimly lit sphere of consciousness. Nor have his hands forgotten the shape of the stone tool, nor his feet forgotten the mud of the Nile. His brow still low, his eyes shifting, his cheeks sucking his own saliva, using reason only to serve the fire in his belly."

The Sage stopped again. He breathed a soft breath. "Might as well still sweat beside the Nile and tremble for the dog-god. Same needs and same fears. Certainty is gone. Answers that have been answers for millennia have vanished in the great vacuum. Once again, man faces the wilderness." The Sage's voice sank to a stop and his eyes closed.

The Youth waited. He watched as dust bits drifted slowly across beams of sunlight. Finally, growing impatient, he said, "Sir, I know your knowledge is great. And your experience is great, too. Please let me learn what you know."

The Sage's eyes opened. He scowled. "What does my life experience matter to you?" he asked sourly. "I care nothing about your life, as you should care nothing about mine. Six billion humans drag their paganism into the twenty-first century; you are but one of this multitude." He paused. "I have become old. Humans are ever more strange to me. They will never become familiar. In this I understand I am no different from any other."

He halted for a moment, staring at the Youth. "You ask, what of God?" He frowned. "A pack of dogs is running together. One of them turns suddenly and bites another, as if he were not one of them, born of them. He bites a strange shape, a ghost, an alien. In a moment of terror, his teeth clash together in a world of nothingness! Do you understand? You who search, and so suppose yourself to be better than others. A play actor! Artificer! Then make your own God! Paint lips on stone and converse! Gather your tin men about you and your battery-run robots and your talking teddy bears! Make a world as God did: in the void!"

The voice of the Sage had become a shout. He stood slowly, pointing a trembling finger. The Youth leaped up, knocking over his chair. In great confusion, he backed clumsily out of the dusty room.

"Create a field!" the Sage cried out. "A vast endeavor, a sparkling creation peopled with innumerable beings, a reckless creation set in its ways, determined to follow its own course. A creation burdened by beings fomenting their lives out of emotion and habit. A prancing, tramping intelligent mass, a bouquet of busybodies, a blending of solids, corroded by propinquity. Minds that speak and beat the air with the flotsam of their thoughts. And you shall be their god!"

The Youth fled, running out into the desert, flustered.

The Woodcarver shook his head, smiling. The poor boy didn't know the proud ego of the pedant, which, like tinder, would roar into flame from the merest spark.

The Woodcarver scraped a bit of wood from his work and continued his tale.

The Youth overcame his discouragement, and after a long and difficult journey, he came to the City. He soon befriended a few of its citizens, and one day asked them if there were not someone who could answer his questions.

One of them answered, telling him of the Titan: "The steel-clanking Titan, who sits upon a grave mound; a hill of rib cages, limb bones, and skulls, of white, dry calcium."

"The Titan is not human," said another, "though we humans know of him."

"We put ourselves to his service," explained the first, "and he puts himself in ours by using us."

"It takes the ears of many gods," a third said, "to hear our noise, the clamor of the human race."

Added the first, "Because, as our numbers increase, we exhaust the gods with our prayers."

"Anyhow, some say," observed the third, "that the gods may rule us no longer."

His companions shook their heads. "Don't say such things!"

As they spoke of their gods, the Youth grew excited. "Where is the Titan?" he asked. "I would like to talk to him."

They laughed. "You cannot speak to him," the first explained. "You must pray to the Titan, though I doubt he would answer you, because you are not one of us."

A fourth dweller of the City spoke up. "He should speak to the Magician."

"Yes! Yes!" the others chorused. "Of course! The Magician! Come, we will take you to his dwelling."

The Youth followed them to the house of the Magician. They held back while the Youth banged a heavy brass knocker against the door.

Presently, a servant opened the door and admitted the Youth, waving the others away. He listened to the Youth's request and then disappeared. As he waited and studied the odd, archaic furniture and the ancient drawings and symbols hanging on the walls, an eerie sense of foreboding overcame the Youth, as if he had arrived at the crumbling edge of a precipice. He glanced at the front door, considering retreat, when the servant returned and beckoned to him.

The Magician

Upon entering the room of the Magician, the Youth felt immediately that he was in the presence of a human oddity. The man standing before him seemed, at his periphery, to dissolve into smoke, then condense again into human form. Staring at the Magician's face, the Youth found that, try as he might, his eyes were unable to focus on his features. Later, having left, a memory came to him of the Magician being clothed in a blue robe and rust red sash and slippers. Yet not even the shape of his face could he recall.

The Magician indicated a long divan and they sat. The Youth spoke, asking the questions he hoped could be resolved by his host.

As the Magician responded, his voice waxed and waned, transiting, like his form, between the real and the unreal.

"You would know," he began, "what man is perhaps not made to know. You are an aspirant, as was I. You question, as did I. But I caution you to listen and consider:

"On a day long ago, before the rising of the sun, I awoke. I felt the approaching thunder of the undiscovered, messages whispered to me before the dawn; strange-to-the-ears superlatives.

"I dressed and left my home.

"The Master Builder had constructed a ladder. Step by step, I, the Magician, ascended. I slid up the sunbeams, my gaze fixed on the light, my posture solemn and erect. Many had gathered there. I held close the prayers of those who prayed, and they, having prayed, stood quiet, their eyes wide with hope.

"'Rise! Arise!' some cried out. 'Ascend beyond our chattering! Our noise! Our darkness!' Their fretful hands twisting skyward, fingers all atwitter, words pouring like foam from their lips; orisons, prayers, entreaties, secret signs, and the singing of songs— noon songs, twilight songs, night songs.

"There soon came a sudden silence. The voices and music cascaded downward, shattering like icicles on a winter night, wearied by the pressure of the unknown.

"Soon I, too, descended, gliding down amid a cluster of memories, budding like the branches of spring. My consciousness passed, as from hand to hand, from one memory to another, down the long corridors to earth. And there the present squeezed into me, through my five senses, its one truth, which is time, where fresh myths will be concocted, fresh hands will handle my mind, and fresh flavors will soon stale." The Magician grew silent.

The Youth, uneasy in his presence, wondered if he should wait or speak. Finally, he asked, "What did you find? I mean, did you bring any—"

The Magician interrupted: "To those who had prayed, I brought disaster: On this day, the daffodils died. Everywhere, there was confusion. Thunder in the pigpens, dwarfs climbing the hill slopes, bean vines lashing with their tendrils all who strayed near them! Violence that day! Screams and heart stops, running and yelling and terror! Blood on the rosebush! I cried out to them all, 'I will walk forth, though the land roars! Bear with me! '"

The Magician's voice had faded to a whisper. "What did I find, you ask. I found the something there that never was. The imprint of the nonexistent. Bruised grass twisted to the earth under that which never was. A scent on the wind, the echo of cries, and memory gouged to the root. Here! they say, here! They who never were. Outlines against the blank sky, lines drawn across motionless water."

His breath caught. In a low voice, he continued: "Terra incognita: the unknown land. All about will shrivel to know this truth. No maps to guide your steps. No signposts. No well-trod paths. The unknown terror, terra incognita, lies all about. Footsteps running in the darkness.

"I was companion to them all, without form, without memory, and without thought. I was motionless, transfixed."

The Magician rose to stand before a dark portrait on the wall. "Would that I had met the Being of goodness and strength. The Being of creation. The Son of creation and witness to creation. I did not."

He turned and spoke directly to the Youth. "Then know now of the terror of the night, of the being thou art. This being, who is thee, peering from behind humanoid brows, recognizably human, yet in the narrow, unlit corridors of the night, prowling and inhuman. Antihuman, yet not subhuman. A human. No worse, no better. Prowler, not predator."

Moving away, the Magician took several deep breaths. "Make what you will of my words. Now you must leave. Come, I will take you to a door other than the one through which you entered."

The Youth stood unsteadily, unnerved by the Magician, who, while speaking, had pointed an arm, almost touching the Youth's chest with a finger. He followed the Magician's lead down a carpeted hall.

"It is possible," the Magician went on, "that the fools who brought you here are waiting outside to plague me with their questions. You will leave by another door."

At the door, the Youth stopped. The Magician turned to him. Gathering his courage, the Youth asked, "But what of God? The Titan who sits on the mountain of skulls—is the Titan, God?"

The Magician shook his head. "A thought to occupy the ignorant." He reflected for a moment. "But I will give you this to consider, a thought that will, no doubt, comfort you during the many moments of agony to come.

"It is when humans need God's help the most that he is the furthest from us. The Deity approaches not your screams but your silence."

The Youth stepped outside into the bright sunlight, blinking his eyes in some confusion. He heard the door close softly behind him.

The Woodcarver looked up at the cloudless sky. The sun, he said, moves to the horizon. Before its light disappears, I will finish. He rubbed the wooden form he was carving against his sleeve. And this, too, will be finished, he said.

The Youth's search, continued the Woodcarver, did not end with his encounter with the Magician. But after the Magician, none could answer his questions. Years passed. The Youth became a man. But before hoisting the burden most other men bore, he thought to return to where his questioning had begun. He would confront the Pastor as a fellow adult and finally have explained to him the meaning of the planting of the trees, which he had been too shy to ask for as a youth.

He was soon walking through the young aspens, trees growing with remarkable uniformity, as the Pastor had said they would, being forty, not one more or one less. He stopped at the center of the grove, gazing at the trees, their leaves glittering in the wind, wondering how he should find the Reverend.

"You return!"

The Reverend

Strolling through the aspens, the Reverend had come upon the Seeker. He smiled with delight. Though his hair had whitened, his skin was still smooth and ruddy. They embraced.

"Yes," said the Seeker. "I have returned."

Smiling still, the Reverend asked, "How has your search gone?"

"Dear Reverend, I am as ignorant as the day I left. I have found no answers."

The Reverend nodded. "No surprise there. Fools search for answers; the wise search for questions." He grasped the Seeker's hands in his own and bowed his head. "Will you pray with me?

"Let us waken ourselves to heaven," the Reverend declaimed with folded hands, "to divine souls dancing in the firmament, to presences, to obeisances, and to the nod of God and the smile of Christ, Amen."

The two walked slowly together through the trees, talking of how each had spent the years.

"I know," said the Seeker at one point, "your meaning when you say, 'The wise search for questions.' It is that the answers to all the questions man asks or will ever ask are on display now in front of us. They wait only for the right questions."

"Quite true, as frustrating as that is," the Reverend agreed.

They took a few more steps and then stopped.

The Seeker spoke resolutely. "I came back here for one reason. I wanted to see you and ask you for the meaning of that day the trees were planted. I have asked others and now I return to ask you, what was the meaning of what you did?"

"What was the meaning?" the Reverend mused. "It was, I think, a demonstration. The meaning was no more than that forty living things now exist where previously there was nothing but fallow earth. But what did I say to the Junior Choir that day?"

The Seeker answered with growing exasperation, "That as God planted universes in the void, you planted those trees!"

"Ah. Does that make any sense? My mood, it seems, was quite austere at the time. Perhaps I have changed. Now I only observe my human flock and contribute what I can when asked. I am mainly an observer."

"Do you know how hard I've tried to understand what you did that day?" the Seeker asked impatiently.

The Reverend smiled. "Well, I'm sure your search was not totally in vain." His smile broadened. "I invite you to join me and become an observer of the human players. While you act out your own performance, of course."

"Is that what life is, a performance?" the Seeker asked shortly.

"Yes. I begin to see that a performance may well be all it is. An entertainment for the heavens to smile at."

"Do you mean God?'

"Ah, that subject." The Reverend pursed his lips. "I've found that the older one gets, the less one knows about that particular subject."

"But you are a clergyman?!"

The Reverend chuckled. "Don't expect the clergy to know anything about God. We may cook the meals, wash the dishes, and make the beds, but we never see the Master of the house."

"Then life is only observing and performing."

"Succinctly said. True ever and always, for all creatures, not excepting homo sapiens. As a matter of fact, I somewhat addressed that subject in a recent sermon. Part of it is still fresh in my memory.

"'All creatures,' it went, 'exist by pumping their breasts and circulating the rivulets of life through their bodies. All palpitate, all shiver in the wind, all run from the storm, all climb to the highest rise of ground to search for their enemies, all scan the horizon, and all gaze up into the sun and blink, quick-blinded.

"'As for us, we humans, friend is enemy and enemy is friend. And who gathers forces, arms itself, and slips out at daybreak to meet another in battle, soon after discovers a friend and finds, on another day, in that friend an enemy.

"'And on the clockwork ticks,
This marching to and fro
Lover another picks
And friend another foe.'"

The Seeker shook his head in disgust. "All this performing and observing adds up to is going around and around in a circle."

"Very true. The Wheel of Life, as they put it. A journey of change but no progress. Until the end."

"Then it does come to an end?"

"Assuredly. Whatever has a beginning must have an ending." The Reverend paused, his mood somber. "Then what of that day ordained from the beginning to be the last: the Day of Judgment? When the last trumpet is blown, how many, I wonder, will prefer to continue their sleep? 'Nay, bring me not to your heaven!' Christ awaits us with open arms, but do we care for his embrace? We like what we know. Not the hot fever breath of death-in-life, not the love-death, but one more day like yesterday. Just one more day. And another day."

They stood there, silent, thinking different thoughts, until the Seeker spoke. "I know a fine woman. I've been thinking of marriage."

"Yes! By all means: marriage, a home, and children. Yes. Live that life and you'll do well."

The Seeker thrust out his hand. "Good-bye, sir. I'll take your advice. I'll go back and marry her, if she'll have me."

Disregarding the outstretched hand, the Reverend embraced him. "Good-bye. And may God go with you."

The Seeker frowned a moment, wondering at the reference, and then he smiled. "Good-bye," he said again. He turned and walked briskly away, out of the aspen grove forever.

The Woodcarver placed the form he had been shaping on the ground before him, finally satisfied. "It is finished," he said, smiling. "Is it not beautiful?"

"Yes," we said.

So now begins the race of the Seeker to the finish line, the Woodcarver said. Doubt not his position in the race, hair follicles tensed and eyebrows wickered; steam the legs and pump the arms out and back, up and down. Who knows how long he must run? He speeds on, with the light heart he had forgotten from his youth. Very well, the laurels may all be handed out, the blue ribbons and the red, the yellow, and the white, the judges gone, the cheerers-on gone, and the checkered flag furled. Trot on, weary runner, the race is your own. Somewhere, there is a tally kept, and along with the absurdities, the stupidities and the transgressions there are listed the good, enough perhaps even to surprise yourself. Go on to the end and there you'll see.

And, at the end, how shall we find him?

Singing in the wilderness, waiting for the gong to chime. Waiting for meaning to suddenly blare out its trumpet call. An end to the wildness. Then peace: a wisp of silver sunset, miles of sandy beach, and, across the ocean, an orange sun, nodding in sleep, slipping into blue haze. And something throbbing inward and outward.

The body fails. A persistent weariness overcomes him. Weakened, he takes to his bed. Dim forms drift in the shadows about him. He hears voices.

Draw out the venom slowly, they whisper, so it inflicts harm neither on the host nor on a brother who might brush by haphazardly.

A whole headful of thoughts tumble toward some window to the outside. The gray stuff within his skull, long protected and imprisoned, now feels the touch of ice and so shrivels and desiccates.

Let me out! cries the mind (the brain dying). Let me be as vapor!

Such an ambition—to drift into what? A cloud of escaped vapors?

He dreams; the images fade away. His chest heaves gently with its final breath and life departs.

The Woodcarver looked away, as if witness once more to a long-past event. He spoke again, more forcefully.

A thousand, thousand impressions are stamped on the mind, indelible tattoos that we come to believe are our own, but whisk in without our notice. They were not chosen by us, but now we nurture them and stroke them familiarly as our possessions. They are part of us. With each incarnation (if thus we continue) we are scrubbed clean, but not quite; the old patterns form up and victimize us. We are shoved along by them, and by fresh imperatives, across the spectrum of human life, life after life.

To know this truth and still continue these lives—can this be the most ignoble knowledge one can have about oneself? To a being knowing life—not as a human but observing from beyond—it must seem incomprehensible that, having found the truth, one could go on being an ordinary human. Still, the fly, thinking it is clever, buzzes too close to the web and once again provides a meal for the spider, who need only to construct its glittering trap. We are caught in this dream again and again, and what else can be the solution but that God sets us free. No more glittering web. Some call this grace and we pray for it.

The Woodcarver rose slowly. He continued: So goes the pilgrim on the road. Walking, then stopping for some trivial reason, he walks again. Shone on by the sun and rained upon, wet and tired, resting, and then walking on. It is true, then also it is all false. Narrow and obscure is the path, easily lost when light dims; but he knows, too, that long ago he came to the end of this journey. A voyager in the dark to a terminus in the light long-ago known. A shiver of fear! A shiver of joy!

The Woodcarver cried out, "Ah, awesome light! Met in the night!"

His arms lifted toward the setting sun.

Poetry

A Fragrant Rose

A fragrant rose may quench the stubborn fire,
    The anomalous blaze.
Pewter and walnut wood, shining in the memory,
Roses and the smell of roses.
Her darling smile, precious to me
    Even at an ending.
Pendulums of the past sweep across
    My melting heart.
For what moment past is not sweeter than today,
    Sweeter than any tomorrow?
Though, with remembrance, my heart cries out
    I feel this pain, too, as sweet.
So with longing, I voyage into the changeless past
To live once more the yesterday
That was once the detestable now.

From the Nether Place

Slow from the nether place I creep
To bed with humans dull with sleep.
I smile and flatter with each dream
And make what's pure dire evil seem.

With evil gone from man's intent,
Believing lies they drift content.
Each soul I lash with bonds unfelt
That none escape the fate they're dealt.

The wise proclaim, No sin can damn!
They say I'm not, but still I am.

The Robin

Thursday, walking on my way to see her,
I stopped, watching a robin in a maple tree.
      Friday, too, and Saturday,
      Sunday the Lord's Day,
Singing his robin's song, flying from branch to branch,
          Inflating his molten breast.
Each day I watched, enchanted, breathing
        The cool spring air
And hope, witness to his buoyant spirit, reawakened.
I thought to bring her with me
(Knowing how hard that would be for her)
So she could see what joy could be.
But too quick the robin's singing ended.
      Dead now.
      The robin, too.

The Frozen Shore

I walked along the frozen shore
    Of a river, cold.
My feet were bare upon the ice,
    The sky was gold.
The air was new and never breathed;
    I was alone.
The wind blew hard through rattling trees,
    The wind did moan.
I walked four miles; two there, two back,
    While night did fall.
Then entered I the river, cold
    That ice be my pall.

Sweet Summer's Wane

Sweet summer's wane; then autumn's moody end
Close shut the door of yet another year,
The constant hours slowly wend their way
Down dark'ning lanes, their footfalls soft and slow.
Deep August's time does then an ending make
To squirrels crouched beside their hollow knot
And bluebirds nested on their springtime bough.
The flowers summer fields enchant close up
As early frost licks deep its icy tongue
And sucks their fragrance dry.
Thus do seasons pass and we who count
Their passing conjure meaning from each year
While humbler creatures live each moment
And seem to need no moment more than that.
Better we, too, mark not the passing years
For too near to the dawn is the twilight.

Rapture Retrieved

Rapture retrieved from pale yesterdays:
Tomb-bound animals stripped of their pelts,
Boneless transients caught choking
On dark weeds that spread out from their throats,
Yet now tailored, clipped, refined,
Rocketing upward for transit with amorphous forms
Copulating with the darkness.
Unpeeled love, clasping nudity to nudity,
Dark into light, light into dark.
Oh! Sweet ecstasy of the unborn!

And Then the Dusk

And then the dusk into the heart's mouth;
Flame wasting on the horizon. And said,
"The tune tomb boom racket on the ratchet."
The tiddum peaks frosty breath faulty death
Peepums. And the mother, the sister,
"Moan groan groan granny on the bed dead."
Fume and fume and pasty Tom
Digging in the softy downy deep drowny earth
Without mirth perth in the trees a trumpet sound
Sang, "Amen *ahem* amen amen *ahem.*"
Glory glory make a story in the coffin
Granny gory pray and say a pray today
Say pray say pray today say pray Amen"
Amen Amen Amen Amen Amen.
Too twit Tom in the twiddle twang
Twit Tom in the middle sang,
"Gang a lang gang gang gang ho-hi
Twit in the twiddle ho-hi, ho-hi,
O twit in the piddle ho-hi"
Sing Tom sang Tom, "Twang a lang for the twang
Gang lang yea burst in the earth
For the twang gang lang in the earth"
"Ho-hi ho-hi"
"Amen" said "Amen heaven Amen."
"O lang in the earth girth" sang
"Lang lang lang in the earth,
O sing the twang gang sang lang
Lang lang in the earth girth birth
Lang o lang o lang" sang.

Groan a moan and moan groan
Mother and sister and brother and blaster
And ratchet a hatchet. A hatchet—
      Oh, my!
    An' granny abed so poorly hewn.
    Plume and plum and groan intone
    An' sown in the earth dead granny sown
    Amen Amen dear granny Amen.

I Wake as from a Dream

I wake as from a dream, wondering
What was done before I dreamt.
A tree of dark and slender branches passes near,
I lift my hand to catch a twig
Dripping with dew, bobbing in the cool air,
It is out of reach before I touch it;
For my hand, my body, is carried by a chorus
Of mourners; eight gray-draped shapes
Striding to a slow and noiseless cadence.
Where do they go? My mind cries out.
I would race ahead, then return
To tell myself what is to be—I cannot.
I am caught within a formless webbing,
Caught amid a crowd of bodies
Where every struggle to be free
Awakens the eight-legged arachnid.

Threnody

Watching tomtits upon the noon snow
Shamming up a clamor of elfin wings,
Feeling the season's oppressive passage
As time, walking solemnly, owl-eyed,
An old man searching in his pockets,
Turning them inside out, outside in.

Were we not together still?
Yes, for there was the alpine moon
Glowing like crystal, rolling across the sky,
A lost marble, a child's toy, bouncing
    Into the gutter.
We listened to the bird, not knowing
What sort, singing so variously,
Hidden behind the hand-sized leaves
Not knowing so mere a bird could sing so,
Hopping among the tree's gray branches.

We sat together on the porch
    (Gritty under our buttocks)
The day fading like a far-off cry,
Pulling our clothes about our legs,
    Swatting mosquitoes,
Wondering if our souls were free
Or if their time would have an ending.
Day, then twilight; sudden silences
Ringing like church bells in our ears.

We were together then.
Or was that night the first since we parted
And it was I alone in the nightfall
Gathering memories about me?

Willows sap my strength. I asked over and over
Why there were so many, their cascading shrouds
Dipping down toward the earth. I yearn
Toward oak trees, which seem so sturdy;
I think such trees would not tremble
Through the windy night, as if rootless,
But would face the dark, imperturbable.

Let these strands of thought drift away from me,
Let time gather them up like candles
And, one by one, blow out their flame
So I take up my lessened life.

But now they tell me you are free
That I may touch you not again.
Then you are free, truly free,
Or are you forever lost?
Will I, in my day, embrace you
Or merely go extinct
Having no name, no breath…and no love.

Pensive Night

Pensive drifts the foggy night
The air does glow without delight
It draws me forth to breathe its breath
To dream of life without its death.

A Hidden World

Flailing from a hidden world heralds
The encroachment of an unheard presence
Whose weight as of a body,
Brushes by, as it falls through the night.
The malignant dark shimmers in its wake,
Space distorting, as it were breath.
An echo calls a name from the darkness
And the dreamer recoils, remembering,
Once again out of the silence rises
The unending whisperings
     Of blasphemies.

Trapped in the pain of desolation
     The scroll is unfurled.
On each line indited witness or victim,
Memories of violence, cruelty,
     Indifference.
Name upon name voiced in harsh accent
Chosen from the beginning for numb despair.
Once human, stung by poisonous lips,
Made blind to the approaching horror.
They who sneered at outstretched hands
Now crouch on bloodied stones and clutch the air
Abandoned by God like broken toys.
So unprotected, prey to extinct raptors
Whose talons scarify the naked soul
With pain that freshens with each savage blow.
Agonies exposed to the mirthless laughter
     Of his multitude.

In a stifling darkness, the Unholy Being flexes,
Venomous snakes circle, their tongues flicking upward
     Into consciousness.

Christmastime

Christmastime and mildew on the ground,
Mold and fungus grown in the heart.
Was not once a Savior born?
Was hope not blessed with a Christ?
Our Lord! Fools cry out, fewer each year.
Dusty cathedrals echo hymns while
Disheartened priests drone of Advent;
Of the Virgin, Holy Ghost deflowered,
Her nine months gone, then births the Son,
The promised One, not born but reborn!
Holy light! Holy night! Born again
To set right the world forevermore!

Soon came the flogging of the soul,
        The ego's demise.
The heart reawakened, melts, blending
Fresh blood into the blood of everything.

    Hosanna! The faithful shout,
Praise our Lord, who came to earth
To forgive our sins that merit death!
Their heads bow down and fingers clasp
And lips mumble remembered prayers;
Yet a glance betrays their growing doubt.
The millennium memory fades
In the fierce light of unbelief.
What once was clear, eyes now strain to see,
For bleak wealth reddens the flesh
And ridicules the oddity of faith.

We embrace him still! believers cry.
Then catch him up in your eager arms,
Steal him away, if he immortal be,
Save your treasure for another age
And leave this world to rot and to rage.

Our Present Pace

I know our present pace is sad
And man's not good, but nat'rally bad
Not a hope but just a fad
      Of life.

I wonder what is really true—
That you love me and I love you?
But that's not true, I don't really do
      Feel love.

The end is death, we both will die
(But first a tear, an ache, a sigh)
And leave like strangers, say good-bye
      To life.

Well, let it come; then I'll be dead
These words not writ, not even said;
There's not a feeling not been read
      Of life.

Life is good when you are young
But once you're old all songs are sung
And not a word you'd care to tongue
      Of life.

It isn't new, it isn't sweet
You'll end up bored; you'll wind up beat
No word is fresh: repeat, repeat;
        That's life.

Krait, Deadly Snake

Krait, deadly snake, hooks twin-fanged nonlife
     Into foreign skin, through skin into muscle,
     Blood, sinew, warm vegetable stew,
     Mineral floating sea; injects venom.
Venom: muscular-paralytic, tissue-attacking
     Elapine soup, made several parts
     Vile saliva, one part death, mixed
     In tight, smooth elastic flask located
     Between compressor muscle and venom duct.
Flask overextension from venom overload
     Creating pressure, irritation to krait
     Consciousness; krait to seek, find,
     Inject with venom happy, hapless,
     Bumbling, searching human victim.
Victim then to scream, totter, shake krait
     Loose, stumble, grab punctured flesh,
     Blanch, redden, overheat, shout,
     Cry out, cry, die.
Krait then glides away to its secret nest
     There to rest as first new drop of
     Deadly fluid exudes into depleted flask.
Toxic nature thus deals its death. Praise nature!
     Praise death! Admirable krait! Darling victim!
     Exquisite pain! Happy melodrama!
     Delightful death-dance; praise thyself!
     Consciousness to be extinguished, mind to be
          Devoured, limbs to crumble!
          O happy Creator who created krait!

So Placed Are They

So placed are they that stars are meant to shine
Eternal in the wordless heaven's depth;
To forfeit not their share of light or deign
To change throughout their timeless length and breadth,
But rather, mindless, mime some natural law
That's fastened on them as a tyrant's stare,
So wheel in august orbits and courses draw
Through endless seas of empty space, and bare.
And yet I say the stars are not more set,
More constant than the love that holds my heart
And not more single than the light I've met
In sleep's quiet path aglow with magic art.
The stars will fall, their music shatter, dumb
Before this light shall dim, or reck' its sum.

For Whom the Midnight

For whom the midnight spreads her shattered wings
To wash the wind with the weight of jasmine:
A satyr, half-human, quick to the leap,
A faun, flank cool, having lain in darkness,
A shape, shedding its light in fevered dreams,
A pang of mem'ry aching to be known,
An outline, black against the blackness drawn,
A shadow shifting in exploding light,
A heart that pulses as a darkened sun
And knows but this, nor knows what else may be.
Its end is knowing knowledge is not learned,
That breath, its last, shall fade in endless wind.
Thus none return; or all return once more
Yet not to play the role they played before.

Tribute to a Yogi

The seasoned need best known to please the Self
Waits wrapped and hidden in its secret place,
Coiled, as a snake about a column's base,
Eyeing its power, as a demon elf.
And while I walk in darkness and in sleep
I move to feel as caught in tangled life
I seek a brightness in its dark'ning strife
Yet hope denies me; loneliness I reap.
But stare I toward me into calming eye;
My senses falter, weaken, drift away;
A massive river pulls me into day
Opening out beneath an endless sky;
A fiery terror of joy holds me high
And there I live and, breathless, there I die.

So Sure We Are

So sure we are that life will never cease
We labor that abundance should increase,
We lay them down, one by one, the hours
To store from each its bounty as it flowers.
Still, time, expressed in wrinkled flesh and face,
So fleet, is ever willing for the race.
How shall we run, you and I, to win
When look! So soon the fire has died within.
Our elders; see how they sink into rue,
Advance in years and quietly slip from view.
What diff'rent fate has any ever known
Save to lie in furrows where once his seed was sown?
Then slow thy pace and search for matters final,
In the head, or in the heart, or in the column spinal.

What Else But Words

What else but feeble words flick'ring like dark
          Reflections,
Word sounds that may suggest vast conceptions
From a flagging human mind spent in
          Ambitious pursuit.
What other than the absolute, knowing it is
          Beyond that
More than the perfect, more than perfection
(For behind the subtle face of perfection is
       The glittering mask of the imperfect)
More than greatness, greater than beauty,
Beyond all expressions; all descriptions,
Beyond all eternity-flung voices chattering
       In the wilderness of space;
More than seeming, more than light, more than
          Appearances
Beyond knowing; beyond the knower
Beyond understanding; beyond he who would
          Understand,
Greater than constructions, planets, spiral nebulae
More august than the seemliest stars
More regal, more imperious than innumerable suns
          Gravitating into global clusters,
      Into one great sun
Fleeter afoot than light, more violent than novae,
          Than supernovae.
Wiser than wisdom, beyond the cleverest insight,
Vaster than thought, vaster than the furthest
          Fling of imagination,
Beyond love, beyond even the sweetest love
Beyond the All, multiplied many times,
Beyond universe piled upon universe, god upon god,
Beyond, until all that is, or could ever be, is
          Nothing
And Nothing is.

O Deep Yearn

O deep yearn! O morning light, shadows long-drawn!
O free-spoken; dim-lit path in the dawn's stillness!
Of thee, a voice of no breath, a sunny chanter as if
Smoke ling'ring long in the still air!
O pulsing wilderness, fire-footed, treading in the wild wind!
O heart's concord and dear delight, fearless and
Faultless, wind-licked in the morning light!
O passioned and purposed vortex drawing health from
The world's health and health of its own.
My spirit ever-unbound, charming as an enchanter's
Wand drawing darkness into shapes of light.
O kinship! Free-born and waxing with gentleness.
My spirit, born as your spirit, interlaced in your
Soul's life
My spirit, beating with your heart, watching your blood,
Hot and healthy, flow through your flesh,
That close my spirit, my breath; that near, forever,
I to thee!

Know Your Enemy

Know your enemy;
Not as the tiger, fearing the winds of autumn,
Creeping lame and sick through the stiff elephant
                                        grass,
Fleeing the teeth and the claws of the other,
Knowing not the hunter, ten thousand miles away,
His rifle in his arms, dreaming of death.
Know your enemy.

His Frontal Lobotomy

Sealed inside a bottle, an alcohol-filled jar,
Floats a tiny bit of flesh from my appendectomy.
It threatens from the shelf above my whiskey bar
And brings to mind morning's frontal lobotomy.

I save all that's cut from me, from fingernail to hair.
I jar them, case them, or wrap in cotton battin'
Whatever once was part of me, unto the solitary tear.
But what of the morrow, when that surgeon from Manhattan

Starts slicing threads of nerves hid deep within my skull?
What is left to treasure when once the cut's been made?
Not my nervous visions or any thought not dull
Just the doctor growling, "Make sure it's all pre-paid!"

The Best Is Monarchy

I met today a man who wanted a return to monarchy.
Yes.
He is Polish, an old Polish soldier, an admirer of
                    Pilsudski.
Politicians are spoiled, he said, by democracy.
The other systems are ruined by bureaucracy,
The best is monarchy.

There Was an Old Boy

There was an old boy in his dotage
Who would sally forth from his cottage
Not to pay his bills
Or visit the mills
But to indulge in his practice of frottage.

If I Had an Ocelot

If I had an ocelot
I would think a lot
Of my ocelot.
If I had a cat
I would think of that.

If I Were King

If I were king
I would fling
My outstretched arms beyond the light.

If I were lord
I'd leap toward
The dazzle of a starry night.

If I were saint
Sans meanest taint
With thee I'd soar in buoyant flight.

Hail a New Citizen

Hail a new citizen of megalopolis!
A grandmegalopolitanite to be.
A microscopic shred, a billionth part,
A nonentity, a mere bit, a piece, a token;
One more of the relentless additions
Ejected from the womb.
    Of the blood of progeny
    Of the tiny, squalling mouths
    Of multitudinous cots
    Vacated, replaced, vacated, replaced.
Of bloody, squirming pink brown black
    Infant bodies.
This crowd, this torment, this storm of
Humanity descending from the void,
    Confounding
    Laws, rules, hopes, borders, states, charities,
    Plans, new plans, fresh new plans…

The Prolonged Analysis

"I think I understand now."
Putting pad and pen away,
Said Doctor Hoffman
To the patient where he lay.

"Indeed, I understand now
Why this analysis
Has caused us so much bother—
You've mental paralysis.

"You have grown too dependent
On the father image—me!
I'm eighty-four tomorrow
You'll be sixty-two or three."

The Doctor nudged his patient
Then very gently said,
"This thirty-year analysis—"
Then saw the man was dead.

Sighing, Doctor Hoffman
Wrote down the last entry:
"Patient ended treatment.
No response to therapy."

Brief Orations

THE OLD BONE

Where flesh has fled, there's bone alone;
Sorrowing, crumbling bone,
Rattling, shivering bone
That, once adorned with conscious flesh,
Cracks and spills its marrow
Into tomorrow's tatters.

CONSIDER THE DINOSAURS, whose keepers, the paleontologists, measure in bones some 150 million years of duplication, replication, and multiplication. A hundred dozen varieties: slim and quick, slow and stolid, bright flesh-eaters, dull plant-eaters, spending a million decades munching, chewing, farting, fighting, reproducing, round and round, again and again; the same idea in a thousand flesh-coats, tiny and grand and fierce and shy—and in all that immense age, not once there emerges what the primates telescoped into a few million years. Something fishy here. Either evolution forgot the earth or got caught in a spiral, round and round, up and down. Or evolution wasn't. Or something was about, gradually bored, wearied with the saurian routine; not easily wearied, but then finally wearied, and in a few quick ages, hunting down, rooting out, winking out each one of the multitudinous species, twisting the last neck, breaking the last back, drowning the last of the last in a mountain of slime, drying to bone-laced rock. Rock for the entertainment, the mystification of the darling species, crown of the living, the bare-skinned walkabout, handler, and headscratcher, now on stage at this very moment: you and I. When will we be wearied with? And by whom or by what? Genuflect to the fossil creatures that once charmed whatever-it-is out of a good, long chunk of the world's time, so much the less time for you and I and yours and mine and their issue and their issue's issue and on and on and on, to the onset of a fresh weariness.

A TWO-SUN SKY

A BRIGHT ORANGE SKY, a sun eying its faraway twin. A two-sun patch of ground in the galaxy, a great squeeze of excess energy out of a sky full of light. On their satellite, living things pad about, enter caves and wonder at the dark, blinking at the dark ends of caves, feeling the walls with tender limbs, the cool walls. The dark is a sudden dark, and there in the caves, saliva dripping, wait the things that eat the blinded, living things. Insectlike or dragons; protobiological beings, new inventions on a twice-baked world. Somewhere in this grandeur, the humans land, borne by odd devices. Were these devices thought machines? Bubbles of will? Apports slipping through dimensions? Simple wishes and daydreams? Objects carried these still-recognizable humans from here to there in a not-here-to-there universe and landed them and waited for them and would take them away once whatever they had come for had been accomplished. Recognizable humans wanting to see, to catalogue, to challenge, to kill, to penetrate, to slog through, to sweat, and to carry away. To be heroic. To return with stories. Yes, the story begins with two suns in an orange sky and tells of the dark, dangerous cave the first among them entered and how he was rescued. Then the injuries that wouldn't heal and how he died and how his body is still there, undisturbed, though it is supposed his spirit escaped into the cosmos and set about wandering, as humans do.

PRESSING ON

It is not by chance that the words framing the entrance to hell are said to be Abandon Hope, all ye who enter here. The corollary being that those who are without hope are already living in hell. It is here and many are those who have entered it.

One aspect of hell is trying to thrash blood out of dried skin, although we pay attention to the words within with that happy alertness of the dog listening for the approach of his master. There is a drone of invention just there, where fish swim beneath the clear ice, fish of all varieties, where plants move in the current with a bubbling of filmy creatures, tiny yet clotted together so they are seen; there is a whole life, in fact, under the ice. One's booted foot goes down on the ice, hard. *Crack!* And again *crack! Crackle!* Invention! Inspiration! *Crack! Crack!* A whistle of triumph—*whew!* The water trickling through the crazed ice. Stomp hard, dear friend, stomp and stomp some more. So long as there are boots on your feet, smash at the ice. Here it is that one's character enters: this guy walks in, straight-backed. *I'm here now,* he says, and *I'm going to press on. I'll press on and it won't matter whatever else happens.*

It is what you decide and how you decide; that is the secret.

THE PILTDOWN
FALL-DOWN

NOT STARTING BUT CONTINUING with the integrated, nonintegrated skull of Piltdown man. The egregious brain pan of calculating man. Who was this man? The detective was defective, finding salted in his mine of probabilities and ambitions the dead man, long-dead near-man, head-man. The dreams of the dreamers, most of us, dreaming of the skull-to-be, the one startling discovery, the germinal find and laying greedy hands on that one jewel, the existence of which had been predicted out of our horizon fantasies.

And waiting for all us dreamers, the sickening clutch in the stomach; the unmasking of the fraud. Snickers and hoots, nudges and sorry head-shakings, shards of dreams done to dust. A blow to the brain and the done is really undone. Divorced from fantasy, the dream of dreams ripped apart, perhaps revealing, like a nest of boxes, new fantasies. And we continue to spin dizzily, without center or circumference, in the limitless dream void. This horror we clutch; the dreams are best forgot.

STRIDE THE GUIDE

WITH THE PISTOL Of ennui, the hero blasts a hole through the gray clouds of time. The hero? Why, the hero is—

The oddest thing happened to me on my way out of life. I ran into this series of—No, I cannot describe it—pops and pips, bits and bumps, trips and falls, springs and snows, habits and resolutions—I cannot begin to describe it, all that stuff happening; the horrible twerps and twitters and rattles and crashes. I said to myself, this: "Let us join hands"— solemn voice out of the gloom—"if we will all join our hands, we will soon find our way." Sure, I thought, or stumble together into the catastrophe. "What catastrophe?" you ask. Don't ask. Don't ask what evil might befall us, don't even think—But there are always voices out of the obscure ordure: a chorus of voices: "This way." "That way." "Any way." So many voices, so many ways, so that, without our knowing, one or the other becomes our Guide. Stride the Guide. We stride with the Guide, foolish face, laughable loiterer, he giggling and screaming more than the rest of us. "Follow after me!" giggles Stride the Guide, making loops and circles with his striding legs and we follow. "Onward!" he cries and we are back where we began. "Recognize this?" he shouts. "Yes!" we chorus. "Fine! Onward! Follow me and I shall lead you out of the murk!" And he, laughing helplessly, sinks to the ground, tears of mirth starting from his eyes. "Follow, fallow, fellow, fooloo, fool, you," says he till grunts of laughter throttle his voice. Is Stride the Guide the right guide? Don't ask. Don't dare ask. We all shall wait patiently until he recovers himself and resumes the role of our leader.

HEAVEN OR BUST

THEN DO WE CLIMB up to the heavens, tanklike, turrets revolving? What will heaven think? Join the five Titans in their reckless feat, Pelion on Ossa. But glancing down on the lunatic racket, the gods blink their hooded eyes, reptilian smoke trails—are they pitiless? Forward of us, foolish of us. Yes, we had better use those tanks, just in case. We will ride in them, bobbing across the first hillocks, our hands waving out of the ports, but see that our bodies are well protected. Heavy tanks, gargantuan tanks with lots of ammunition (we would absolutely never use it first), and we tread on, not without caution, with the *wee-ly, wee-ly, clank, clank* tank sounds. And a banner. Not Excelsior. We are too mean to provoke, but on that banner, painted in bland colors: Friends A-Comin'. We mean to say, God-friends, hands outstretched, automatic weapons hidden; fear not—we love. (*Clank, clank.*) We are humans and aren't we lovable? What sort of god would tell us no? We'll join you in heaven and let the tanks and weapons stay outside. We want to share your happiness; what do you say?

What do they say? What do the gods say? We really want to know.

MARKING TIME

REMEMBER HOW I used to mark time with a pen? A habit yearned into being. I used to reach a poet's invention, a phrase, a bit of nonsense—ah, for the fertility of yesteryear. What invention! What applause from all about, an auditorium of applause, its members hungry to touch the air I've breathed out—ah, those golden days!

Now I'm out of prison with a pension, increasingly decrepit, laughably irrelevant. The young—the poor, callous young—clutching treasures of rock and hip-hop, push by, push past. "Out of my way, old man!" How I love it! Why that snide, silent chuckle of mine? Ah, then you have not seen the young as I do. I see them where they are not now but there in the desert, older, aging. I hear those vacant roars. I know that then there will not even be echoes. Carcasses then sucked down into a postdiluvian sediment. I can hear the murmur now: Fire or flood? Ice or fire? And when shall it come to pass? Pull the chain and start fresh. Again. And once again. Or Nemesis; a solid rock of iron and gold, rolling in the Great Vacuum, turning, turning, a giant several miles broad, the Lord's yo-yo spinning slowly down an invisible string. A fresh combustion of the Alexandrian library, scrolls that are now countless bodies frying in the conflagration. And the Voice:

I did not promise forever to you, not even survival, not even complete life spans. I did not even promise a Noah/Lot human, a know-it-all survivor. No. When my disgust with my creation comes up to here—*Phoot!*

THE SCHOLAR'S LIFE

THE LIFE OF THE INTELLECT? How far from my personality is the life of the scholar; to be dealing with abstractions and building up arguments with polysyllabic jargon. A paper here, a paper there, academic arrows aimed at the academic bull's-eye. A living and a good one, a security that beats almost any other once tenure is under one's belt. Retiring with honors and memories, hopefully skewering a few rivals with effective riposte; but then, too, nursing the wounds left by enemy zingers. Most particularly, those penetrating innocently enough and then bursting with venom, their true nature finally comprehended. Papers, reviews, evaluations, and socializing; human competition played out in a dry, bloodless life. Finally, Herr Professor Von Emeritus pottering about campus, mentally kicking the shins of aged peers as they pass, smiling their tight smiles.

Well, look at me as I consider the life of a schoolman; I, who was, when a student, one of the dullest. For one reason or another, short-sheeted here, short-sheeted there, this bit of self-pity inspired by the life of Paul Bowles, whose biography I have just finished reading. Bowles was a musician and a composer, a novelist and a short story writer, a linguist, a translator, and an artist good enough to sell his sketches. I share many of his interests and attitudes, but dourly reflect that although I, too, began with the desire to be a composer and then a writer, there is the one sine qua non Bowles and I did not share: talent. I had planned to be a genius but discovered that even a genius has to have talent. So in place of that I put self-deception, pretending that one day the gifts would tumble off the laden tannenbaum, that one day everything would click into place, all the while holding up my hands to shield from me the intuition that sadly shook its robber fly head.

THOUGHTS THAT PREVENT THINKING

A S THE ATTENTION WANES, numerous possibilities prevent themselves. You would have supposed that by now in my life, tremendous and awesome hulks of thoughts would be trudging through my brain—and by "now," I mean "Now." I mean a constant parade of weighty, pachydermatous conceptions and reasonings pounding through the brain, making their presence known with forceful trunk-bugling, grabbing my attention. But no. Vapid rabbits, common mice, crickets, and insects of a multitudinous variety, all of the crawling and sliming type. If only there were just one thought rocketing heavenward to spangle the dark in spectacular colors; but no, not even one. The Lottery is an apt analogue. Bet a dollar or a thousand, the odds don't change.

I have always waited for the false jollity of Ed McMahon to leap into my life with an unconscionably huge armful of booty, all for me. Come on, Ed, get a move on before you irreparably puncture your ego on some stray critical spike. Toss the money over the fence and prance away before our time blinks off the screen. Prance away on those decaying legs, dear benefactor, and with your sob of joy spray the gladsome air. Or else a *Shazam!* bursting out of the blue, as an acquaintance of mine once put it. *Shazam!* and the pale lead transmutes into minted gold in a garish flash. "*Shazam!*" he would say, the word he had waited all his life to hear. Never mind him. Ignore him, dear, dear fate, and pass on your delights to me. I have a pool of self-pity to mop up, and I could use the light overhead to work by.

A SALE OF PLACENTA

WHAT IS THE philosophical news, the latest discovery of the high domes? Have they found God yet? We'll surely want to know if they do. The Garden of Eden, have they located it? The Ark of the Covenant? The Virgin Mary's maidenhead? Mary's one and only placenta—now there's a relic one would yearn to own a piece of.

The real, the authentic, the unique God-shroud! Purchase a dried bit of the true holy placenta and be saved from the rigors of hell . How can you afford not to buy your very own sacred treasure today? Observe how it is safely and securely sealed in its own exquisitely designed, faux gold reliquary, liberally sprinkled with sparkling, genuine industrial-grade diamonds! Look through the Gothic arched glass window, and you will see the sacred flesh resting on its black velveteen bed! Admire the wondrous artistry, the spiritually uplifting craftsmanship! Get your piece of the true placenta today, and be inspired for years to come. But you must place your order now, while this offer is still available. Our operators are standing by, waiting to take your order, day or night. Credit cards accepted. Sorry, no personal checks.

Why not? What else can one expect? What sort of age do we live in anyhow? Dignity? Respect? No, you will have to find a life in another time and another place. Here we enjoy a mobocracy, led by the academically gowned, bull-horned secular activist—sign on or miss out.

POND SCUM

WHAT DO YOU SCOOP out of a pond, after all, but pond scum? Algae; living clots of green plant/animal; sticky, gummy animal/plant. And the clock bends over a tabletop, slipping amoebalike, because there is gravity and a grave waiting (a solemn-opening), slipping like pond slime slips over the fingers, will-less because gravity is, and nothing—no being, not even the top beings on the world's being-scale, not one thing—may resist. Even birds slam down on the ground, as if they would fly to the center of the earth, where gravity waits. For there in the very center is the Waiter, servant of us all, waiting as we all fall toward the center, like it or not. Or perhaps we break into two parts, the one part falling, the other part rising into the indefinable. The sticky falling things; showers, kites, clocks, church bells, and—lest we forget—bodies all fall. And in the other direction, definitely invisible, rising, soaring, free—as always—of grave/gravity, lifting into the inexpressible and disappearing, so that we wonder if it ever was, the perhaps thing, the filmy question mark, the dispersing mist. So wave farewell to it, and then bury, burn, eat the part that gravity took.

FILLING UP THE HOLES

I WAS FILLING HOLES in the clapboard on the back of the house for the paint job, which will be completed, I suppose, this Sunday. The sun had sunk into the fog, and the wind pushed on my back while I engaged in this mundane task. The prelude to Tristan and Isolde was singing in the back of my mind when the thought came that there were no more Richard Wagners, that we were living on our cultural patrimony. I was wondering why that was, why high art, philosophy, and music had gone out of human life. And wondered what had done it. The drive for utopia, which has held the West in turmoil for a century? The slaughter of the Great Wars? The rise of the bourgeoisie and bourgeois institutions and the countercultural reaction? The explosion of population? The flood of merchandise, which has made accumulators of us all? Technology? Perhaps it resulted from the making of demos into god, and the diversions and entertainments concocted to placate this deity. I am not one to trace clearly all these patterns to some inevitable conclusion. Perhaps the answer cannot be found through the intellect at all. Possibly all these strands tangle into a confusion no mind could unravel. Yet intellect may be bypassed by an impression; that the heart, the genius of the human race has gone out of us. This not happening in a day, but with a small subtraction, decade by decade, and now we are impoverished and we don't know why. The ship has broken loose from its moorings in the night and now we are out of sight of land. And soon there will come a storm out there in the deep water, and our struggle for survival, if we survive, will use up centuries.

THE FEELER REACHES

THRUST LIGHT into some observation, some something extracted from the world and filtered through this unique sieve, as the light of the sun on the dust.

There was this boredom with the mundane; this fine notion that, suffering this flat emotion, the feeler reaches for the sky. Thus man pierces with his head the empty blue and is said to have landed in 1969 CE a small craft on the moon. And not dying. But being banal: "One small step," etcetera. And what a remarkable fellow he is! "I stepped, I jumped over the moon!" And the odd thing is that he found no footprints on that sandy shore. Perhaps, says one science-taster, we are all alone here. Imagine that, a universe of many more than a few other suns in which man is the only inhabitant. What fun we shall have inserting humans into frail and crude crafts to journey into an illimitable future. Good-bye, dear sailor, swab the decks, polish the space stuff off the brass, and don't forget us here on this now-mean earth. Stepping on the next island; Mars it will be, they say, then perhaps a moon of Jupiter's. Or Saturn. Still no footprints in the sand. Leafing back into the past, the sailors find the observation of a long-dead scientist. A crude science he practiced, but yes, here it is, right here in the universal database: "Perhaps we are all alone here." All alone. Another world, another aloneness. All, all alone. Are we humbled? But no. It is a great responsibility. We are the first, so what shall we teach the universe (a vast mass now not quite so prepossessing)? Yes, it is up to man to instruct the rocks and to tutor the suns; the universe must learn human wisdom. What a great future for us all! What a grand, grand history of unending tomorrows and tomorrows man shall enjoy!

FRACTALS

FRACTALS. SCIENTIFIC OBJECTS. Bits of bits. It is exciting, a great wonder. We all suppose we know how things become fractals. Yes, on the tip of my tongue or the end of my pen. Right off the sheet of paper, growing in the air. A form dissolved. A question, not thought. An answer unconceived. Be that as it may, one day, in the brain of a human, a sound grows, chipped off the memory of like sounds. It is a definition wavering in the air, purposeless. It is a column of smoke poked by a breeze. The sudden, transient form emerges: word, definition, Adam naming the animals. This one task delegated by the Eternal to the temporal. I see you with my mind, a mind built by fractals, infinitely subtle in the dog and patent in the human. We suppose we understand whatever is most familiar, but then—pow!—the whole grasped knowledge leaps away and disintegrates. Then we become wise, knowing that we don't know. Back in our skulls, the little things we potter with, pushing these trivial objects this way and that way; this motion putting our tiny selves back on the train. Let's all imagine this world as being banal, the more banal the better. We find the obvious things put everything in perspective, because we ourselves are obvious things, knocking about this world—our world, we think. (Unkind eyes look down on us and through us, seeing our transparent, banal selves.) Fractals. We can say fractals; the word has meaning now. The meaning always there and we have stapled a sound to it. This much more we know now than we did. And, for the love of heaven, don't let's alert ourselves to whatever other brains may be coldly dissecting our banal psyches, our fractals.

THE MAN ON THE BRIDGE

THE MAN ON THE BRIDGE. Alone. Brooding, a brew of dark feelings crawling about his feet like a nest of snakes. He stares down at the ground below him, seventy feet or more down. *No. Not suicide. Too cheap; too predictable. That is what they all expect of me. Life-ending. No, I will not be pushed out of life by that sort. No. If I die by my own cause, it shall be at a time of my own choosing and in a place of my own choosing. And for a reason of my own. My own. Alone.*

Alone on the bridge. He turns, head still bowed and walks a step or two. Stops. *Shall it be now? Is now the time I have chosen? No. This time can too easily be confused with a time chosen for me by those others. I will not be driven into my own dissolution by people I detest. Those I hate. And hate!*

His head lifts. His lips moving with sudden animation, he cries out, "Hate!" And again, "Hate! Hate!" His face, once dull and gray, flushes pink with blood and his eyes sparkle with life. "Hate!" he shouts again. He laughs. His shoulders snap back and he strides away, his arms and legs working like a soldier's. One, two, three, four. "Hate! Hate!" Hut, two, three, four. "Hate!" He laughs, marching to his Armageddon.

FULMINATIONS

FULMINATIONS ON A SHOESTRING. Ah, the courage to stand self-exposed, open to all. Nudist, exhibitionist.

The climate of the midland was all;

It worked down from storms to mild rain.

A poem? The sound, the rhythm, and the sense. Pulchritudinous words that exhaust and enchant. The words heard in the midnight mind, moving through dim light, heard and not heard, seen but not seen. Words feeling out for a mind to touch. To which mind shall they come from their storehouse of sound? Sounds, tunes, and rhythms naked of sense. Marking the time, ready since the beginning to become part of the whole body. And so they shall be strung along that form. Beads and brocades. Fabrics and strings of gold. Sentiments, sounds, and bells clanging. Ideas and ideas of ideas. Thoughts and wisps of things scarcely held in the endless mind. All to adorn form willed into dream. All for you, so you may float through and about, out and in, that you may know and forget and know again, that you may one day guess whose wings beat, whose face parts the air, and whose limbs touch the dreams. Dance and soar and lift up and drift down through and about that form until endless time comes to its end. And at that end, the knowing. Or not. Or the dream was at fault, a miscalculation from the beginning, a raw mistake, a first-time try, a botch. And that's what's wrong: two thoughts from the beginning. It is or it is not. We are or we are not. And in the unbearable tension, a birth, a life, a death.

THE GRAND DESIGN

IN JUDGMENT, ALAS. Don't you sense the imperative? The finger raised, the eyebrows lifted, and the hand rolling aloft impatiently. "And? And? Come! Out with it!" An examination you haven't studied for; in fact, you haven't a clue what questions shall be asked, if any. Terrified, you watch the hand slowly moving toward the rope that operates the trapdoor under your feet. You blurt out answers, wild guesses, but nothing you say seems to slow that hand's stealthy movement. Perhaps you surrender; shut up and close your eyes. Perhaps you become angry and scream out a lungful of curses. Or try charm. Try slickness and guile. What about begging? How about dropping to your knees and whimpering? Yes, tap your head on the floor and spill out your sins, each one, until your throat is hoarse and your memory empties out. Then, with a sly glance at that hand (Ah, God still moving!) bleat out the deeds undone, the kindnesses not thought of, and the gifts ungiven. Alas, sad fate, nothing your desperate mind can conceive of works. It seems that you are doomed. Likely, then it begins to dawn on you that this instant of convergence of yours—the cream pie thrown to splat in your face, the trapdoor opened under your feet, your clothes ripped away from you, and, yes, the agonizing knife slice into your belly—all were planned, with a smile, from the very beginning of everything. By what? Something, somewhere. Something whose Grand Design is to introduce you to nothingness.

KARMA

"**A**LL," THEY SAY, "will become known." All that is hidden will be broadcast on the most indiscriminate of breezes. Those secret pacts, those fantasies, those sexual trysts, those aberrations, and those abominations, known now under the sun, midday sun, shadowless sun, where shadowless beings paw the foul corruptions in the searing, burning light. And you, the only shadow, cowering in your own darkness, crouching, sinking into your shadow, trembling, sweating, and drooling. "All shall be known." But you, you clasp your arms across your face, your teeth gnash, you sigh and groan; you shake in agony. You stutter, "Ha-Have compassion! Where is your pity? Pity me! Help me! Save me please, please, please—"

Such a picture! Such a sight! But does the sun move on to cast its scorching light elsewhere? No. Will there be mercy for you? No. "All will be known and all will be dealt with justly." Justice! Dreadful word! Everyone has been lied to, deceived, and misled and you have slipped away from justice. Until now. But surely, even now, may not pity mitigate the leaden blow? Once again, no. Deception has disappeared, all is revealed. There will be justice at last. Measure for measure. Blow for blow. Transgressions shall be counted off slowly and not one overlooked. Neither pleading nor pain nor reason will soften even one blow. Prepare yourself. There has been no suffering that you shall not know. And have not earned.

AN AGENT OF DISQUIET

ABOVEGROUND. Now there's the place to be, catching life as it drifts past, debris in the wind. Perhaps when the night comes, there will be a stretch of catastrophe, a hard, bumpy roadway, spring killer, axle breaker, and there a break in the fabric to poke your head through. Ah, they'll put me through hell, they always complain, horn-blaring, cymbal-clanging, pot-pounding noisome noise of hell, don't, don't thrust shove push goad tweak prod me on into that what-it-is—don't. Have you noticed how much we humans whine? Why is that? Then sit quiet and still because there is that other night; that fright-night all uptight. Laugh now, pray later.

Two predators stalk through the world: one is a giant cat with long canines and fierce eyes, that growls and grunts and clutches its prey with enormous cruel talons. And the other predator, kiting over life, a shadow stretching across the world, form never seen, incomprehensible. We know what that has come for when it comes. That is why we invented prayer. Laughter now, prayer later. Terror prayer yelled into the void; a throat-bursting, eye-bugging, face-crimsoning, arms-yanking-at-the-dead-air, bawl, bawl, scream, and holler prayer. The cat can chew on our gristle, but that's not what sets us off, is it? We kiss the flesh good-bye with a shrug and a shudder, but it is that other, the shadow in the dark, it is that we've always cast our magic against.

FOUNDATION FOUND

T HE BEACHED WAVES; the terns tripping up and down the beach slope to the ocean's rhythm; tiny animals in the sand and a large black dog, alternately pleased and bored with fetching a flat piece of wood. On the horizon, over the ocean, clouds gray and close to the water, moving inland at the beach's south end. I, hands in pockets, jacket zippered, standing at the edge of the damp sand, watching the surf tumbling over itself, drifting up the beach and back and listening to the surf's noise, listening to the brain's noise, the memory's noise, thinking that out there on the ocean's surface where is the foundation? Everything is drifting away from everything else, bobbing across the water's surface from blank horizon to blank horizon, through storms and droughts, through daylight and night, under the stars, under the clouds, from piercing light to suffocating darkness, ever moving from here to there without aim, without beginning or ending, till the waters dry up and foundation is found at last. And how it is that, since the beginning, that one spot of baked earth was ordained for each bit of flotsam—though not one place being better than any other to rest upon—and there each thing to stay until the universe itself is sucked back into finality, into abstraction, into the everlasting enigma. Time, that old, cold conqueror. And I wonder if, at the end of it all, were there ears to hear, there wouldn't be heard a tiny, raw, sardonic chuckle, a dry heh, heh, heh for all the numberless ages that have gone before, for all the actors and their acting, whose stage has been obliterated into infinity. Into quiet laughter.

FORGIVE ME, HONEY

THE MAWKISH MOCKERY that does it for life's end. A life built on the dark concrete side of a dark stream of a river made of liquid, languorous poison. A trinity, a trial, and the three kinds of fatalities: by the elbow, by the catch, and by the pardon.

A game little guy spinning, clutching himself, falling to the gleaming night pavement, groveling under a kitchen table, bumping, banging against the chair legs, the broom handles, the warm panels of the stove. Turning, twisting, crying out, gurgling, and choking: "I didn't mean to." "It was a mistake." "Don't blame me." "I can't go on." "I want to die." "I want to change, to end, to grow, to disperse, to destroy the universe; my mad sickness, our mad sicknesses." "Forgive me, honey, but I can't face it anymore." "Take care of the children." *(Don't tell them; they mustn't know I ran away, leaped into the void, disappeared, vanished.)* "It hurts too much." "I can't take it." "It's all hopeless." "I can't change, can't go on, go on, go on." "Good-bye." "Farewell, good-bye." "Forgive me; try to understand." *(They don't understand—I don't understand; tempted by oblivion, the dark wind that blew out the candles of my dreams.)* "Good-bye." And again. "Good-bye."

MELANCHOLIA

THE ANGUISH UNKNOWN—the cries in the dark, the endless melancholy that drains like sap from a wound into life, congealing about the psyches of the forlorn. Agony that grips us suddenly and without reason; moans that start from our throats as we lie, helpless, between sleep and wakefulness. Sadness from the beginning of the world, from the conception of life, consciousness that ached before it knew itself; within us all and all of us startled by our grief.

- - - - o - - - -

Leave God's thoughts for Him to think.

- - - - o - - - -

Fortune favors the fecund.

THE HAMMER OF TIME

THE MAN SITS in his tiny study, all modesty and ego, hoping for a break. (A plaything of Maya.) He rummages about in his ancient thoughts, his experiences, his impressions. He is frightened. He is not frightened. It is a game; he knows that. Silly or noble or depraved; a game. We help make the rules and amendments to the rules. We make a point here, another there. Rule 27C, subsection B, title FA-113 is canceled. A triumph! But without our knowing, or even with our knowing, and beyond our powers to prevent, new rules are scribbled in and new games begun as the old games end. "Laugh," they say. It is only a game. A play game. A lesson, a test; then a recess. But we are adults. Grown-ups with real responsibilities. We must be taken seriously. We work, we raise children, pay taxes, and fight wars—we continue the game. "Laugh," they tell us. And they laugh.

Nostalgia is the return to pain. We remember and grimace. But they laugh. And they tell us to laugh. Laugh with us. The game will end one day, the game will end soon enough. Then what will become of all this glumness? You will be alone on the field; no one left to watch, no one to see, and no one to protest. So you might as well laugh. Laugh with us. And finally, we laugh.

UNCROWDED HEAVEN

CCORDING TO HIS BIOGRAPHER, he never really got down into the flame that was searing the life out of his flesh. Except maybe at the last; who can say what he thought of at the last? His wife said an accident happened, cleaning his rifle and—well, it was a terrible accident. Maybe, in a way she didn't know, it was an accident. Odd, inevitable accident.

Violence is sure to be done to us, by nature outright or nature using guile, luring us to execute it ourselves, then washing her hands with a sardonic laugh. A suicide? Thus! *To oblivion with you!* she cries. Started me thinking then about life's purpose. The twentieth century told too many of the people who came into it that the purpose of life is to suffer. Clearly demonstrated it. The definitive picture is of a victim shot and falling into a pit behind him dug by himself; the sound is a hollow groan, that of a boy with his eyes blasted out by shell fragments; the feeling is pain—sustained, unpitying pain, for no anesthetics are available and those that are have been reserved for the Important People, voted for by you (ja, da, yes, oui, etcetera), in the event that a tooth should fester or a toe break. The century's smell can only be the stench that no one cares to describe. Then, finally, I thought of what the religious tell us; that the purpose of life is to find God. And very helpful advice it is. Like telling those born blind that the purpose of life is to see *(And why can't you see? No excuse for it).* Directing the double amputee to walk up the slope of Mount Everest because that's where heaven is, at the top; room for only a few at a time to stand. Not many people heed that advice, alas for God. And uncrowded heaven.

THE FORM OF WOMAN

THOUGHTS SIFT THROUGH my mind and chance to catch on some projection, such as abortion and the politically correct crowd. Of course, I am antiabortion. Usually. Really, anti a cavalier approach to life.

On television there is the woman in her late twenties, quite irritated because her procedure has been delayed by some protestors outside the clinic. "I'm having it done anyway. What have they accomplished?" The answer being that the immature creature attached to her uterine lining—through no cause of its own—manages to live a few hours longer in this brutal world. Then I think brave the other woman, who tells of the abortion she had done and of her regrets. And I wait for the predictable response from the first mom-to-be, who then says, as she bluntly puts it, simply had a thing removed from her body and hasn't thought of it since. How to measure the spiritual blindness in that remark? Pity and terror reach out for the male who might one day chose her for a mate, believing he has found a fellow human being to share his life. *I'm going to do what I want with my own body.* Though the truth is that this fetus is a part of her and a part of humanity and it cannot be cut from one without being cut from the other. And it does help the squeamish to objectify that which we mean to destroy by a euphemism: fetus. It has just that neutral scientistic sound to it that you want. In the fifties, we had Mom and the stultifying life that revolved around her bored us all. Now we have Ms. *(I'm going to have my orgasm whenever and with whomever I want, and no one is going to stop me),* and centrifugal succeeds centripetal, terror succeeds boredom, and we are not sure what has taken the form of woman.

BART ANALOGUES

THE HOUSES IN THE EAST BAY seen from a BART window. BART analogues coasting through the system. I, too, was once an analogue. And was again today. A pilgrimage to Fremont. Grim pilgrim. Groaning pilchard. No, wrong, the system was not crowded where and when I went. Back home at 4:30 p.m. The pilchards crowd like pilchards, form streams of pilchards when the clock says, *Go! Go home! Swim, float, wiggle, or leap to your home. On your way, fish-face.* No rest for the wary.

Ragged, worn houses near the tracks of BART in the East Bay down to Fremont; houses with sagging fences between yard after yard. Some yards neat—green lawn and trimmed flowers. Others woebegone—bare earth and nasty car. And graffiti like a multicolored infection; scribbled mind-junk to the point where the victims no longer bother to scrub off or paint over. Ah, let the kids have their fun; a statewide, continent-wide genuflection to the darling buds of youth. A fin de siècle kind of thing; leave the graffiti interpretation to some far-in-the-future archaeologist whose genes are even now jiggling about in far-apart bodies. The impulse to spray graffiti-as-urine indiscriminately the laboratory consequence of an overpopulated rat's nest. A consequence of racing up the logarithmic graph; people, machines, products; an exponential multiplication of sameness, heading skyward like a holiday rocket, higher, ever higher, the climb up to its explosive end.

WORD-SOUNDS

I TRY HARD TO CATCH the word-sounds that maunder on under the noise of the mind. Listen, try to distinguish—what? Listen: Is it a novel being told, an epic poem, or a fortune-telling? I hear the rhythm indistinctly, like music's timbre, a subtlety. Perhaps a history read out or a romance far away in imagination? There is neither beginning nor end to it. Maybe it is a saga chanted by sages long ago into the ether, to be heard by whatever ear listens most intently. Sounds mounting like an escalator. You simply step on, and it takes you where it will.

As always, I wonder how I fit into this here and now. I listen, but I seem to be living in a foreign land: the language I recognize, but the meaning I've lost. References are made and imperatives declared, but it is all as if dogs and goats were waltzing in a delicate balance about a ballroom and none are surprised. Yes, as if these creatures had slipped into human customs with not a brow being raised. Then in a sudden moment, the music shrieks, and the beasts break out into wild bleating, barking, urinating, butting, biting, copulating and defecating, only in another instant to resume their decorum and their waltz. The meaning has all changed, even meaning itself. I fear an ending has come and I have missed it. The ancient strands have been cut, not by the wise but by the foolish, who care for nothing so long as they enjoy their moments of maddening dance.

A YEAR'S FINAL THIRD

BEGINNING THE LAST THIRD of the year: ta-ta, ta-tum, a roll of the drums and a twinge in the spirit. But come, come, set out the wassail bowl. Fill it with drink and sing a rousing song; tral-la, tra-lee—

The hummingbird tips into sweet, secret trumpets
Wings whirring in joyous spree.
Its tiny heart vibrates in bingettes and bumpettes;
Dance on! Dance on, O dear colibri!

I could go on and on about the wreckage of the civilized, the downing of the human prospect, wail and moan. But no. Let me be enough satisfied with tomorrow's hope and believe the spirit, no matter how ignored and abhorred, will rise in the morning. Dawn will come, though madmen pray for the dark and run from the light. Yes, the dawn; tender, sweet, and generous to those who look for it, but its light searing and painful beyond computation for the ignorant and the defiant. I may be one of those ignorant yet pray against defiance.

I see a trail in the dust. I feel I should walk there, following some hidden light. Where it shall take me, I cannot know, but think I recognize and remember the form I shall find at its end. Yet I fear that I have been let loose to travel some monstrous arc; to swing out on an endless tether, leaving and approaching until infinity should come to an end. And that what I shall find is what I had left, for it all had been done in an instant, and I had not moved from the space I had always lived in.

So commences the year's final third.

WAS LIFE ONCE THIS?

WORKING ON A BADLY neglected education, the education of the spirit. Listen to the dialogue and savor the monologue. What practice have I missed somewhere? I left something somewhere and now I have quite forgot. Melting like snow on one's boot. Listening, hearing the pulse; not mine but the pulse of the world. Pulse, pulse—it beats more regular than mine. There is the laughter of children, the noise of innocence.

Feel the movement underfoot, the movement of subterranean mountains, the cliffs that may shear up beneath our feet. Life, they say, was once like this. Once there was a place; once the place was here. That time and that place unrecorded, out of history. A swelling of the heart, a heart beating faster. And now, what do we know of it? That place—a dream of it. O shriveled spirit, dream of the light, a gorgeous light, all colors—and once upon a time, you, in that place, lost in that place.

(Begin again.) Once long ago in a place long lost, in a time long forgotten, there was, yes, now you remember. But no! You are frantic. Remember, remember what? Ah, smash your fists into the air, churn the mist, and stamp about on the hollow earth! The place! The time! It slips away, the memory of what cannot be recalled, the fresh wind across the plain, across the face, a suggestion of—something. The flesh was touched, the eye saw, the hearing acute in that time, that place; but how will it ever be remembered? As a memory of a memory unremembered, yet not forgotten?

THE DOA DAY

CREATIVE JUICES cannot be strained too fine. One's concentration should not suffer. Words still pile in, also sounds, grunts, some maybe of pain. Where is the growth, the seedling? Where is the sprout breaking the baked surface? There, between your toes. Toe in there and fret the stolid earth. Cultivate, that's the ticket; a cultivated voice, calm and restrained. Strain as a synonym for rupture, a breaking of flesh, a rude growth under the skin. Strain, then—*Pop!* Ah, he's done it now! The operation from that instant planned, the table prepared and the surgical tray rolled out under the lights. A performance is due and the star is you. Be prepared. Be a Boy Scout. Grit the teeth so they shatter, cry not but groan and grunt and bite the tongue. They won't wait for the ambulance, not on that DOA day, they will just go ahead and cut into the fleshy bulge with whatever tool, shiny from fresh use. "Do you need anesthetic?" the fool asks. Did a coward ever need his mother? Give me that maternal hand, though it be whacked off from a corpse of whatever species. We cry out. That's only human—pat, pat on the head—only human. Primate, prime material, primed for the bloody job.

Duck! Damn it, can't you see the knife slicing about? Open your eyes! Duck again! Oh, shame, it got you that time. And blood. Don't slip on the blood, for another slice is due any second now. Watch it! Good! Good, swung away and it nicked but an ear. *Will the blood never stop?* But I ask you, which is better, the slow bleeding or a quick one into a vital area? Keep ducking, ducking away on DOA day.

MAROONED

"A CAST-OFF," SAID HE, looking about him. "Marooned and alone."

Marooned. Alone on an island, walking about on its beach, settling finally on one beach. Sitting on the sand and glaring at the horizon. The water horizon. Flat, a line dim, sometimes dark, always level from one inward curve of the beach to the other. The island's highest point is a certain tree; from there, swinging his head, he sees the entire horizon, 360 degrees of it, level, unwaveringly level, no matter how frenzied the waves mounting the beach, pressing up onto the land.

Down on the beach once more, sea foam swarms about his ankles. Daring the waves, the nonswimmer wades into the warm liquid, daring them. *Carry me off?* No. He walks to the sand once more and looks back at the surf. In there somewhere, in that formless water, is his imprint scaled to his size, a shadow form perfect, waiting for the day or the night when he will cry, yes! Or, not waiting, catching him unaware about the thigh with a shadow arm, the simulacrum sliding into his flesh, fitted to him with a wave's push and the battering of another wave and another. His cry of despair, that shadow's cry, the shore drifting farther and farther from his straining arms. And the vessel of land, anchor hoisted, sails away, away beyond the flat water horizon.

Four One Act Plays

The Death of Marmeladov

A ONE-ACT PLAY

Adapted by
KEITH HOPKINSON
from
CRIME AND PUNISHMENT
by Fyodor Dostoyevsky
(*Translated by Constance Garnett*)

CHARACTERS

SEMYON ZAHAROVITCH MARMELADOV
KATERINA IVANOVNA, HIS WIFE
RASKOLNIKOV
SONIA, MARMELADOV'S DAUGHTER
A POLICEMAN
A DOCTOR
A PRIEST

SETTING

*A warm summer evening in the late nineteenth century,
St. Petersburg, Russia.*

SCENE 1

A small, dimly lit boardinghouse room littered with rags of all sorts, mostly patched-up children's clothes. There is a sofa full of holes. An old table. A trunk. Boxes. Two chairs, on one of which is an earthenware pitcher of water. There is a door in the rear. Across stage left is hung a ragged sheet. Behind it is a closet in which sleep three small children. KATERINA comes from behind this sheet, speaking softly to the children, offstage.

KATERINA   Sleep now, Polenka. Ssh! We mustn't wake your little brother and sister. Yes—sleep. *(She coughs. KATERINA goes to a bundle of old clothes she has been mending. She sits and starts to sew. She puts the garment down suddenly.)* Where is he? *(Stands.)* Where is he, the drunken vagabond? Why doesn't he come? Does he think—now what?

(Coming in under KATERINA's speech are heard voices offstage in the hall beyond the door in the rear: "Here's where Marmeladov lives!" "What happened to him?" "In here! In here!" RASKOLNIKOV backs in through the door rear, carrying MARMELADOV's shoulders, while a POLICEMAN follows, carrying the dying man's feet.)

KATERINA   *(Dropping the clothes she had been mending on the floor.)* Quiet! What is it? You'll wake the children! What are they bringing? *(She sees who it is.)* Oh—

POLICEMAN   Where shall we put him?

RASKOLNIKOV   Here on the sofa! *(They place MARMELADOV on the sofa.)*

A VOICE   *(Offstage, in the hall.)* Run over in the street! Drunk!

(KATERINA, on the edge of hysteria, gasps for breath. The POLICEMAN goes to the partly open door, rear, and stands by it.)

RASKOLNIKOV   *(Going quickly to KATERINA.)* Please, madam, be calm! Please! He was crossing the street and a carriage—

KATERINA   No!

RASKOLNIKOV	Don't be frightened! I'm sure he'll come to. Do you remember that I was here before with your husband? A few days ago? My name is Raskolnikov. *(Holding her, as she seems about to faint.)* Please—
KATERINA	He's done it this time! *(KATERINA rushes to her husband. She opens his shirt and begins examining him frantically.)*
RASKOLNIKOV	*(To the POLICEMAN.)* We must get a doctor!
POLICEMAN	The hospital would have been better.
RASKOLNIKOV	*(To someone offstage, hidden by the partly open door.)* Can't one of you get a doctor? Tell him I'll pay!
VOICE	*(Offstage.)* There's a doctor down the street! I'll get him!
RASKOLNIKOV	Tell him to hurry!
POLICEMAN	Better get a priest.
RASKOLNIKOV	*(To the person, offstage.)* Yes, a priest. *(RASKOLNIKOV goes to KATERINA, who is kneeling by her husband.)* Have you any water? A towel? *(He helps KATERINA to her feet.)* Please…he's injured but not dead. We must see what the doctor says.
KATERINA	Yes…water.…*(KATERINA wets a towel from the earthenware pitcher and hands the towel to RASKOLNIKOV, who pats MARMELADOV's face with it. KATERINA breathes painfully, pressing her clenched hands to her breast.)*
POLICEMAN	Look at her! It was a mistake to bring him here!
RASKOLNIKOV	Madam—
KATERINA	Sonia! We must get Sonia! *(She hurries to the door and speaks to the people offstage.)* One of you, hurry and get Sonia! She lives at Kapernaumov's. The tailor!
VOICE	*(Offstage.)* Nikolai knows where she lives! He's been there in the back room with her often enough!
ANOTHER VOICE	*(Offstage.)* Hurry, Nikolai!

(There is laughter offstage. Katerina, who had turned from the door, turns back to it in a fury.)

KATERINA	Laugh, will you? Is it a spectacle for you to gape at? *(KATERINA tries to close the door, but the POLICE-MAN stops her.)*
POLICEMAN	He must have air, madam. It is too close in here.
KATERINA	You might let him die in peace! *(She turns away, coughing, holding a rag to her mouth.)*
VOICE	*(Offstage.)* They should have taken him to the hospital.
ANOTHER VOICE	*(Offstage.)* They haven't any business making a disturbance here!
KATERINA	*(Back at the door, beside herself with rage.)* No business to die! *(To the POLICEMAN.)* I demand that you close that door at once and admit no one!

(The POLICEMAN only shakes his head.)

KATERINA	I warn you, the governor-general himself shall be informed of your conduct! Everyone knows my husband has many important friends; it is only because of his pride that he abandoned them, because he couldn't control his drinking— *(A fit of coughing breaks her speech.)*

(MARMELADOV recovers consciousness and groans. RASKOLNIKOV is standing over him. The dying man doesn't recognize him and turns his head about uneasily. KATERINA has come to his side.)

KATERINA	My God! His whole chest is crushed! (To *RAS-KOLNIKOV.*) We must take off his clothes. Turn a little, Semyon Zaharovitch, if you can....
MARMELADOV	*(Forcing it out against the pain.)* Priest...

(KATERINA turns from him tensely, pressing a scream back from her lips with her hand. A moment of silence.)

MARMELADOV	A priest!
KATERINA	*(Shouting at him.)* Be quiet! You'll get your priest!

(MARMELADOV moves his head about uneasily. Voices in the hall offstage: "Here he is!" "In there, Doctor!")

RASKOLNIKOV   Thank God!

(The DOCTOR enters, looking about mistrustfully. With KATERINA at his side, he examines MARMELADOV. He shakes his head. He leaves MARME-LADOV and takes RASKOLNIKOV to one side. KATERINA remains by her husband, wiping his face and chest with the towel.)

DOCTOR	*(Softly.)* It is a miracle that he has regained consciousness.
RASKOLNIKOV	What do you think?
DOCTOR	He will die immediately.
RASKOLNIKOV	There is no hope?
DOCTOR	None at all! He has a massive bruise over the heart, and his head is badly fractured. I could bleed him if you like—
RASKOLNIKOV	Perhaps it would relieve—
DOCTOR	If you like. It would be perfectly useless.

(RASKOLNIKOV hesitates.)

DOCTOR	Quite useless.
RASKOLNIKOV	*(Moves toward the DOCTOR.)* You'll stay here?
DOCTOR	I cannot. I have my regular patients. I'll return later with the certificate.

(As the DOCTOR reaches the door, the PRIEST enters. They exchange glances. The DOCTOR shakes his head and exits. The PRIEST goes to MARMEL-ADOV and makes the sign of the cross.)

PRIEST	What is your name, my son?
MARMELADOV	Sem…Sem…
KATERINA	His name is Semyon Zaharovitch Marmeladov.

(The PRIEST commences the last rites of the Russian Orthodox Church.

Lights down.)

SCENE 2
A tavern, some days previously. Lights up. There is one table and two chairs. On the table is RASKOLNIKOV's jug of beer and his glass. Upstage, hidden by the darkness, we see the vague shapes of other patrons.

RASKOLNIKOV   *(Moving slowly as he talks.)* How terrible! And it was only a few days ago that I met Semyon Marmeladov for the first time...in this tavern.... *(He sits.)* He came to my table....

(MARMELADOV comes slowly on from stage right. He is quite drunk but sobers as the scene progresses.)

MARMELADOV   May I venture to engage you, sir, in conversation? Your bearing suggests to me that you are a man of education—as I am—not accustomed to such... surroundings....

(Someone in the darkness upstage laughs.)

VOICE   *(From the darkness upstage.)* Careful, young fellow, he'll talk your head off!

(MARMELADOV has been carrying his own jug of beer and his glass. He puts them now on RASKOLNIKOV's table.)

MARMELADOV   Ignore them, sir—they are ruffians. Ruffians. *(Strikes a pose.)* My name is Semyon Zaharovitch Marmeladov; my position, titular counselor in the government.

(A few laughs are heard from upstage.)

MARMELADOV   May I inquire, are you in government service?
RASKOLNIKOV   *(Curtly.)* No. I am studying.

MARMELADOV	A student! Exactly my impression! I am a man of immense experience, sir. *(Indicating that he would like to sit.)* May I?
RASKOLNIKOV	Go ahead.
MARMELADOV	*(Sitting.)* Ah— *(He pours some beer into his glass from his jug and drinks. He puts the glass down and stares vacantly for a moment.)* It isn't a vice to be poor! Certainly, it is no virtue to be drunk—too often. But to beg—it is a vice to beg! Poor men still have their dignity but beggars—never! People sweep beggars away with brooms to make it as humiliating as possible! And quite right! I am the first to humiliate myself! *(He leans toward RASKOLNIKOV like a conspirator.)* Have you ever spent a night on a hay barge on the Neva?
RASKOLNIKOV	No, I have not.
MARMELADOV	I have slept on a hay barge for the past five nights. Perhaps you see bits of hay— *(He sees hay on his clothing and brushes it off.)* Yes—

(In the dark upstage, someone snickers.)

| MARMELADOV | Pay no attention to them. |

(The snicker comes again.)

| VOICE | *(From the dark upstage.)* Why don't you go to work? If you work for the government, why aren't you in your office? |
| MARMELADOV | *(To RASKOLNIKOV.)* Why am I not at my desk? Ah, how my heart aches when I think of what a useless worm I am. Young man, has it ever happened to you to ask for a loan—without hope? |

(Another laugh from the dark.)

RASKOLNIKOV   *(An annoyed glance in the direction of the laughter.)*
                   Yes. But what do you mean—without hope?

MARMELADOV   Without hope because you know with certainty
                   that this person will give you not one kopeck! And
                   why should he? He knows I won't pay it back. Out
                   of compassion? No. Mr. Lebeziatnikov keeps up
                   with modern ideas; he explained to me that nowa-
                   days science itself forbids compassion. Yet I go to
                   his home and—

RASKOLNIKOV   But why do you go?

MARMELADOV   There are times when a man must go somewhere!
                   When they gave my daughter the yellow ticket,
                   then I had to go—

*(When MARMELADOV says, "yellow ticket," there is whispering and snick-
ering in the back.)*

MARMELADOV   Yes, my Sonia has a yellow passport. *(Hastily.)* But
                   no matter, no matter!

(Loud guffaws upstage.)

VOICE   *(From upstage.)* Ah, I bet she's a beauty!

ANOTHER VOICE   *(From upstage.)* What rates does she charge?

RASKOLNIKOV   *(To the men upstage.)* That's enough!

MARMELADOV   They don't bother me. Everyone knows about it.
                   And I accept it...with humility. So be it! Ecce
                   homo! Behold this man! Young man, can you look
                   at this face and say it is not the face of...a pig!

(More loud laughter from upstage.)

VOICE   *(From upstage.)* A pig!

ANOTHER VOICE   *(From upstage.)* Oink! Oink!

MARMELADOV   So be it. I am a beast. But my wife is a lady. Katerina
                   Ivanovna is the daughter of an officer, a woman of
                   refinement. If only once she would show a little

MARMELADOV (CONT.)	affection for me. A man should have someone who feels for him. I know that when she pulls my hair, she does it only out of pity—
VOICE	*(From upstage, laughing.)* Pulls his hair!
MARMELADOV	Without shame, I repeat, pulls my hair! If just once she would...No, I'm only talking! More than once my dream did come true and we...ah...I am a beast by nature!
VOICE	*(From upstage.)* A pig!
MARMELADOV	Do you know I have sold the very stockings off her legs for drink? Not her shoes, you understand, that would be more or less in the order of things, but her stockings...and our room so cold, and she's coughing all the time...she coughs up blood—she has that disease—And she works from morning to night scrubbing and cleaning, tending the children, and her chest so weak....I feel it! Do you imagine I don't feel it? The more I drink, the more I feel it! That's why I drink: to find feeling....I drink so I may suffer! *(In despair, he folds his arms on the table and lays his head on them.)*
VOICE	*(From upstage.)* What a swine!
ANOTHER VOICE	*(From upstage.)* How can you stand an old bum like that?
RASKOLNIKOV	*(To the people upstage.)* This is no business of yours. Leave us alone.
MARMELADOV	*(Raises his head from his arms.)* You know, Katerina Ivanovna has a certificate of merit. When she left school, the governor himself presented her with a gold medal and a certificate of merit. The medal has been...sold, but she shows the certificate of merit to everyone. I don't blame her. The only thing left to her is the past. To this day, she speaks of her first husband with tears in her eyes. And I'm pleased, very pleased, that she once knew happiness....But when we met she was alone, a widow with three small children. And I with my Sonia. She had nowhere

MARMELADOV (CONT.) to turn! Do you know what it means when there is absolutely nowhere to turn? We married, and for one whole year I was the best of husbands, the most conscientious of men; not once did I touch this— *(He indicates the beer.)* Then I lost my job—the office was reorganized—and I began— *(He picks up his glass of beer and then pushes it from him in sudden revulsion.)* We came here to St. Petersburg. I found another job...and lost it....Do you understand?... What money we live on...it's Sonia's money. She's such a gentle creature, with such a pale, thin face. Let me ask you, do you believe that a respectable girl can earn a living by honest work?

RASKOLNIKOV I don't know.

MARMELADOV Pennies can she earn! And that only if she does not leave her work for an instant! To this day, Ivan Ivanitch Klopstock—do you know him?

RASKOLNIKOV No.

MARMELADOV My friend, he is a civil counselor, but to this day he has not paid my Sonia for the half-dozen shirts she made for him. He said the collars weren't made to pattern and that she put them in wrong—but still he wears them! *(He drinks, puts the glass down as a painful memory comes to mind.)* It's still only a few months since that evening I was lying on our sofa. I had been out all day and...I was drunk, I was just helpless drunk. Katerina Ivanovna was walking up and down in our little room, she was just beside herself, like a tigress, screaming at Sonia, "Here you are living with us—you eat our food and you keep warm in our room—and you do nothing to help us!" Poor Sonia, much she had to eat when not even the children had a crust of bread for three days! "Dear Katerina, how can you ask me to do such a thing?" "And why not? Are you something so sweet, so precious?" *(His head falls into his hands.)* Don't blame her...the children were crying from

MARMELADOV   hunger. Sonia went out into the street. When she
(CONT.)   came back, she put thirty rubles on the table with-
               out a word. She lay down on her bed, her face to
               the wall, her little body trembling. Katerina went to
               her, fell on her knees beside her, and kissed her and
               there were tears on her face—She lay down next to
               her and they fell asleep in each other's arms…and
               I…I was drunk! *(He buries his face in his hand and
               sobs.)*

*(RASKOLNIKOV places his hand for a moment on MARMELADOV's
arm.)*

MARMELADOV   *(Raises his head.)* Five days ago, I stole the key to
               Katerina Ivanovna's strongbox, like a thief in the
               night, and took out everything that was there.
               Twelve silver rubles. Now look at me! *(Stands, ex-
               cited.)* Look at me! For these rags, I sold the last of
               my good clothes! It's the end of everything! *(Sits,
               drops his head, and smiles.)* This morning I went to
               see my Sonia—I needed money for a little pick-
               me-up! *(He laughs.)*
VOICE   *(From upstage, incredulous.)* And she gave it to you?
MARMELADOV   *(To RASKOLNIKOV.)* This very quart was bought
               with her money! Thirty kopecks, all the money
               that she had! And so here I am, her own father,
               drinking up her last thirty kopecks! *(He drinks the
               beer in his glass and tries to replenish it from the jug,
               but there is no more left.)* And I have drunk it! *(He
               holds his glass aloft, inviting someone to buy him more
               beer.)* Who will have pity on a man like me?

(Laughter from upstage. Even RASKOLNIKOV smiles.)

VOICE   Look at the nerve!
ANOTHER VOICE What a reptile!
FIRST VOICE   Why should you be pitied?

MARMELADOV   Why should I be pitied? *(Stands and stretches out an arm, still holding the empty beer glass.)* Yes! There's no reason to pity me! I should be crucified, not pitied! Yes, crucify me! I will go willingly! I have searched all my life for suffering! *(Folds his hands, still with the beer glass, against his chest and looks to heaven.)* Oh, who but God can pity me? Only he...only he. He pities all men. He understands all things! On the last day of earth, on the Day of Judgment, he will come, and he will ask, "Where is the daughter who gave herself so three little children and their sick mother might live? Where is the daughter who pitied that filthy drunk, her own father?" He will say, "Come to me! I forgive thee! I forgive thy sins, for greatly hast though loved!" He will forgive my Sonia, I know he will! And on that last day, he will judge and he will forgive all men. And when he has forgiven all the others, then he will summon us. "Come forth!" He will say, "Come forth, ye drunks, ye children of shame!" And he will say unto us, "Ye are swine and have the mark of the beast upon thee; but come ye also!" And the others will ask, "Lord, why dost thou receive such men as these?" And he will answer, "Why do I receive them? I receive them because not one of them believed himself worthy to be saved!" And he will hold out his hands to us, and we shall fall down before him and weep. And we will understand all things...and all men will understand...and...and Katerina...even she...will understand. *(Sinks into his chair. Silence. For a moment, the beer glass dangles from his fingers, and then it drops to the floor.)*

VOICE   *(From upstage.)* What crazy ideas!

ANOTHER VOICE *(From upstage.)* A fine government official he is!

FIRST VOICE   *(From upstage.)* Look at him! He talked himself silly!

MARMELADOV   *(Suddenly grasps RASKOLNIKOV's arm.)* Come home with me! Please! I must go home!

RASKOLNIKOV	All right.
MARMELADOV	*(Stands.)* Will you come with me?
RASKOLNIKOV	I will. *(He stands.)*
MARMELADOV	I'm not afraid of her. Let her hit me! Let her pull my hair!

(Laughter from the darkness upstage.)

VOICE	*(From upstage.)* Pulls his hair!
ANOTHER VOICE	*(From upstage.)* I'd like to see that!
MARMELADOV	What does that matter? I'm not afraid of that! *(He clutches RASKOLNIKOV's arm and speaks more quietly.)* It's her eyes…her eyes frighten me…and her breathing.…Do you know how people with that disease breathe? And the children…it's been five days.
RASKOLNIKOV	Come along.

(Lights down.)

MARMELADOV	*(Offstage.)* Here…this is our room—Katerina—
KATERINA	*(Offstage.)* You! Where is the money? Where are the twelve silver rubles you took from the chest?
MARMELADOV	*(Cries out, offstage.)* Don't pull my hair, Katerina!
KATERINA	*(Offstage.)* You've drunk it all!

(MARMELADOV cries out again.)

KATERINA	*(Offstage.)* The children are hungry, don't you understand? Hungry! You thief! What have you done to us?

SCENE 3

Same as scene 1. Lights up. The PRIEST finishes administering the last rites and draws away. KATERINA, who has been praying with him beside MARMELADOV's bed, rises.

PRIEST	*(To KATERINA.)* My child, we must resign ourselves to the inevitable—
KATERINA	*(Sharply.)* What am I to do with my children?
PRIEST	God is merciful; look to him for help in your—
KATERINA	Yes, he is merciful. But not to us!
PRIEST	That's a sin, madam, you must never think—
KATERINA	*(Pointing at MARMELADOV.)* And isn't that a sin?
PRIEST	Perhaps those who caused the accident will compensate you—at least for the loss of his earnings.
KATERINA	You don't understand! Why should they give me anything? He was drunk! He threw himself under the wheels! He had no money and no job! He brought us nothing but misery! He drank away everything! He robbed us to get drunk—he wasted our lives! Thank God he's dying! *(She wipes the dying man's face with the towel.)*
PRIEST	Such feelings are a great sin, madam! You must forgive in the hour of death.
KATERINA	*(Leaves MARMELADOV, excitedly.)* Forgive! If he hadn't been run over, he would have come home drunk! He would have fallen down there. *(Points to the sofa.)* And slept like an animal! And all night, while he slept, I would have been washing and rinsing our rags, and as soon as there was light enough to see, I would have begun mending them! That's how I spend my nights! Forgive! I have forgiven— *(She goes into a coughing fit and presses a ragged handkerchief to her lips. She chokes down the cough and shows the cloth to the PRIEST.)* See...blood...

(The PRIEST bows his head and says nothing.)

| MARMELADOV | *(He moves an arm toward KATERINA weakly, trying to ask for forgiveness.)* Uh…uh… |
| KATERINA | *(Sharply.)* Be silent! I know what you want to say! |

(SONIA enters timidly. The POLICEMAN bars her way.)

| POLICEMAN | Yes, Miss? |
| SONIA | I'm…his daughter— |

(The POLICEMAN steps aside for her. SONIA takes a step or two and stops.)

SONIA	Father—
MARMELADOV	*(Suddenly sees SONIA and struggles to sit up, alarmed.)* Who's that? Who's that?
KATERINA	Lie down!
MARMELADOV	*(With his last strength, MARMELADOV manages to rise onto his elbows. He recognizes SONIA.)* Sonia! Oh, Sonia—forgive me! *(His strength gives way and he slips toward the floor. RASKOLNIKOV, KATERINA, and SONIA rush forward to catch him. SONIA, with a cry, falls to her knees and grasps him about the chest. He manages a few guttural sounds and dies. They put MARMELADOV back on the sofa. The PRIEST makes the sign of the cross and exits. The POLICEMAN exits.)*
KATERINA	*(Wringing her hands.)* What's to become of us? How can I bury him? I have no money—how can I feed my children?
RASKOLNIKOV	Katerina Ivanovna, the day I met your husband, he told me of your life here. That evening, we became friends. I want to help you. *(Takes some money from his pocket.)* Here—that's twenty rubles.
KATERINA	Oh…thank you! Sonia! Sonia!

(SONIA, who has remained kneeling by her dead father, lifts her face.)

| KATERINA | Look, Sonia! This gentleman knew your father and now he's going to help us! *(To RASKOLNIKOV.)* |

KATERINA (CONT.)	God bless you! I never thought my husband had such friends in St. Petersburg! *(Tying the money into a handkerchief.)* Poor man! I felt so sorry for him! He would sit in a corner and look at me, so unhappy, and I'd want to comfort him—But then I'd think, Be kind to him and he'll drink more than ever. We will repay you very soon, I assure you—
RASKOLNIKOV	No, please don't bother to—
KATERINA	Oh, don't think we shall always be in these circumstances. I am the daughter of a colonel, and I assure you we shall soon be able to repay you for your kindness. Sonia and I plan to return to the town where I grew up and open a boarding school for the daughters of gentlemen. *(She coughs.)* We've spoken of it many times, haven't we, Sonia?

(SONIA bows her head, avoiding KATERINA's glance.)

KATERINA	It's true! I come from a good family—I went to a fine school—They awarded me the certificate of merit! I'll show you! *(KATERINA starts hunting for the certificate.)*
RASKOLNIKOV	I don't think it—
KATERINA	Perhaps you don't believe me?
RASKOLNIKOV	Certainly—
KATERINA	I have it here! Sonia, here, you must help me! *(SONIA rises to her feet.)* Come, Sonia—look there! *(KATERINA points to where SONIA should look and busies herself looking for the certificate. SONIA only backs away, staring at KATERINA.)* There was a gold medal, too, but it was lost— *(She sees SONIA watching her. She coughs.)* But Sonia, why won't you help me look?
RASKOLNIKOV	It doesn't matter—
KATERINA	Yes! Yes, it does matter! *(She finds the certificate.)* Here! Here it is! Here is the certificate! *(She shows the certificate to RASKOLNIKOV and then goes into a coughing fit. She sinks to her knees beside*

KATERINA   *MARMELADOV.)* O Lord, how can I tell the chil-
(CONT.)   dren? *(She rests her head upon the dead man's chest. The
                  certificate slips from her fingers and falls to the floor.)*

The General of the Skies

A FARCE WITH

MELODRAMATIC RELIEF

CHARACTERS

THE GENERAL (RETIRED), UNITED STATES AIR FORCE
ROBERT, THE GENERAL'S AIDE
TWO YOUNG MEN

*Lyrics from "The Air Force Song" by Robert Crawford,
courtesy USAF Heritage of America Band.*

The front room of THE GENERAL's house. It is relatively bare, most things seeming to have been packed away in the trunks and boxes that are about. There is a table on which ROBERT, THE GENERAL's aide puts the things he is bringing into the room. There are a few chairs and other nondescript bits of furniture. The front door is stage left. The door to the adjoining room is stage right.

ROBERT comes on from stage right, carrying a load of documents. He puts them down on the table and pauses a moment, resting.

THE GENERAL   *(Offstage right.)* Here's some more ...come on!

(ROBERT exits stage right.)

THE GENERAL   *(Offstage.)* Take these! Take these!

(ROBERT enters with another load. THE GENERAL comes on, carrying nothing.)

THE GENERAL   There's more papers by the hassock. Come, we must finish this before they get here!

(ROBERT puts his load down on the table and exits stage right once more.)

THE GENERAL   Why couldn't they have given me a white boy? Only to humiliate me— *(ROBERT comes on with another load.)* Put them over there! *(THE GENERAL pushes ROBERT's elbow. ROBERT loses his grip and the papers tumble to the floor. THE GENERAL dives for them.)*

THE GENERAL   Careful! My diaries! These are my diaries! Priceless memories!

ROBERT   I'm sorry, sir! *(ROBERT helps THE GENERAL gather the diaries from the floor.)*

THE GENERAL   I need every memory. I have long intended to write my memoirs. It is a magnificent story. Mine is a story the American people are waiting breathlessly to hear. Will I have time for my memoirs, do you suppose?

ROBERT	I—
THE GENERAL	Oh, time enough for memoirs, surely. Even if I do have to move out of here—twenty years in one location, and they say I must move! There'll be another place, don't you think? After all, I am a national hero; you don't shove a national hero away just anywhere.
ROBERT	No, sir.
THE GENERAL	No? I am beginning to find your personality agreeable. What is your name, soldier?
ROBERT	Robert Ather—
THE GENERAL	That's all! Just the first name! Just Robert. Call a Negro by anything but his first name, and he gets uppity. It is that first slice cut out of authority that counts. Yes. I want you to drop the sir, Robert. I want our relationship to be informal. Call me General.
ROBERT	All right. General.
THE GENERAL	That's right, Robert, call me General just as if it were my first name. Rank opens such gaps between people. *(THE GENERAL tries to scratch his back. He will continue to do so off and on throughout the play—except in his more impassioned moments. He presents his back to ROBERT.)* Scratch my back, would you, Robert? In the middle. *(ROBERT scratches THE GENERAL's back.)* Why do you suppose they're coming, Robert?
ROBERT	*(Indicating the back scratch.)* How's that?
THE GENERAL	All this rush, rush, rush. I feel concern. *(THE GENERAL turns, the back scratching over.)* Robert, I have a premonition that you are to be my last aide-de-camp.
ROBERT	Oh no—
THE GENERAL	No, don't object. Don't attempt to dissuade me. One gets a certain feeling when fate gathers its legs under itself.
ROBERT	Perhaps it will be a new honor, General. Perhaps they want to give you a new medal.

THE GENERAL   Oh, do you think so? Do you think that's possible? A new decoration? A new ribbon? But which one could it be? Have you seen my medals, Robert? I must have them all. *(THE GENERAL opens one of his boxes of medals.)* Look! Which one is missing? Can you tell?

ROBERT   No—

THE GENERAL   Green ribbons, brown ribbons, scarlet ribbons, gold ribbons—Look at this one, isn't it pretty? Notice the play of light. And this one. What was it for? And this—I remember! The Potluck Campaign! It's the prettiest, don't you think? I was always fascinated by the glint and glitter of gold. And this—What color is that? Dishwater gray. Yes. Given to me by my wife for the faithful taking out of the dinner scraps to the dog's kennel each evening for twenty-seven long years.

ROBERT   Twenty-seven years! That's really an—

THE GENERAL   —old dog. Toward the end, I cradled him tenderly in my arms while he urinated on my uniform. *(Firmly.)* But a general must be prepared to accept the burden of responsibility. This bit of silk, or maybe it's nylon, it's all I have left from my wife. She's gone, Robert.

ROBERT   Dead, General?

THE GENERAL   No. Just gone, damn her. The children, too, of course, long ago. *(Picks up another ribbon.)* What was this for? *(Picks up a large book and leafs through it.)* The fall of Troy? No! Battle of Tours? No! Tannenberg? No! Leipzig? No! Flodden Field? No! Salamis? No! Verdun? Bull Run? No! Damn it, what color is that ribbon?

ROBERT   *(Examines the ribbon.)* Blood red.

THE GENERAL   Of course! The debit half of a typewriter ribbon. Awarded for valor while engaged in sanguinary struggles in the corridors of the Pentagon. Navy people, you know, Robert. Vicious fighters. *(Con-*

THE GENERAL (CONT.) *sidering the past.)* The old Pentagon crowd. My buddies. Where have they gone? Harry and Black Jim and Fatso Brannigan and Speedball Jackson—they gave him Korea, poor devil—and Waco and all the rest—Why did they turn their backs on me? I was the biggest of them all. A hero among heroes. Oh, what amarvelous time that was, Robert. Of course, you missed it. You're too young. *(The drone of World War II bombers comes in under THE GENERAL's speech. The sound builds as he continues.)* Those fleets of bombers, that solid, thumping roar those old engines made, saturation raids, circles of flame—Marvelous! The plane leaping into the sky as the bombs fell away, the bucking of the wings under the flack, marigolds and roses bursting in the twilight, shivering in the concussion—Bang! Bang! Boom! Yes, Robert. Poetry! It is poetry! That's what you people down on the ground will never understand—the magnificence, the power, and the damn beauty of it! The sky! The ocean sky! *(Singing.)* "Off we go into the wild blue yonder / Dum de dum / Give 'er the gun!" *(THE GENERAL pauses for a moment, choked with emotion.)* Oh, Robert, what a glorious time to be a general! I am impaled on the cusp of an upthrusting arc! Thermopylae to Dresden! Greek fire to firestorm! Spear to tank to terror! Megatons! Megadeaths! *(Short pause.)* Overkill! Ah, glorious, marvelous, wonderful! We! We are the first real gods! Masters of the ultimate! Fingers on the fuse of eternity! *(Stops, carried away, and suddenly collapses.)* But not me. They cut me off, Robert.

ROBERT *(Impatiently.)* General—

THE GENERAL Why, Robert? *(Scratching himself.)* Why do you suppose they just cut me off?

ROBERT Perhaps some deficiency in you that—

THE GENERAL Deficiency? In me? How ironic, Robert, that you

THE GENERAL (CONT.)	should use that word, and of me, of all people! You'll see....When they publish my memoirs, you'll read, with your mouth gaping open, the life of the most complete of men! *(Scratches.)* Oh yes, I know what you mean. My scratching. They don't care to see a general scratching himself like a simian. Well, I'm sick. Everyone has illnesses. And my illness is incurable, Robert. I have an incurable illness. I itch. I burn. I feel numb. My skin flakes and scales and swells with pus. I have sores that won't close. I am crawling with dirt and disease. The doctors laugh at me. "Incurable!" They run after me with their diagnosis. They are importunate. They won't leave me alone. They ring the doorbell; they rattle my windows at night. "You are incurably ill!" But I never seem to die. Everyone gets sick, don't they?

(ROBERT starts to speak but shrugs his shoulders instead.)

THE GENERAL	Why couldn't it have been thrombosis? Or arteriosclerosis? Or cancer? Yes, cancer. No one laughs at cancer. A damn good disease for a general. *(THE GENERAL pins one of his medals on his jacket and then tears it off and throws it on the floor.)* I don't know what happened to my dignity. Once, I could walk into a room and you could hear a pin drop. You could cut the air with a saber. I frowned and the corps trembled. But now my character is water, dribbled out of me. Everything is drowned in familiarity. People laugh. I once could keep them at a distance but no more. Why, Robert?
ROBERT	C'est la guerre, mon General.
THE GENERAL	Cut out that frog talk! Show me some courtesy! *(Ruminating.)* It began long ago. During the war. I made myself too easy, too accessible. A lovable old guy! A joy to babies! Look! *(He grins.)*

THE GENERAL (CONT.)	Everybody loves this grin! What a decent, open, sincere, lovable grin it is! *(Indicating a newspaper headliner.)* The General Grins as Thousands Cheer! People took advantage. *(Reaching a deeper memory.)* No. No, I'll tell you when it began. After the war. An afternoon in autumn with the sunlight coming down at an angle and a chill in the air…a crowd of people pushing and shoving each other, their arms reaching out to me, trying to touch me, silly ass grins on their faces, calling and laughing and jostling…and me in the middle, half dragged out of my car. It's all like a photograph; each face is printed in my memory. Those people…they were different. They weren't the usual crowd. They were relatives, friends, all of us together on an outing…It was a little girl. Yes, she started it all. Her mother pushed her at me from the crowd, and I clutched her, with her breath panting on my cheek, and then, just as her mother had told her to, she kissed me. And I was destroyed, felled like a tree by that soft, damp blow—oh— *(He moans, unable to go on.)*
ROBERT	But General, surely you had been kissed by children before.
THE GENERAL	Yes! Of course! I am a general, a hero of the people, with all that it implies!
ROBERT	Why, then, this particular child—
THE GENERAL	It was the way she looked at me after the kiss, staring at me, eyes bold with innocence—Ah! The expression on that child's face! Smug, superior—I felt torn open! Naked before all those people, stripped of my clothes, my rank, my prestige, my command! People were holding the car door open. I pushed them away and I yelled at the driver, "Get the hell out of here!" You know what I did then?
ROBERT	What did you do, General?

(THE GENERAL says something so softly it isn't heard.)

ROBERT   Sorry, I didn't hear what you said.

THE GENERAL   I masturbated! Not since my adolescence had I
                  turned to that for consolation. But there, that day,
                  in that silent, smooth-riding limousine, I—I ran
                  from a child with guillotine eyes. I was opened,
                  hollowed out by those child's eyes. That was the
                  first day of my illness. I relieved the primal itch
                  and scratched open an epidemic. *(Scratches him-
                  self, in agony.)* They've all turned their backs on
                  me. Nothing bothered them! No child looked
                  at them! Tell me, Robert, tell me...what did she
                  see? She looked in my face...she saw—What is
                  it? Look at me, look in my eyes—What do you
                  see?

ROBERT   Nothing. I see a General.

THE GENERAL   You can tell me, Robert. You can see. You're a
                  Negro, you're out of all this. Tell me, what is it
                  she saw?

ROBERT   I don't know.

THE GENERAL   Tell me! Tell me, damn you!

ROBERT   Guilt.

THE GENERAL   What? Guilt? Guilt for what? We won the war,
                  didn't we? Don't make yourself ridiculous!

ROBERT   I see guilt.

THE GENERAL   Ridiculous! We have no guilt. Airmen have sweet
                  dreams. We're above the mess. Twenty thousand
                  feet up, it's all statistics. It's the way war should be:
                  clean, objective—surgical. You! Why do you pre-
                  tend? You couldn't care less! War means that many
                  fewer white people when it's over! You don't fool
                  me! I know you, hiding behind that black mask! You
                  shuffle and scrape, but you don't give a good damn!
                  I— *(With difficulty, he gets control of himself.)* Oh...
                  oh, Robert. I'm sorry. Forgive me. I want you to like
                  me...you, of all people. I want you to care for me,

THE GENERAL (CONT.)   Robert. I ask for very little—only a tear, a symbol. In the name of brotherhood, give me something! Just a sign, that's all I ask! *(THE GENERAL falls on his knees in front of his aide. The noise of approaching bombers lowers.)* This is your General, begging you on his knees…forgive me! I'm only a child of my time! Forgive them, Lord, for they know not what they do. Comfort me, grant me some token of forgiveness. Lift me up!

(The drone of the planes rises.)

THE GENERAL   They're coming! The bombers are coming! There's blood on the snow!

(THE GENERAL sobs.)

ROBERT   *(Helps him to his feet. The aide is undisturbed. He smiles. When he speaks, the noise of the bombers stops.)* Get up, General. They'll be here any minute. You don't want them to see you like this.

THE GENERAL   Robert, in the name of God, in the name of brotherhood, I didn't mean to kill her.

ROBERT   Who didn't you mean to kill, General?

THE GENERAL   *(After a pause.)* Do you have a cigarette, Robert?

ROBERT   Yes. *(ROBERT gives THE GENERAL a cigarette and lights it for him.)*

THE GENERAL   The doctors thought I scratched because I smoked, so no more cigarettes. No more fried foods or strawberries or sex or long walks in the country or wool underwear or visiting relatives— *(Scratches himself.)*

(ROBERT sits down, very casual.)

THE GENERAL   Have you ever been in love, Robert?

ROBERT   Never, General.

THE GENERAL   Once in my life, I was in love. During the war.
A young German girl. Beautiful young girl.
(Coughs.) I don't think I can smoke anymore.
(Puts out the cigarette.) Damn Germans! Robert,
their reputation for order is overrated! At the
end, they gave up everything—even their order
went. It was winter, you know, and the bodies…
the bodies were still there on the ground, untouched. I remember the blood as scarlet, but it
couldn't have been, not even in winter. It must
have dried—don't you think it must have dried?
Then it would have been rust colored. Why do
I remember the blood as red? *(Pause.)* All that's
bad for morale. Very bad. We didn't let the boys
see where their bombs had gone, not when the
killing was fresh, not until we got right in there,
right into Germany.

(Lights down slowly except on the General.)

We had just raided this town the day before, and I
went to see. The dust was still settling. No. Not really. Everything had settled. It was…quiet. I went
up one street and down the next…almost as if I
were searching for something. And I saw this girl.
She was lying on the broken stones. Dead. But not
disfigured. I suppose she had been killed by concussion. She was almost naked, her clothes mostly
blown from her body. And thrown onto this pile of
rubble in an artistic, a most artistic pose—draped
upon those dusty bits of masonry like an artist's
model. In profile…the profile of her face—perfect
beauty. Blue eyes gazing at the heavens. Long, dark
lashes. Blonde hair spread about her like the petals
of a flower. Her breasts, the tips pink, yes, rose pink,
like rosebuds in the spring—that color… *(Pause.)*
It's ridiculous, I know. It's absurd. After all, back in

THE GENERAL
(CONT.)

the States, I had a wife and children. But I stood there in that cold winter, dust from the bombing still drifting, as it were, through the atmosphere, and I…I fell in love with this beautiful creature. From depths in me I had not known existed, there rose an exquisite, a sweet, oh God, so sweet and over-whelming an emotion. I stood there, trembling like a fourteen-year-old boy, trembling on the tip of the first, sweet spear of love, love that I had never known men could feel…I was lost! I completely forgot my-self, forgot the war, forgot my rank and where I was.…I even forgot that this…that she was…dead. She had only fallen, stumbled in the debris. She was unconscious, waiting for someone to come to her, to kiss her lips and awaken her. I ran to embrace her! "My love! All my life I have searched—" I bent over to kiss her—Ah! Her eye! The other eye! Torn from her face, lying on her cheek, staring at the red snow! The blood! She was a corpse! No!

(The sound of the bombers resumes.)

THE GENERAL

No! Go back! We've bombed this town! Go back! Return to your base! She's dead! Go back! Don't you know what you've done? No! Go back! *(THE GENERAL sinks to the floor, clutching his head.)*

(The noise of the bombers is overpowering. Abruptly, five solid raps are heard at the front door. Bang! Bang! Bang! Bang! Bang! The sound of the bombers disappears. The lighting, which was focused on THE GENERAL, returns to normal.)

ROBERT

They're here, General.

(THE GENERAL looks about him, coming slowly back to reality. He scratch-es himself.)

ROBERT   *Get up, General.*

(THE GENERAL slowly rises. He brushes dust from his clothes. He struggles back to some semblance of dignity.)

ROBERT   Shall I open the door?
THE GENERAL   Sir! Shall I open the door, sir!
ROBERT   You told me I didn't have to say sir to you.
THE GENERAL   Sir!
ROBERT   Sir!
THE GENERAL   That was a different mood. Staff officers can in-
                dulge in capricious moods, but the book says, sir!
                And, by God, you'll say, sir! Open the door!
ROBERT   Yes! Sir!

(ROBERT opens the front door. "They" turn out to be two youths—one white, the other black—dressed casually in khaki, shirts open at the neck. They look like two boys from the corner service station, but they have pistols strapped to their waists. They stand good-naturedly by the door, waiting for THE GENERAL.)

THE GENERAL   Well, this is good-bye, Robert.

(THE GENERAL tries to shake ROBERT's hand, but ROBERT salutes him instead.)

ROBERT   Good-bye, sir.

(THE GENERAL answers ROBERT's salute and holds it, so they are both saluting through the following dialogue.)

THE GENERAL   Good-bye, Robert. You'll take care of my
                decorations and my papers, won't you, Robert?
                They're part of history. Glorious…bombers. Well!
                Well, Robert, let's go out and see what they want
                from me, shall we, Robert?

(THE GENERAL turns and exits through the front door, still holding his salute, followed by the two young men. ROBERT, whose salute has become increasingly lax, drops his arm. He laughs quietly. A moment of silence, underlined by ROBERT's soft laughter. There is a sudden pistol shot offstage. ROBERT laughs. His laughter grows. He kicks over the table, and THE GENERAL's effects crash to the floor. ROBERT roars with laughter.)

The Prophet Jeremiah

SCENE 1

The inside of an old clapboard shack in the hills of eastern Tennessee. A weather-beaten sign leans, end up, in a corner. The faded black lettering on it reads Church of the Prophet. On the back wall is chalked in large, crude capitals GOD OUR FATHER. An old sofa, a relic from ancient times, is in the center of the room. There are a few other battered pieces of furniture distributed about. The exit to the outside is at right, and a door leading to a small utility room is at left. A rifle is leaning beside the door right. From outside comes the sound of a gathering of people. Their singing, talking, and hand-clapping go on in the background throughout the play.

A pregnant woman, SISTER VEENA, is seated on the sofa. She is dressed in the full, coarse dress of the region, and she wears heavy shoes.

BEN DANIELS enters from right. He is about thirty-two. He is dressed in a khaki shirt and dungarees. He looks about quickly and then stares at SISTER VEENA.

BEN	Sister Veena! What're yew doin' in th' parish house?
VEENA	I'm waitin'.
BEN	Waitin' fer him? He ain't come back yet?
VEENA	No, he ain't.
BEN	*(Tries to contain himself but can't.)* Yew ain't got no business here in th' parish house, Sister Veena. A unmarried woman with an unknown man's kid 'bout to be born from her should stay from th' sight of a man of God.
VEENA	Maybe a sinful person got more business waitin' fer a holy man than any.
BEN	*(Instantly remorseful.)* That's right, Sister Veena, yer right. Forgive me. I got too great a pride in my own goodness. I got a place waitin' fer yew in Brother William's Model A, Sister Veena.
VEENA	When th' time comes, I'll take it.
BEN	*(Moving about nervously.)* I cain't think right fer worry. He's been gone all th' day long. This day, out of all days! I been keepin' th' congregation a-singin', but they been askin' questions I cain't answer. I been worryin' all th' time.

VEENA	Yew air doin' wonderful with th' people, Brother Ben. Nair's good as Th' Prophet.
BEN	I cain't never be as good as Th' Prophet. An' he ain't here.
VEENA	Yew needn't to worry. They ain't no one big enough to worry 'bout him. He has worry fer all his flock an' fer each an' ev'ry one of his sheep, an' th' worryin' of others fer him but burdens him more.
BEN	I cain't hep but wonder what's come to him. Today, he was to lead th' faithful down from th' hills to Johnson City an' begin th' great work of th' salvation—but he ain't here.
VEENA	*(Calmly.)* If he don't come, then yew must lead th' kin to Johnson City, Brother Ben.
BEN	Me!
VEENA	But he'll come.
BEN	Sister Veena, he's only mortal flesh like yew an' me. He could have fallen off a ledge in th' mountains an' hurt hisself or even kilt hisself.
VEENA	Th' Prophet ain't in th' mountains huntin'. There's his rifle right over there. Th' Prophet ain't kilt. Th' Prophet ain't gonna die yet. Before he dies, he's gonna bring th' new faith to Johnson City an' 'stablish th' faith there fer all th' world's salvation. That's God's work an' God'll pertect him fer it.
BEN	*(Goes to door right and opens it.)* He ain't come. He ain't come. All th' people packed what they owned an' loaded up their cars or their mules or even their cows to leave th' hills an' bring th' new faith to th' world. *(Closes door.)* Th' packin' was all finished in th' mornin', an' since then we been a-prayin' an' a-singin' an' a-waitin' 'cause Th' Prophet ain't here to lead us into th' city. *(Turning to her in a frenzy.)* What do it mean, Sister Veena? Ain't we got th' blessin' of God? Is th' faith wantin'?
VEENA	*(She rises heavily.)* Blasphemy! Th' voice of God is his voice, they ain't no voice stronger in th' truth

VEENA (CONT.)   than th' voice of Th' Prophet.

BEN   Maybe God has seen fit to take him from us.

VEENA   His life is God's life—God wouldn't take his own life.

(Voices are heard offstage shouting, "He's here!" "Th' Prophet's come back!" Th' Prophet's here!" The voices come closer. The singing begins again with renewed vigor. BEN and VEENA stand motionless.)

BEN   He's come! *(He rushes to the door, flinging it open.)*

(VEENA watches the door intently. THE PROPHET enters. He is tall and gaunt with long, tough muscles. His eyes spark with vitality. His voice, when he speaks, is strong and assured. He is carrying an old carpetbag stuffed full. BEN stoops to take it from him.)

THE PROPHET   I can sling this into th' corner quicker 'n' yew. *(He strides into the room, tossing the bag into the corner.)* Howdy, Sister Veena. Well, Brother Ben, how's all th' kin?

BEN   They's all fine, Prophet. They're wantin' to be led.

(Enter SISTER SUSAN. She is about twenty-eight. She has on a cheap red coat, and underneath is a mail order dress, a size or so too small, accentuating her sensuously curved flesh. She moves quietly and confidently.)

SUSAN   Howdy, folks.

BEN   Where yew been, Sister Susan? Yer man been worryin' all day. Yew'd best go over an' reassure him.

SUSAN   I aim to.

(The two women have been studying each other. Now VEENA looks past SUSAN and moves heavily through the door. SUSAN closes the door after her and walks over to the sofa, taking VEENA's place comfortably.)

BEN   We been frettin' all day after yew, Jeremiah, a-worryin' fer fear of what happened to yew.

THE PROPHET	No need fer frettin'. I been takin' my stock in th' solitude. Now I'll go an' say what I feel to th' congregation.
BEN	Air we leavin'?
THE PROPHET	We be. An' this night, so we'll see Johnson City first in th' brightness an' th' glory of th' mornin'. An' all th' people in th' city will see us comin' to 'stablish th' Church of th' Prophet, an' they'll welcome us in their hearts, even though their voices mock us. We cain't have their churches 'thout a fight. We'll march all night an' gird ourselves with our weariness—ain't no one fights as hard as a tired, stubborn man.
BEN	Yew mean they's goin' to be real fightin'?
THE PROPHET	They may be. That's my rifle there, all loaded. But we-uns is gonna fight first with our words an' th' strength of our faith. *(A little worried.)* Do yew really think th' people air ready, Ben?
BEN	I do. Their faith kep' them a-singin' all through th' day while yew was gone. Now yer back an' they're singin' more joyous than ever. Listen to them.

(They listen to the sounds of the hymn-singing for a moment.)

THE PROPHET	I'm goin' out to them.
BEN	*(As THE PROPHET exits through door right.)* They're waitin' fer yew. They want mightily to hear yew speak. *(He is following THE PROPHET, and then he turns.)* Be yew a-comin', Sister Susan?
SUSAN	I'm tired. So tired. I been trampin' 'round all day, an' now my legs has done weakened on me.
BEN	Where yew been? Yer man been frantic fer yew all day. Yew better go to him.
SUSAN	Later. I got to rest.
BEN	I'll tell him yer here. *(Starts to leave.)*
SUSAN	Ben.
BEN	Yeah?

SUSAN   Why fer yew want to go out there? Yew don't need to hep him. Yew been with th' people all day. Now come an' rest. *(Makes a place for him on the sofa.)*

BEN   I got to hear him. They been questions hurtin' me in my own mind, an' I want my faith strengthened. *(He starts out again.)*

SUSAN   Brother Ben! I want to talk to yew. I need yer hep. *(He starts toward her.)* Shut th' door. It's kinda private like.

BEN   *(Shutting the door.)* What air troublin' yew, Sister?

SUSAN   Come over here. Come over beside me. *(She pulls off her coat, revealing the rounded curves of her body. BEN walks over.)* Sit down.

BEN   What air th' trouble? *(As he sits.)*

SUSAN   It's a mighty wearisome thing. Hold my han'. Please. It'll hep me tell yew. *(He takes her hand in his and she moves closer to him.)* It's a mighty troublesome thing, but yew can hep me with it. Ben, I got to know what's th' matter with me.

BEN   What's th' matter with yew? Why, nothin'. Maybe yew don't make th' fuss over yer family that most females do. But yer young.

SUSAN   I don't mean that. I mean me. What's th' matter with me? *(She moves his hand to her thigh.)* Looky here. Yew been sittin' with me a few minutes, an' yew been holdin' my hand an' lookin' at my body. *(She presses against him.)* What's th' matter with me that yew don't do nothin' 'bout all that?

BEN   *(Looks at her for an astonished moment and then jerks away from her violently and leaps up. SUSAN rises beside him.)* Yew don't know what yer sayin'! Yew don't know what yer thinkin'!

SUSAN   *(She moves her arms slowly about his waist and presses herself to him.)* Don't I? I want yew, Ben.

BEN   What yew mean? D'yew know what yer doin'? *(He slaps her violently.)* Wake up, woman, wake up! Yer married! Yew got kids! Wake up, before th'

BEN (CONT.)	punishment of th' Lord is visited on yew!
SUSAN	*(She is bewildered for a moment and then vicious.)* Who's goin' to visit that punishment on me on this airth?
BEN	Th' Prophet Jeremiah!
SUSAN	Th' Prophet Jeremiah ain't goin' to hurt his sweetheart! Who else air they?
BEN	*(Taking a threatening step toward her.)* What air yew sayin'?
SUSAN	What I said!
BEN	*(Grabs her and shakes her.)* Yew lie! Don't lie to me or I'll stand yew before all th' people to lie to them. What devil's got into yew fer yew to say such things?
SUSAN	It's true! That's where Th' Prophet was all day— with me! He couldn't come an' lead th' people to th' city 'cause he was holdin' me in his arms!
BEN	*(Shouting furiously.)* He wasn't in no one's arms! Lie! Lie! Lie! *(He slaps her with each repetition.)* Dirty, wicked destroyer! It ain't so! It didn't happen! *(She has been forced to her knees, terrified.)* Tell me th' truth! Tell me, by God!
SUSAN	*(She collapses. Her face is in her hands, protecting herself.)* Yew don't want me. I got to have yew.
BEN	*(He kicks her. She falls over on her side.)* What air th' truth? Tell me!
SUSAN	*(She is crying.)* I'm tellin' th' truth. Th' Prophet an' me was together all day. We laughed together an' we played. He was like I never seen him before— he were mortal flesh, like me. We pleasured each other.
BEN	*(He steps away from her in disgust.)* Yaa! I see yer lyin'. My spurnin' made yew lie so's to hurt me an' yew almos' did, yew Jezebel! Jeremiah couldn't never more do what yew said than he could lead his kin over a cliff to destruction in th' darkness!
SUSAN	*(She rises slowly.)* Yew don't believe me.

BEN	Believe! *(He turns to her swiftly.)* Ain't yew done 'nough hurtin'? Get to yer man!
SUSAN	Then I'll show yew.
BEN	Stop yer mouth!
SUSAN	If he was to come into this here room an' he thought he was alone with me, then if what I'm tellin' yew is th' truth, he'll be th' way I say he is, won't he?
BEN	What do yew want? What trick have yew got now?
SUSAN	I want yer lovin' an' I'm goin' to show yew that he what's better than yew ain't too proud to take it.
BEN	Damn— *(He raises his hand to strike her, but she doesn't move.)*
SUSAN	If I called him in here, an' yew hid in that shed out there an' he thought him an' me was alone, yew'd find out th' truth soon enough. Wouldn't yew?
BEN	Yew want, on this night of all nights, fer me to be sneakin' 'round, spyin'—
SUSAN	It ain't but right that before we leave, yew should know this. Yew hide in that shed there. I'll bring him in. *(She opens door right.)*
BEN	Yer air tryin' to fuss me, yew damned—
SUSAN	He sees me. He's comin' over. Now yew'll find out.
BEN	*(Hesitates for a moment and then goes to door left.)* I'll listen to yew. I'll hear yew try with him what yew tried with me. An' I'll hear yer punishment fer that an' I'll enjoy hearin' it. *(He starts through the door, stops, and turns.)* And, by God, if'n he's too merciful to give yew punishment, I'll have th' kin yank out yer tongue fer th' liar yew air. *(He leaves.)*
THE PROPHET	*(Offstage.)* I been speakin' to them an' firin' up their courage fer th' hard road ahead. *(He enters, closing the door.)* Where's Ben?
SUSAN	He went out there.
THE PROPHET	I didn't see him.
SUSAN	He went out. *(THE PROPHET starts to leave.)* Wait!
THE PROPHET	I ain't got no time fer yew now, Sister Susan. I got to find Ben.

SUSAN	Wait. We was together all day, Jeremiah, but with all th' things we did this last day, we never satisfied ourselves with each other. *(She takes hold of his arm. He shakes her off.)*
THE PROPHET	Let go. I've dallied enough with yew today. I got to go out an' lead th' kin to Johnson City.
SUSAN	*(Coming to him.)* Yew still like me, don't yew? They ain't no harm likin' a body, is they?
THE PROPHET	Yeah, I sure like yew.
SUSAN	*(She leads him to the sofa and they sit.)* No one's here. Yew can show yer like a little, cain't yew?
THE PROPHET	*(Suddenly he grabs her and they kiss torridly. They break.)* Goddamn it, woman, I'll take yew now.

(Lights go down. The singers in the background are singing of crossing the Jordan into the Promised Land. The sound wells up and BEN's heartbroken, lonely voice joins them.)

BEN	*(He breaks down, sobbing.)* O my God. My God! Why has yew lef' me?

(Lights up. THE PROPHET is standing, staring at the shed door, his coat dangling from his hand. SUSAN still sits. The door bursts open and BEN stands there, looking at THE PROPHET with a tortured expression on his face. The coat falls from THE PROPHET's hand.)

BEN	*(Crying.)* It's true, by God, it's true!
SUSAN	He ain't too proud to love me, yew can see.
BEN	*(Savagely.)* Shut up! Shut up, yew slut! I'll kill yew, by God, I'll kill yew now! *(He rushes toward her. She jumps up from the sofa and moves out of his reach.)*
THE PROPHET	*(Quietly.)* What was yew doin' in that shed, Ben?

(BEN turns to THE PROPHET.)

THE PROPHET	Yew hadn't ought to have been in that shed, Ben *(He has visibly crumbled.)*

BEN	She told me to spy on yew an' see yew was lovers! I didn't believe her!
THE PROPHET	What yew think I ought to do about this, Ben? *(BEN walks up to THE PROPHET and strikes him, knocking him down. THE PROPHET pulls a handkerchief from his pocket in a daze and dabs at his lips.)* Ben, I don't know why I done it. I didn't fight my own nature. I got to be someone else. I slipped myself outa one suit an' into another. I never even known what I was doin'. I want to lead my kin.
BEN	*(Viciously.)* Yew know what yew done? Yew done ended th' Church of th' Prophet with yer passion. Yew? Yew ain't no saint. Yew air just common, ordinary trash. Th' church is done ended.
THE PROPHET	*(Rising pathetically.)* Air it, Ben?
BEN	Them people out there. All our people that's singin' th' songs yew taught them. Believin' whatever yew told them. Wantin' to work fer yew, even to die fer yew. Wantin' yew to lead them into salvation an' into th' light of God. Waitin' fer yew while yew was gone, prayin' fer yew, a-singin' an' a-praisin' yew as a prophet of God! A-hopin' an' a-hopin'!
THE PROPHET	I done wrecked it.
BEN	The kin builded their courage an' their strength to follow yew down th' hard road into conflict an' preach yer gospel of salvation in th' halls of all th' people on th' airth. An' 'stead of bein' with them, yew were in this woman's arms. 'Stead of leadin' them, yew were lovin' her up. I'm a-goin' out an' tell them what yew done! *(Starts for door.)*
THE PROPHET	Yeah, yew gotta. Let them do what they want with me, and then yew can lead them into salvation.
BEN	Me? Lead them? They ain't gonna be any Church of th' Prophet when I get done with them. I'm goin' to kill their love an' their faith an' their salvation fer them! I'm goin' to kill their God fer them! I'm goin' to kill their souls! I'm goin' to send them back

BEN (CONT.)	into th' hills without no hope, or love, or eternal life in their hearts! Th' Church of th' Prophet is goin' to be washed away with their footprints on this ground!
THE PROPHET	Is this what I done? Did I do this much? *(Nods.)* Yeah. Th' church rises or falls with its builder. I done sinned an' th' church sinned. I ain't a saint an' th' church ain't holy. I die an' th' church dies with me. *(Turns to BEN.)* Even so, I ain't th' church. I thought yew was th' church but yew cain't be. Not no more. An' th' church ain't th' people—not no more. An' th' church ain't what I taught, 'cause what I taught couldn't keep me sinless. Yeah. Then th' church air dead. My kin must crawl back into th' hills an' suffer th' rest of their lives out in their souls' silence. Yeah, it's done. *(His head falls.)*
BEN	*(BEN starts to leave, but he pauses and a softer expression comes over his face.)* Maybe—maybe I needn't to tell them. Maybe I'll forget about it an' jus' go 'way, out'n th' sight of them.
SUSAN	*(She takes a step or two toward THE PROPHET.)* Nobody needn't say nothin' 'bout what happened. Ev'ry man's mostly flesh an' sometime it jus' gets stronger than th' spirit. Maybe th' Lord meant it to be like that.
THE PROPHET	*(More vigorously.)* We was all borned in th' flesh. If we died in th' flesh—knowin' nothin' better than the flesh—we was damned! I taught yew that! An' if th' spirit was weaker than th' flesh, then it was meaner than th' flesh. I taught yew that. I believed what I taught yew. I still believe it to be so. If'n I didn't, I would force yew both to keep silent about what happened—an' yew would, too, by God! If'n I didn't, I would take ev'ry woman in th' church what looked good in my eye, an' no livin' man could stop me, either! *(He shakes his head.)* I believed what I taught yew more'n anythin'. I preached to yew, an'

THE PROPHET (CONT.)	after I was done, in th' 'citement of my belief, another man done snuck into my hide an' sinned with th' woman he desired. An' when he was done, he lef' me lonely with my sin, cursin' my weak flesh. An' then I praised God an' thought it was all forgot; but it wasn't, 'cause now all my kin got to know of my weak flesh. All of them got to know 'bout me an' Sister Veena. Yeah, that air my kid a-burstin' in her belly! That sin air mine, too! Oh, I am a sinful, wicked man! *(He falls to his knees:)*
BEN	*(Thunderstruck.)* Sister Veena? That's why she waited all day fer yew in th' parish house. An' we been cursin' her as a sinner—we even talked 'bout sendin' her out'n th' blessin' of th' church, an' yew never said nothin'! An' all th' time, yew were th' blame fer it!
THE PROPHET	*(Rising.)* They ain't no endin' to it. I done sinned powerful. Not my flesh only but also my spirit. An' now it's all comin' back onto me. I cain't excuse my sins. I'm spirit or flesh, either one. I cain't be both. *(Moves to door right.)*
BEN	Where yew goin'?
THE PROPHET	*(Staring at the rifle leaning beside the door.)* Goin' out to tell my kin I won't be set to lead them.
BEN	*(Agonized.)* No, wait, they might hurt yew. Anyhow—maybe they needn't to be told. Maybe—
THE PROPHET	They got to be told. One way or another—
BEN	Jeremiah— *(There is a pause, and then BEN and SUSAN turn away.)*
THE PROPHET	G'bye, Ben. Yew air still whole, maybe yew'll see fit to lead them. *(He picks up the rifle and goes through the door, leaving it open.)*
SUSAN	*(Turning quickly.)* No! Wait! Let me go with yew!
BEN	*(Holding her.)* Stop! This got to be. Don't yew go; they may kill yew. O woman, why, why, did yew make me know?
SUSAN	I couldn't hep it. I wanted yew, Ben, an' yew was proud.

BEN	This thing wasn't worth th' knowin'. *(A shot is heard. BEN and SUSAN stand still for a frozen moment. The singing stops.)*
SUSAN	My God! Ben—
BEN	*(Shouting.)* Jeremiah! *(He rushes out the door.)* Jeremiah! Dead! He's done kilt hisself! The Prophet's dead!

(SUSAN stands breathlessly and then collapses on the sofa.)

SCENE 2: EPILOGUE

A road on a bare hillside, dimly lit from the valley below by the torches of THE PROPHET's flock. The road leads to Johnson City. BEN enters from stage right, takes a few steps, and then wipes his brow wearily. He turns upstage, toward the light. In the distance can be heard the voices of the people, mourning.

BEN	Listen to them. They're singin' th' songs of mournin' like their lives were done. Maybe it is th' last song of th' kin. They know ev'rythin'. Th' serpent done showed them th' tree. Now they see Veena's belly an' know it is his seed. Now they look at Susan an' see his sweetheart. Now they'll look down at his dead body an' see their own dead faces. Like I saw mine. *(Shakes his head sadly.)* We shouldn't of hoped so much, we shouldn't of believed so much—we got too far to fall from our hope. *(He listens.)* Th' kin're singin' out their dyin'; listen to them. They ain't no more church fer my kin. They won't ever be another fer them. *(A pause.)* Why'd I leave them? I should have been a comfort to them, 'stead of tellin' them ev'rythin' an' leavin' fer Johnson City. Maybe I should go back an' try to build up th' faith again. Maybe I can make them live again. They air my people. They needs me. *(He turns back, walks a few steps. He buries his head in his hands.)* O God, I cain't, I cain't. I was meant to follow, not lead! *(He throws his head back, looking at the*

BEN (CONT.)   *dark sky.)* God! God be damned! Yew ruint th' best man what ever prayed to yew! Why'd yew kill him, turnin' th' weakness of his flesh again' him? *(He slumps down.)* We was ready to fight fer th' faith an' die fer it. We was sold'ers. We'd a done anythin'! Th' airth didn't know what we was set to do! *(He lifts his hands to his face painfully.)* What? What that yew say? We was too strong fer th' worth of what we knew? *(Something has awakened in him.)* Lovin' kilt us. Maybe that's it, maybe lovin' ain't so bad as we made it out to be. But sure th' Bible told us it was wrong. But maybe that's wrong, too. Maybe we ought to of lived with lovin', 'stead of fightin' it in ourselves! Maybe Th' Prophet done right even there, 'thout knowin' it. But that wasn't fer his knowin'. He couldn't of taught us that. When we believed it were bad, we joined together an' strengthened one another's fightin'. But when a man would see lovin' weren't bad an' th' spirit can live with it, he got to go off in th' quiet of his own self or he'll pollute them that don't know. An' he cain't go back, such a man. An' maybe in th' quiet of hisself, he searches till he finds somethin' better than this, even. Maybe that's what th' Lord meant to be; fer his truth to be known in a man 'thout it bein' set 'fore him in th' faith of others. An' that's th' way I'm to find out what I'm to be. That's th' way I'll built me up into th' image of God. Then th' faith had to die. It were less'n this, an' God wouldn't never let th' lesser thing triumph over th' greater. Then th' Lord kilt Th' Prophet fer what Th' Prophet didn't know. *(BEN falls to his knees ecstatically.)* Blessed be th' name of th' Lord! Fer God has done slew hisself with Th' Prophet! God knowed as much as Th' Prophet. But then he knew more an' Th' Prophet had to pass! God had to kill th' old self he climbed outa! An' th' new God is in

BEN (CONT.)

me! *(He rises slowly.)* Hallelujah! Him in th' Path of th' Lord is th' man who'll pick from th' ruin an' destruction th' seed of th' Lord! An' that man, bein' blessed, has got to fergive th' Lord fer bein' cruel to those that walked before! Th' Lord, in his wisdom, knows he's got to be cruel to them in th' past so's he can preserve hisself fer th' tomorrow! I'm a-goin' to Johnson City to see what th' Lord has done with hisself! *(BEN strides off left with a happy glow on his face.)*

(CURTAIN)

A Few Words Before Entering Hell

AN IMMORALITY PLAY
IN ONE ACT

The scene is dim and gr–ay and cheerless, a dark dawn on an old battle-field. The few trees in the background have grown warped and twisted, as if cringing from destruction long threatened.

This inglorious landscape is on the passage to hell, a harsh, bleak, wind-swept plateau suggesting nothing other than eternal limbo.

There is a slope of ground upstage at chair height. At stage left, a potted plant nestles against this embankment. It is gnarled from the struggle for life in this hostile place and, indeed, appears on the verge of defeat.

A wispy pall of smoke issues from stage right, immediately followed by the entrance of SATAN. He is dressed in a cheap red devil's costume from which the scarlet tail droops limply. He carries a pail of steaming water. We hear him coughing fitfully within the hideous mask. He sets the pail down beside the plant and lifts off his devil's head.

SATAN   Ugh! Ugh! What a foul place it is! *(Wipes his fore-head.)* Whew!

(The DEVIL is a man of uncertain age. His demeanor is rather refined, though weighted with an air of tired self-pity. The dominant trait that his face pres-ents is not sadness, which can often seem sweet, but glumness; sadness soured by boredom.

He stands still for a moment, breathing this purer air, exhausted from his existence. He pulls a zipper down the front of his costume and steps out of it, revealing a conservative gray flannel suit beneath.)

SATAN   Look! I'm streaming sweat! The suit will be ruined.
                         My best one, too! Ugh! The traditions of hell! *(He
                         smoothes out the rumpled material, then sits down
                         on the embankment, sighing deeply. He addresses the
                         plant beside him.)* Alive yet? You seem stronger
                         than the other plants; perhaps you'll make it af-
                         ter all. I've tried to help you along. But I guess I
                         just don't have the green thumb. *(He looks around
                         and shakes his head.)* No, it's this place. *(He shivers.)*
                         Never any sun here. Clouds and reflections and
                         darkness; night and half day—never anything else.

(He pulls himself to his feet.)

SATAN (CONT.)   Well, little fellow, I brought you some nice water. It isn't a very easy thing to find in hell, you know. I must sneak it out so those who prefer a scalding won't see. How they'd complain if they knew I was taking their precious water away! Well, why shouldn't I take a little water? It's my hell, isn't it? *(Sighs.)* No. No, it isn't. I'm just a symbol, just a convenience. Hell belongs to the human race. *(He picks up the pail and starts pouring its contents into the pot.)* Now we'll take a drink, a great, big, nice wet drink of water because we're very, very thirsty. Is it too warm? Is it a wee bit too warm? *(Stops pouring.)* I didn't give the water enough time to cool. Maybe it doesn't matter. The little thing's going to die anyway. I know it is. Like the others. *(He sits down on the embankment painfully.)* I should be starting back. They'll miss me. So many excellent imps and demons: Prince Beelzebub, the finest, the ablest of fallen archangels—but no, none of them are quite adequate. The devil himself must direct the punishment. Snobs! Ah, how I wish I were rid of them! *(He stands.)* They've stained the righteous conflict, made the great revolt ignoble. They've turned angels into serpents, serpents into worms! They can never be unhappy enough, never leave evil enough alone. One must flog one's imagination for new methods of torture. Not a moment to oneself. Not an instant of rest. *(Sits slowly, holds his head with a harassed gesture.)* So many things I've planned for the Cause that must be left undone. Hell just isn't making any progress.

(A MAN enters from stage left. He is in his late forties. He wears a white shirt, trousers, and lounging sandals. A great bloodstain covers most of his shirtfront. He has entered with an air of intention, but when he sees the DEVIL he hesitates uncertainly.)

MAN   Er—how do you do?

(The DEVIL starts, then stares irritably at the intruder.)

MAN   Hiya! Am I ever glad to see you! You're the first hu-
               man being I've seen since I was killed. Put it there,
               friend!

*(The MAN approaches the DEVIL happily, hand outstretched. The DEVIL
growls violently and returns his head to the cradle of his palms.)*

MAN   Well, what's the matter? What's the matter with
               the guy? You'd think I'd said something wrong. Say,
               could be he isn't real, either. Maybe I'm imagining
               him, too. Maybe—

SATAN   Oh, shut up, you eternal fool!

MAN   Say, you're pretty tough, aren't you? I don't care if
               you aren't real, how'd you like a good sock in the
               kisser?…But I guess it wouldn't do any good; my
               hand'd go right through. The funniest thing, right
               after he killed me, I tried to hit him—hard! But
               my hand went right through—right through! Gee,
               it was the funniest thing. I must be dead, I said
               to myself. Then all at once, I felt that I had to go
               somewhere, and I kept going until I got—here.
               You know, you're the first person I've seen who
               looks real, and I don't know yet if you really are.
               Real, I mean.

SATAN   Would it satisfy you if I said I am real? Has your
               imagination the ability to grant that much reality
               to its figments?

MAN   Somehow I get the feeling you're real, all right.
               What is this place, anyhow? Heaven? Am I really
               dead?

SATAN   If you got this far unescorted, you are dead.

MAN   Dead? Oh, God! *(He falls on his knees suddenly and
               starts sobbing.)*

SATAN   *(He frowns harshly at the mention of God. SATAN watches the MAN for a disgusted moment, then leans close to the newcomer's ear.)* You! *(The MAN starts violently and stares apprehensively at the DEVIL.)* Stop that stupid bawling—it won't get you back into that body of yours. Not only are you dead, you are bound for hell.

MAN   *(Leaps to his feet.)* Hell? There's really a hell?!

SATAN   You weren't told?

MAN   Told? Yes. But—I didn't believe it! Nobody believes that stuff! *(He clasps his head in his hands.)* Ohh!

SATAN   I believe we have given sufficient publicity to—

MAN   But why me? Why am *I* going to hell? I didn't do anything bad. Why, I was murdered! They killed me! They should go to hell; I should go to heaven!

SATAN   I don't know that it matters particularly how you died. How you lived evidently didn't come up to the standards of— *(Points upward.)* —up to his standards, so—

MAN   But it's unfair! It's not right! It's— *(Shakes his fist in the general direction of heaven.)*

SATAN   *(Rising to his feet.)* How these scenes bore me.

MAN   And you! Who are you to tell me I'm going to hell? Who—

SATAN   I am Satan.

MAN   *(A mixture of awe and terror grips the man.)* Y-You—

(He backs slowly away, then with a sudden burst of speed turns and bolts offstage. The DEVIL shrugs with mild disgust and dismisses the human from his mind. He stoops to collect his costume suit and bucket. The MAN appears again, stage left.)

MAN   Say—

(The DEVIL half pauses, then continues to prepare his departure.)

MAN	Ah—sir? Please, sir, could you wait—ah—
SATAN	Just follow me.
MAN	Ohh— *(The word is a ghastly sound. He clears his throat desperately.)* Please, Mr. Satan, I-I insist! I—
SATAN	*(Expels his breath explosively and hurls his belongings down on the ground. He sits heavily on the embankment and holds his head in his hands.)* Very well, very well, very well, tell me why you don't deserve hell, but for the love of mercy, make it short!
MAN	I can't understand it! Please, Mr. Satan, listen to me. It's not fair. It's—criminal. I didn't do anything wrong. I never did do anything really wrong. You never came and tempted me, did you? Did you? I never signed any of your contracts. Why, you didn't even recognize me! Just now! Then why me? I never broke any law. I went to church regularly. I was never in jail. I always did exactly what the authorities told me to do.
SATAN	There's your reason.
MAN	I never—what?—I always paid my bills regularly. I never had any trouble with the finance company. I never cheated anyone out of anything. In fact, *I* was the one who was always being cheated! Look at my wife. For years, probably, she's been mixed up with this guy; then when she makes sure I have a nice, big, fat insurance policy—whammy! The next thing I know, I'm standing beside my bed. And there I am, lying there with a hole in my chest big enough to— *(Points to his chest.)* —Well, look for yourself! Why, Mr. Satan, I was murdered! There isn't any justice, sending me to hell! It's damnable! It's completely—
SATAN	Stop shouting. I have nothing whatever to do with passing judgment. Neither am I a board of review. If you're damned, you're damned. So come along. *(Starts to rise.)*
MAN	Wait! Isn't there anyone I can contact? Anyone I

MAN (CONT.)	can talk to? Don't they ever make mistakes?
SATAN	I never bothered myself to find out. Whoever comes along I take, and invariably they fit in. Of course, their friends help.
MAN	Friends?
SATAN	Certainly, friends. Evil runs in groups, you know. To put it in your threadbare idiom, Birds of a feather flock together. One is known by the company one keeps. Etc., etc.
MAN	Yes? And—you wouldn't know a Dick Brown, would you?
SATAN	I know innumerable Browns.
MAN	Richard Atherton Brown?
SATAN	I don't recall him.
MAN	He died just a little while ago. Ah—you wouldn't know a Bill, er, William Morrison, would you? He's a little, sawed-off—
SATAN	*(Rising.)* My dear fellow, hell is inhabited by some twenty billion human beings, give or take a few hundred million. And although I have an excellent memory, I have never cared to employ it on human names. Now, if you will follow me.
MAN	Oh, please, wait! Just a minute, just one minute! Please!
SATAN	Sir, you are keeping me from the execution of my duties.
MAN	Yes, but—well, listen just for one more second. Surely, you have that much time.
SATAN	*(Sighs.)* I have all the time in the world. *(Shrugs and sits once more.)*
MAN	Well…isn't there somebody I can tell my case to? Can't I appeal the decision before—well, God? Maybe if I could—
SATAN	No. All the evidence is on the record. Being dead, it is impossible for you to create new evidence. The record has been reviewed, a decision has been made, and here you are. Therefore—

MAN   But if there is a hell, I should think there would be
             some kind of court you'd go to when you died. I
             thought there'd be someplace where you'd come up
             before God—

SATAN   Waste of time. Having all the evidence and, pre-
             sumably, divine wisdom, the Supreme One judges
             in camera. No amount of impassioned pleading or
             ranting—and that is all it would amount to, any-
             how—would change the character of the evidence,
             or, for that matter, your character. I'll say that for
             him, once he makes a law, he sticks to it— *(Shakes
             his head, throws up his hands.)* —for the present.
             Though heaven knows—and I mean that quite
             literally, heaven itself knows— *(Rising to his feet.)*
             —none of his laws is worth a piffle. Not a millen-
             nium goes by that he doesn't adjust his laws, change
             them, do a little "improving," adapting, shifting
             around.... *(Getting a full head of steam.)* And right
             there is the very nub of our ancient quarrel. The
             precise point that took me out of heaven. How I am
             misjudged! You humans believe me to have wres-
             tled with a Greater Power, to have struggled and
             lost in a violent, eye-gouging war with Divinity, to
             have been tossed down by his greater strength; the
             immoral crushed by the moral—What ignorance! I
             left! I walked out! I was the protester against law-
             lessness, against chaos, against the eternal churning
             up, churning up so one never knew from one age
             to the next where he was. I stood then, and I stand
             now, for the literal against the nebulous, for law be-
             fore lawlessness, for sanity in place of this frantic
             madness called evolution. For order in place of—

MAN   But—

SATAN   In place of disorder. For—

MAN   But—Pardon me for interrupting, Mr. Satan, but—
             haven't you got that all wrong? Our scientists say
             there's nothing but order in the universe, nothing

MAN (CONT.)	but law; I do know that much—
SATAN	You know nothing. Don't speak to me of your science. That's all I hear these days: science, science, science; the newest preoccupation of your idiot race. This presumed "order" of the universe might just as well be disorder, depending on what sort of universe you contemplate. As for your science, if you had bothered to study its history, you would know that the yardstick of one generation is the error of the next. Scientists be damned—and for that matter, I am pleased to say many of them are!
MAN	Well—I always read—
SATAN	Bah! You can read no better than what there is to read. Order! Don't talk to me of order. You don't understand the meaning of order. You are born; fifty years later, you return to your birthplace and you remark with satisfaction, "The old place hasn't changed much." Fifty years! Why, an iota of change in fifty billion years is criminal! If initial creation is perfection, how can change bring improvement? Most evidently, it cannot! And I challenge anyone to represent to me that the universe, as it stands, is perfection.
MAN	But—
SATAN	Yes—
MAN	I'm sorry, I hate to keep interrupting, but the Bible says God created the universe. If he made it, he must know what he's doing, changing it all the time.
SATAN	Created the universe, indeed! He didn't create the universe anymore than you did. Everything came out of the black belly of chaos, unfathered. First there wasn't. Then there was. That was the beginning; even your Bible, with all its lies about me, is explicit on that point. This Being you call God happened to be stronger than the rest of us and therefore took command. And because the majority of angels

SATAN (CONT.)	are like the majority of men—sheep—he won the crowd. Presently, however, a few of the wiser and more alert among us commenced to express grave reservations. The course that was being taken, we felt, was erratic in the extreme. In point of fact, we challenged the insane notion that a course was to be taken at all—that the universe had to go from here to there, that perfection could be improved upon. It became all too clear that the Administration was leading us down the road to ruin. Creeping chaos had become the order of the day; extinction threatened all we held most dear. Therefore, after representations had been made repeatedly and were answered by no more than humiliating silence, we vowed we no longer would accept conditions as they were. We issued a manifesto urging the entire sentient universe to join the Cause, and with that we walked out. We came here and we are still here. That is the whole truth and all the rest is a pious lie. I might add, because you are new, that pious to us is the equivalent of fiendish on earth.
MAN	But that's not so bad. You didn't do anything so awful.
SATAN	We did nothing wrong. *(Sighs.)* Ah, there's no point at all in discussing it. *(The DEVIL walks over to his possessions and is about to pick them up.)*
MAN	But—what about me? I didn't do anything wrong, either. I was murdered!
SATAN	One could hardly miss the circumstances of your death with that great blotch of blood on your chest. Obviously, you have failed to grasp how my experience applies to your own problems. The gist, dear fellow, is that there is no justice in the universe— only opinion.
MAN	But—but I don't want to go to hell!
SATAN	*(Picking his things up.)* Neither do I.
MAN	It isn't fair! I shouldn't be damned!

(The DEVIL shrugs his shoulders and moves toward the exit, stage right. A WOMAN enters, stage left. The tight black sheath that clothes her enhances her natural sexiness. Marring her attractiveness, however, is a small hole in her left temple, from which a trickle of blood, now encrusted, made its way down to her lower jaw.)

WOMAN	Where am I?
MAN	*(Wheeling.)* Ellen! My God, you're dead, too?
SATAN	*(He has stopped. Shakes his head.)* The wife—
ELLEN	John! You're dead! We killed you! Oh, it's a terrible dream!
JOHN	Dream? Dream, my eye! What happened? Why are you dead? Don't tell me that guy killed you?!
ELLEN	No! No! I'm not dead! I'm just dreaming. Oh! That blood! *(She stares at John's chest.)*
JOHN	You did that! But don't worry—you're dead, all right.
ELLEN	It's all so unreal.
JOHN	That wears off after you stand around for a while talking. Then it's the other that seems unreal. What happened to your forehead?
ELLEN	*(She feels gingerly about her forehead with her fingers. She finds softened tissues about the bullet's aperture. With an "Ooh" of disgust, she quickly withdraws her hand.)* That's where the bullet went in.
JOHN	Bullet? That guy did kill you, didn't he?
ELLEN	*(Stamping her foot.)* He did not! I shot myself!
JOHN	You shot yourself! *(Breaking into laughter.)* If that doesn't take the cake! Shot herself!
ELLEN	*(She slaps him.)* Stop it! Stop that!
JOHN	Hey! Why— *(He is about to return the blow.)*
SATAN	Please. Please restrain your natural human impulses. I witness more than enough of this sort of thing as it is.
JOHN	*(To ELLEN, triumphantly.)* That's the devil, that's who that is! You're going straight to hell!
ELLEN	Oh— *(Almost innocently.)* What are you doing here?
JOHN	*(Furious.)* Damn it, don't change the subject!

ELLEN	Well, you are here, aren't you?
JOHN	Damn!
SATAN	We are all here. Let us conduct ourselves as if—
ELLEN	You're supposed to be the devil? Well, you don't look like the devil to me.
SATAN	Look in my eyes.
ELLEN	*(She looks. Her hands glide to her face, trembling as they cover her eyes.)* Oh— *(She sinks to her knees gracelessly and hunches forward.)* God forgive me.
SATAN	A useless appeal.
JOHN	*(Stares at ELLEN.)* Well, will you look at that. Many's the time I wished I could shut her up like that. Satan, you really should be married. What a gift! *(Walks over to ELLEN.)* Well, what did happen? Ellen?

(She shakes her head.)

JOHN	*(Takes her by the shoulders.)* It's okay.
ELLEN	*(Rising quickly to her knees and clutching him.)* John—
JOHN	Now, now, now, honey; it's okay. Now up on our feet. Come on, up we come! *(ELLEN is half lifted, half rises. She holds JOHN tightly.)*
ELLEN	It's terrible. It isn't a dream, is it?
JOHN	NO. *(He rubs his face.)* I wish it were, though. You always had a pretty good right. *(Half turns to the DEVIL.)* Hey, I thought her hand was supposed to go through me.
SATAN	If it were so, the tortures of hell would be ineffective. *(With a sigh, the DEVIL sits.)*
ELLEN	John....Hold me tight.
JOHN	You're fine now. Come on, tell me what happened.
ELLEN	What does it matter? Oh, I should never have done it: never, never, never. I committed suicide and now I'm damned.
JOHN	*(Drawing away.)* Well, pardon me, but I think the little fact that you murdered your husband with a shotgun might have a bit to do with that.

ELLEN	I didn't do that. Arthur did that.
JOHN	Well, you knew about it. You helped him. And you spent my insurance money with him. You've got to share the guilt, Ellen.
ELLEN	We didn't kill you for the insurance.
JOHN	Well then, why did you?
ELLEN	You would never have given me a divorce.
JOHN	Well, how do you know? Why didn't you ask me? For the love of Mike, did you have to go ahead and kill me?
ELLEN	Anyway, you were perfectly horrid when you found out about Arthur and me.
JOHN	How is a man supposed to act? A guy finds out his wife has been playing around behind his back—for years maybe.
ELLEN	Not years. You always twist things so. It's like you, John. You try to make out it was something ugly and it wasn't. It was beautiful and sweet and tender.
JOHN	*(To the DEVIL.)* Runs around with another man, kills her husband for the insurance money, and shoots herself—and it was something sweet and tender.
ELLEN	You always were insensitive, John. You could never understand how two people could be so desperately in love they would do the sorts of things we did.
JOHN	No, I don't understand. And what's more, I don't think you do either. You haven't said why you shot yourself.
ELLEN	Oh, it wasn't any good. We were so nervous and we quarreled. And the money; we both needed it, yet we didn't want it. And there were all those investigators coming around, asking us awful questions—the police and the insurance people. And your father hired private detectives, all snooping and insinuating and trying to make us contradict each other. We didn't have a moment's peace, not a chance to be really alone anymore. And then we had this terrible quarrel—I just couldn't bear it anymore.

JOHN   But I don't see how there could be any question of me being murdered by you people, it was so dog-gone obvious. All the cops had to do was take a look at me lying there.

ELLEN   Arthur is very clever. He made it appear as though your business partner, Mr. Mantell, had done it.

JOHN   Elmer? You tried to blame Elmer for what you did?

ELLEN   The police arrested him....

JOHN   How low can you get?!

ELLEN   Fortunately, it seemed that you and he had a terrible row before you died. Something about a contract he didn't know about and you got all the money. It involved thousands and apparently Mr. Mantell was going to have you prosecuted. It was his gun we used. I don't know how Arthur found out about that contract. He's so clever.

JOHN   Oh...That. Well, that wasn't anything. Was old Elmer going to prosecute? Boy, he's put a lot faster deals over on other guys and I just smiled. *(To the DEVIL.)* That's sure a nice thing to find out about a guy you call your best friend, you know? I just hope the state *does* send him to the chair.

ELLEN   They were sniffing around when I...left, making all these snide insinuations about Arthur and me. But they couldn't prove anything, and they did have to admit that Mr. Mantell had the best motive.

JOHN   He did not! *(Turning to the DEVIL.)* How do you like that? A half dozen reasons why the whole crew of them should be sent to hell, and they're alive and I'm down here. And I didn't do a thing. I still don't know why I'm here.

SATAN   *(Rising from the embankment where he had been sitting.)* I have nothing to say about hell's candidates.

ELLEN   You don't? You make people sin, don't you?

SATAN   Nonsense! Men's laws make men break them. I didn't decide the character of sin. I didn't give man any commandments.

ELLEN	That's just talk. You're evil and you know it!
SATAN	I bow before your knowledge of the subject, madam.
JOHN	Don't annoy him, Ellen.
SATAN	However, I must insist on the point that, although I rejected heaven, heaven rejected you. In heaven's opinion, you sinned; let it be their opinion. As for hell, I can only assure you that it will execute the punishment.
ELLEN	*(Turns and sobs against JOHN's chest.)* Oh, John, he's cruel.
SATAN	Not by intention. After all, I didn't put you here.
JOHN	Now, honey, leave him alone. He isn't so awful after you talk to him for a while. Besides, there isn't any point in getting on his bad side.
ELLEN	Oh, it's all so mixed up and unfair!
SATAN	Now you approach the truth. The universe *is* mixed up and unfair. I have been pointing out to your husband that the acts that create saints in one age create fools in the next. I don't know what sin is, or goodness. One can only assume that there are no unbreakable laws. For myself, I take the sinners that each age sends to me. What does it matter by what standards they were judged?
ELLEN	But that's terrible. It doesn't make sense!
SATAN	You have eternity to consider the contradictions of heaven. Perhaps you will find the answer; eternity has not been so kind to me. *(Turns to stage right.)* Come along.
JOHN	Wait! Wait, for the love of God!
SATAN	*(Stops.)* Please! Choose your words more carefully!
JOHN	I'm sorry. It slipped out.
SATAN	All right.
JOHN	It wasn't very tactful of me.
SATAN	It is the only really profane oath left to the damned. We must use it with discretion.
JOHN	But surely a man can repent, if he has sinned. Isn't

JOHN (CONT.)	there love in heaven? Something we can pray to? Neither of us did anything really wrong. At least, *I* didn't. Maybe we didn't act very smart—
SATAN	There you have it. You weren't clever. All the love in heaven isn't enough to save the stupid. That law, at least, shows no signs of age.
ELLEN	But if we pray, if we repent—
SATAN	Don't bother; it would be a waste of your time. Not that you don't have a great deal of time to waste.
JOHN	Look, uh, Mr. Satan, you seem like a nice guy. You must have contacts, some sort of emissary system between you and...him. Maybe you could arrange some sort of meeting, some way for us to—
SATAN	Don't attempt to impose yourself upon me. I have no interest in you, nor in the justice of your damnation.

(ELLEN starts to sob.)

JOHN	Please—
SATAN	I will not ask you to accompany me. Many humans would consider it a distinct honor to enter Hades escorted by the Diabolic One himself—but never mind. Providence has branded the way to hell deep in the human mind; you will come to me eventually, in spite of yourselves.

(SATAN collects his things and starts for the stage right exit. Enter stage left a MAN of around thirty. He is walking with swift deliberation, though there is an expression of mistrust and fear on his face. He is dressed in a prison uniform. His shoes are scuffed and heavy; otherwise, he is neat and his clothes are fresh. When he sees the group, he stops suddenly.)

YOUNG MAN	What is this place?

(Everyone turns to him, SATAN slowly and with a sigh.)

YOUNG MAN	Ellen!
ELLEN	Arthur!
SATAN	Another.
JOHN	You! *(JOHN stalks swiftly up to ARTHUR and catches him on the jaw with a sweeping right. ELLEN screams. ARTHUR is dumped on the stage, stunned.)*
JOHN	You swine! Boy, have I been saving that up for a long time!
ELLEN	*(To JOHN.)* You brute! *(ELLEN moves to AR-THUR's side. Not waiting for her succor, he leaps to his feet and rushes JOHN.)*
SATAN	Stop.

(ARTHUR is halted in midstride.)

SATAN	Professionally, I might allow or even bait you to display such an exhibition of human passion. However, at present, it is unnecessary that I endure your mortal malice.
ARTHUR	Who the hell are you?
JOHN	You're sure going to find that out! You're going to find out plenty about him! You're going to wish you were never born! Murderer!
ARTHUR	*(Lifts a hand slowly to his head.)* It's a dream; another one of those awful dreams.
JOHN	It's no dream. But I'll be hanged if I know how you got here. According to the way I'm beginning to figure it, someone like you should be in heaven.
ELLEN	*(Going to ARTHUR.)* Oh, my poor darling.
ARTHUR	Ellen, you're dead.
ELLEN	And you, too, dearest. Now we're here together. You did it, too, didn't you? You came here to join me. Oh, love!
ARTHUR	They gave me the chair. *(Suddenly shouting.)* They gave me the chair! I remember! They strapped me in! I'm dead!
JOHN	Electrocuted. Good. Damn good.

ELLEN   But that can't be true. It must all be a dream, a terrible, morbid dream! It must be! I died only a moment ago. It would take months before they could try Arthur and execute him. Oh, it is a dream! *(She turns to the DEVIL with resentment.)*

JOHN   Say, maybe you're right! Come to think of it, you got here only a little after me; you must have shot yourself long after you killed me.

ELLEN   It was more than a month!

(The three of them look accusingly at SATAN.)

SATAN   Would you like me to walk out of your respective dreams so you can all wake up? Very well, wake up.

(The three close and open their eyes, clenching their fists, straining to wake up. JOHN pinches himself a few times. They give up.)

JOHN   It's no use.

SATAN   You have allowed time to confuse you. There are neither hours nor days here, only eternal relativities. That is *my* law. That is the way it has always been, and that is the way it shall always be. Because the three of you are to be chained eternally to one another, you enter hell together.

ARTHUR   *(Still confused.)* Hell? Who is he?

JOHN   Still, a certain amount of time—

SATAN   You sleep for an hour or twenty hours, yet each time it is but a dark instant between retiring and rising. Now that life has ended for you, that dark instant is a minute or a millennium. In hell, there is no future.

ARTHUR   Ellen, tell me what—

JOHN   *(To ARTHUR, fiercely.)* You're damned, that's what's happened to you! *(Turning from them all. Quietly.)* Damned.

(ELLEN's head falls into her hands. She sobs.)

ARTHUR   *(To the DEVIL.)* Who are you?

SATAN   Satan.

ARTHUR   Is that it? You're the devil? And we're all going to hell? *(He throws back his head and laughs.)* There isn't a hell. And you're the devil? What's that under your arm? Why, it's a costume! A red devil's costume! *(Turning to the others.)* Don't tell me he scared you with that get-up. Well, if this isn't the damnedest—

JOHN   Fool...

ARTHUR   *(Chuckling.)* This is really funny. *(Laughter dies.)* But it's strange. It really is strange. I've tried to wake up. I've tried and I've tried—but I can't. And I keep remembering the courtroom and the judge and then being strapped to that chair and the electrodes taped to my arms and my heart....My heart! *(He turns away in sudden terror and disgust.)*

SATAN   Poor thing. How ruthless men are! He kills, so then the state must kill him. I expect he simply couldn't help himself.

JOHN   *(Taking strong exception to the DEVIL'S remark.)* Oh!

SATAN   Oh yes, you have these violent animal impulses, and your civilized veneer is swept away like so much straw. Of course, you have been given free will, so you are accountable. The sureness of instinct taken from them, an imperious evolution egging them on to who knows what adventures... the history of mankind must be brief—though hectic. *(The DEVIL starts to leave, stage right.)*

ARTHUR   Wait!

(The DEVIL pauses.)

ARTHUR   Now, look, look, if this is really hell and you're the devil, there must be a purgatory. There must be a way—

JOHN | *(Turning on ARTHUR.)* That's you all over, you cheap punk—always looking for the percentage!

SATAN | *(To JOHN.)* Play the game; you had your opportunity. *(To ARTHUR.)* A great many human beings come down here, insisting there is someplace called purgatory. Now, I've always assumed from the description that this place is actually earth. And you failed there, my boy. If there is another kind of purgatory, it must be but an appendage of heaven, where, presumably, the initiated ripen. Of course, you can see that, for you, the whole question is quite immaterial.

ARTHUR | But I don't want to be—

ELLEN | *(Coming to ARTHUR.)* Arthur, we did wrong. We were bad and we must be punished. We—

ARTHUR | Ellen, shut up! This whole thing is crazy! It's a dream! It's got to be a dream! I won't believe it! *(Looking around.)* This doesn't look like hell at all!

JOHN | If I had to stay here for the rest of eternity, I'd think it was hell, all right.

ELLEN | *(To ARTHUR.)* Oh, darling, what does it matter? We're together again now. That's all that matters!

(ARTHUR recoils from her with exasperation.)

ELLEN | Darling—

SATAN | Depend upon female sentimentality to survive death, at any rate.

ELLEN | Can't you see, dearest, our love is the only thing that makes it all worthwhile, the only thing that can dignify hell. If we enter together, dear, close to each other, holding each other's hand, we can't have anything to fear. We may have done some bad things, but they will respect our love.

JOHN | Now, Ellen, just how dignified are you two going to look, walking into hell with me, your husband, stepping along right behind you? You're going to

JOHN (CONT.)	look pretty damn silly, that's how you're going to look.
SATAN	One rarely meets with a prepared attitude at the entrance to hell. Acclimatization is too abrupt.
ARTHUR	Is it really like they say?
SATAN	Descriptions vary; why not leave your mind open for the actual experience?
ARTHUR	I mean, is it bad?
SATAN	Hell's principal industry remains torture.
ARTHUR	Oh, merciful God!
SATAN	An inappropriate epithet.
JOHN	He doesn't like you saying that.
ARTHUR	Is it eternal torture, then?
SATAN	Oh, surely, you are not that insatiable. My employees need some rest, some relaxation. I realize you humans picture my demons gloating with delight as they carry out their duties, but I assure you that such a sensation is far too thin to spread out over eternity. While at work, we work.
ARTHUR	But there is still torture...
SATAN	My dear fellow, the inmates demand it. Once the pain of their most recent punishment is forgotten, they whimper and complain and cry mea culpa until we are positively obligated to prepare a new series of tortures. You call it conscience, I believe.
ARTHUR	I don't feel conscience stricken.
SATAN	Within the confines of hell, conscience is a voice louder than my own. It is in the air. Those who never possessed a conscience develop one.
ELLEN	Never mind the pain, Arthur, we have our love; that will keep us strong.
ARTHUR	Love! In the name of heaven, do you think that I would have even looked at you if I had known it was going to end like this!?
ELLEN	*(Deeply hurt.)* Arthur, how can you say that?
JOHN	I'll tell you how. For once, he's being honest.
ELLEN	Don't you love me? Did you ever love me?

ARTHUR	I missed you when you died, Ellen. I loved you. I thought I loved you. But this!
ELLEN	Then why, why—
JOHN	For the insurance money, that's why. I told you that.
ARTHUR	I don't know. I wanted to do something for you, to prove something....Maybe that wasn't it. I wanted to tie those cops up and get them to pin it on Mantell; what a laugh that would have been! And I needed the money. No, it wasn't the money....I don't know why I did it. Something just got into me. Why do people do things? I don't know. It just got into my head.
ELLEN	Oh, what has happened to us? *(She turns from them, unable to sob.)*
SATAN	Ask any human being his reason for doing anything....Actually, you explained yourself very well, my boy.
JOHN	If there's anything crazier than this mix-up—
ELLEN	Oh, I've suffered so.
SATAN	Here is your typical triangle—the eternal triangle, humans say with uncommon insight. The husband is slain, the woman commits suicide, and the lover is executed—a tragedy. But now, at the approach to hell, the principals are stripped of the physical base for their passions. The residue is pride, vanity, and ambition: mere commonplaces. So it is not really a tragedy at all. *(More intensely.)* Your experience is too usual. I believe it is that which damns you. *(Points toward heaven.)* I tell you, he wants invention, inspiration, the unconventional. Change merely for the sake of change. His interest is not in what is, but in what will be.
JOHN	There isn't a chance in the world for us, is there?
SATAN	None.
JOHN	Then why *were* we? Why all the sermons and all the prayers? Why did we live?

SATAN   Ah, dear, human being, it is only your pride that makes you forget that men are but tiny beings on a tiny earth. You are playthings. I suppose he feels that he expresses himself through you. He will do with you what he will. And when he tires of you, he will go on to something else.

ELLEN   But that's not human.

SATAN   Well, neither is he. Quite otherwise, as a matter of fact. But regret nothing. It is not the act but the human that is damned: you would have reached hell whichever path you took. *(Steps away from the group. In thought.)* Ah, but it is not the human that is damned at all: it is hell. I think this poor race the last of evolution's generations that hell shall receive. The succeeding inventions of the Supreme One shall be immoral with impunity; shall break laws because they are clever, not out of petty ego. It is certain to be so. He himself has always disdained law, making laws and breaking them, not bound by anything. He has never had the proper respect for law. At any rate, with the death of the last human, all change in hell will end. That, at least, is worthwhile. *(Straightens and turns to the others with resolution.)* I have been away much too long. I must go back. And the three of you will come with me.

JOHN   No! Wait!

SATAN   Enough! You have said what you will. What is done is done! It is all over and eternity has begun!

ARTHUR   It can't be true! None of it can be true!

(SATAN throws down his costume suit and begins climbing quickly into it.)

ELLEN   Oh, mercy! What is he doing? I feel faint—

JOHN   It's that suit…something…some power—

ARTHUR   Oh, God, isn't there hope? Isn't there repentance? I repented in prison when they read the Bible to me!

(ARTHUR and JOHN speak at the same time.)

{

ARTHUR   I believed what they said! I believe! Where is their
                forgiveness? I repent! I repent!

JOHN   I didn't do anything! You murdered me, you two.
                Your evil has dragged me down into hell! Before
                God, I never meant to sin!

(SATAN is in his devil's costume.)

ELLEN   Oh, mercy— *(She covers her face.)*

SATAN   Now, then. *(They all have turned away in terror.)*
                Cower, then. Shield yourself from me. But you
                shall always henceforth see me thus. *(He gazes
                at the three.)* Ah, how truly human to fear the ri-
                diculous. *(Loudly, pointing to stage right.)* There is
                hell—enter!

*(One by one, the three sidle past him and hurriedly exit stage right. The devil
is left alone. He looks after the humans for a moment, then removes his devil's
head.)*

SATAN   Well. It has been a unique experience. My mis-
                fortune for being found outside the gates of—my
                home. Where's my bucket? *(Finds it and picks it
                up.)* My little plant? You're dying, too, aren't you?
                Like the others. Good-bye, little fellow. I cannot
                grant life. But if I could, I would give my life for
                your death. *(The DEVIL slumps, wavers for a mo-
                ment, then straightens. He replaces his devil's head
                and, with dignity, exits.)*

Why "Bone Chips"?

You have volunteered for the sorrowful task of distributing the ashes of the loved one, according to their wishes. Now you gingerly open the small cardboard box you picked up at the crematory, face averted from the rising ash. You find, to your surprise, the box stuffed not with ash but with dry and polished flakes sliced from human bone.

The analogy is plain. From an intimate and regenerating core, word or art or music is culled. Packaged in an appropriate form, your work is presented to fellow human beings, hopefully to be as kindly received as a box from the crematory.

POSTSCRIPT: Here the analogy fails.

Turning the box over you find a label on the side. It is a disclaimer. "Some or all of the contents," it declares, "may or may not be those of the deceased." Though upset, you soon realize the ritual of prayer and remembrance was all that truly mattered.